REMEMBER LOVE

Sweet Lord, he thought, *this is unbelievable.* Never in a million years did he think he would have another chance with Dominique. Still, she was alive. As beautiful and vibrant as she had been. If only she knew him, that would make things alright . . . maybe . . .

Trin felt a hand on his arm. There was Dominique, watching him with concern in her fantastic light eyes.

"Are you okay?" she whispered, a small frown pulling at the natural arch of her brows.

Trin looked at her small hand resting lightly on his bicep and willed himself not to pull her into his arms. Tentatively, he placed his own hand over hers. "I'm sorry, I didn't mean to scare you. You just . . ."

Dom leaned forward. "I just what?"

Trin took a deep breath and traced her delicate hand with his strong fingers. "You just remind me of someone."

"Oh . . ." Dom breathed, then smiled deviously. "The love of your life, I take it?" she teased.

BOOK YOUR PLACE ON OUR WEBSITE AND MAKE THE ARABESQUE ROMANCE CONNECTION!

We've created a customized website just for our very special Arabesque readers, where you can get the inside scoop on everything that's going on with Arabesque romance novels.

When you come online, you'll have the exciting opportunity to:

- View covers of upcoming books

- Learn about our future publishing schedule (listed by publication month and author)

- Find out when your favorite authors will be visiting a city near you

- Search for and order backlist books

- Check out author bios and background information

- Send e-mail to your favorite authors

- Join us in weekly chats with authors, readers and other guests

- Get writing guidelines

- AND MUCH MORE!

Visit our website at
http://www.arabesquebooks.com

REMEMBER LOVE

AlTonya Washington

BET Publications, LLC
http://www.bet.com
http://www.arabesquebooks.com

To Masee, my little man.
Mommy loves you.

One

"I'd be more than happy to take an early break so we can go have that talk," Hal Lymon called out as he leaned over the counter of his corner newsstand. His twinkling blue gaze held a touch of mischief as he appraised the undeniably lovely young woman.

Dominique Carver's sparkling champagne stare narrowed and she sent him a knowing look. "I wouldn't dream of taking you away from business," she teased, strolling up to the counter.

Hal waved his hand in the air and let out a grunt. "Dear girl, I assure you I don't mind. It ain't every day an old geezer like me gets to go out with a young beauty like you. Even if it's just business."

Dominique's lilting laughter lent a radiant glow to her flawless cocoa skin. "Mr. Lymon, have any of your female customers ever accused you of being a flirt?"

"Certainly, but at my age, you can get away with anything," he informed her, his bushy red brows wiggling up and down suggestively.

Dominique only shook her head, her short, bouncy curls lifting against the brisk March breeze. "So, you've been in business over thirty years. How long are you planning to stay?" she asked.

"Sweetheart, they'll have to drag me out," Hal promised.

"Well, according to sources inside Morton and Farber, it seems they may be prepared to do just that," Dom replied, casting a glance toward the stark, foreboding Manhattan high-rise.

"Sources, shmorses," Hal said with a grimace. "I was here on this corner before they moved in, and here I will remain."

"And that's exactly why WQTZ wants your story," Dom said, referring to the cable TV station for which she worked. "It's time to send a message that a small business is still a business."

"And worthy of respect," Hal added, slapping his gray cap against his wooden folding counter.

"Still," Dom said, pushing one hand into the back pocket of her short, ice-blue skirt, "I'm sure they're offering a very generous sum to get you off this corner, aren't they?"

"They are," Hal confirmed, glancing over his shoulder. "Money doesn't matter to them, they've got so much of it. What they don't know is it doesn't matter to me either. What they're concerned about is appearances. They think it's more appropriate for people to walk all the way inside that building to some swanky news store to purchase their goods. But, believe it or not, Miss Carver, people still like the personal, simple touch."

Dominique tapped one perfectly manicured nail to her chin and nodded. "Besides, being on this corner gets you to the customers first."

Hal pressed his hand to his heart. "Damn, I love a smart woman."

A few customers arrived and Dom walked away, chuckling as she browsed through the periodicals displayed around the stand. Just as Hal finished his transactions, a tall young man walked out of the Morton and Farber building and approached the stand.

"Good morning, my man!" Hal said, greeting his regular customer. "I tell you, son, I still can't believe you work for those scum. I think you're probably the only decent soul in that whole damn place."

The man's double dimples creased his honey-toned cheeks the instant he grinned. Devastatingly handsome, he stood there shaking his head. His slanting onyx gaze was as vibrant as his dazzling white smile. "Hal, don't you think you're being just a bit hard on everybody in there?"

"Bah!" Hal replied, waving off the possibility.

"Anything new in today?" the man asked as he selected his daily business journal and searched his pocket for change.

"My usual skin magazines, but you're never interested." Hal replied with a devilish chuckle.

Dominique strolled back around the corner. When she spotted the sinfully gorgeous man leaning against the counter, a soft smile touched her full lips and her champagne gaze sparkled. She propped one hand on her hip and waited.

Hal was first to notice her there and quickly gave her his complete attention. "Sweet lady, please forgive me for keeping you waiting," he said, clasping his hands as he sent her his most charming smile.

The man turned as well, his expression growing inquisitive when he saw the incredible dark beauty not ten feet away. "Hello," he said.

Dom offered a slight nod. "Good morning," she replied, shivering a bit at the soft quality of his raspy deep voice.

Hal grimaced when he noticed the set expression on the man's face. "Hands off, man. I'm tryin' to scoop that," he whispered.

The man laughed shortly, never taking his eyes off Dominique. "I don't think so, Hal." He left the stand and slipped one hand around Dom's small waist.

He dipped his head to take her mouth. Dominique gasped, giving him the entrance he wanted. Her body arched against his lean, muscular frame, her fingers curling around the stylish silver tie he wore with his black suit. The kiss only lasted a few seconds. Then the two shared a warm hug.

Hal pulled the gray cap from his head and scratched his sandy red hair.

Dominique noticed and smiled. "Trin . . ." she whispered, silently urging the man to put Hal out of his misery.

Trinidad Salem pulled away, but kept his arm around Dom's waist. "Hal Lymon, my wife, Dominique Salem."

"Salem?" Hal questioned, surprise coming to his face.

"Carver's my maiden name and the one I use on TV," Dom explained.

Suddenly, Hal appeared uneasy. "Mrs. Carver, I hope you can forgive me for being forward."

"Oh Hal, please," Dom replied with a wave of her hand. "It's okay. There's nothing to apologize for," she assured him with a laugh.

Trin turned back to his wife, settling both arms around her waist. "Did you need me for something?" he whispered.

Dom's unforgettable eyes narrowed. "Oh yes," she told him, smiling when he appeared embarrassed and switching to a more businesslike tone. "Actually, I'm down here working on a story."

"You have time to come up to my office?"

"What do you think?" she asked, love and desire radiating from her bright eyes. "Hal, I'd like to talk to you another time, if that's alright?"

"I'll certainly be here for you, lovely lady," Hal called, smiling as Dom walked on toward the Morton and Farber building. "You're a lucky man, Salem. Very lucky," he noted.

Trin clapped Hal's shoulder. "I know," he said, and followed his wife.

"Didn't you have enough of me this morning?" Dominique asked, already unbuttoning her cream-colored satin blouse.

Trin closed and locked the heavy mahogany office doors. "Never," he replied, tugging his tie loose as he closed the distance between his wife and himself.

Dom's blouse hit the floor just as Trin pulled her close. His big hands moved to the simple yet provocative black cotton bra she wore. He unhooked it as Dominique tugged his shirt from the waistband of his trousers. Trin cupped her full breasts in his palms and leaned forward to nibble at her earlobe. Dom shivered, her hands moving to caress his cheek before testing the softness of his dark close-cut hair. She rubbed her fingers through the gorgeous silky curls and shivered when he massaged her back.

In a matter of seconds, it seemed, Trin had removed the skirt and was sweeping her into his arms. Dominique pulled the tie from his collar and tossed it to the floor. The stylish black suit jacket followed.

"Mmm . . . is this what goes on in the office of the CEO?" she teased as he carried her across the plush office.

Trin lowered her to a long, cushiony pearl-gray sofa. "It is when I'm in here with you," he admitted, his dark gaze steady and intense.

"Ooooh . . ." Dom cooed, slowly undoing the row of buttons along his shirt. When the material parted, she eased her hands inside to splay them across his wide, muscular chest. She encircled his lean waist and pulled him closer.

Trin grunted at the action and cupped Dom's chin in one hand while the other disappeared into the thick, dark curls that bounced over her head. He outlined the curve of her lips with the tip of his tongue, before delving inside to sample the sweetness of her mouth. Dom uttered a low moan when he ended the kiss to trail his sensuous lips down the line of her neck and collarbone. As he dropped tiny, moist kisses across her chest, he unfastened the garters she wore and tugged the black panties off her hips and over her long, shapely legs.

Dom located the impressive length of his manhood and squeezed the hard, throbbing ridge where it rested beneath his trousers. When she moved to undo his pants, his hand folded over hers, urging her to stop.

Trin helped himself to all the delights of his wife's body. His lips suckled and tugged at her firm nipples and then he smoothed them with his tongue. Dominique gasped and squirmed beneath him, arching more of that portion of her anatomy into his mouth. She tried to hold him there, but soon he was moving onward . . . downward. His fevered kisses found the flat plane of her stomach and he spent several seconds exploring her bellybutton.

"Oh," she gasped, her eyes widening slightly when she felt his breath against her femininity. Trin's thumb stroked the extra-sensitive dark petals of her womanhood as he favored her inner thighs with slow open-mouthed kisses. Finally, his tongue delved deeply into her body and he pleasured her shamelessly.

Dominique was almost overwhelmed by the delicious sensations coursing through her. Her throaty cries of pleasure only spurred Trin onward. He pressed her thighs to the sofa and increased the pressure of the scandalous kiss.

Soon, Dom was caught in a rush of orgasmic waves that washed over her and had her gasping Trin's name. While she was in the throes of pleasure, he released himself from the confines of his trousers and boxer shorts. When he thrust into her body, she couldn't even cry out.

Trin lowered his handsome face to the side of her neck and inhaled the soft scent of Red that always clung to her skin. Low sounds resonated from his throat as he lost himself in the feel of her body. He managed to keep his thrusts slow and deep, marvelling in the moisture that engulfed his maleness. Her soft, breathless pleas that he not stop were almost his undoing.

"So, what's this story you're working on?" Trin asked later, while they lounged on the sofa.

Dom, still nude in her husband's arms, turned over and leaned against his chest. "Actually, it involves your friend who owns the newsstand on the corner."

"Hal?" Trin remarked, his long, sleek brows drawing close. "What about him?"

"Your company's trying to force him out of business, that's what."

"I don't believe it. Hell, I'd know, wouldn't I?" Trin argued. "I know Hal would've told me if something were goin' on."

Dom shrugged. "Not really. He probably wouldn't want it to seem like he was using your friendship to save his business. Feel free to ask him yourself. *Or,* you could wait for us to air the story."

Trin uttered a short laugh. "You can't put somethin' like that on TV."

"You're right. We can't put this on TV, until the situation is resolved. Then we can wrap it up with Hal Lymon winning out against the big dogs to retain his livelihood." Dom announced triumphantly.

"This is crazy," Trin whispered, his attractive features radiating amusement. "You people . . ."

Dominique took no offense and cuddled closer to her husband. "I know—sexy, huh?" she teased.

Trin couldn't help but chuckle. "Only you," he assured her, moving to feel her beneath him again.

Much later that day, Trin was wrapping up a meeting with company President Henry Thornton, Chief Operating Officer Jarvis Hamrick, and Chief Financial Officer Gordon Samuels.

"I heard we were trying to get Hal Lymon off his corner," Trin mentioned after the other business had been discussed. "That can't be, since I wasn't informed, right?"

The other three men in the room exchanged quick glances.

"Trin, we know Lymon is a friend," Henry Thornton said, "but I'm sure you'll agree the best interest of the business does come first."

"So, it's true?" Trin replied, disbelief clear in his rough voice. "Hmph. I guess I owe my wife an apology."

"Your wife?" Gordon asked.

"You guys should be expecting some negative press in the next few weeks. WQTZ is airing a human interest piece featuring my friend Hal Lymon," Trin announced as he gathered his things. "Oh, and forcing a man to leave his life's work is not in the best interest of this company. I'll stop any attempts made to run him off that corner," he promised, before leaving the conference room.

Silence filled the room for several seconds. Jarvis Hamrick leaned over and pressed a silver button on the phone that sat on the table.

"Bring me the CEO file," he instructed the person who answered.

"Jarvis . . ." Henry Thornton warned.

"We should've done this a long time ago," Jarvis argued, his deeply tanned, weatherbeaten face holding a guarded look.

"We've revealed enough from that damn file," Henry said.

"Obviously not." Jarvis countered. "Our Mr. Salem is still consorting with people who could expose things we don't want exposed."

Henry was appalled. "She's his wife!"

"She's a reporter," Gordon Samuels reminded him.

"Don't do this, Jarvis."

"It's done, Henry," Gordon decided, running a hand through his graying blonde hair. He reached for the receiver and pressed it to his ear. "Have Trinidad come to my office at five."

Trin was already on his way home. He had left right after his meeting with Thornton, Hamrick and Samuels, eager to get home to Dominique. He had called her office and had been informed that she had left for the day, A soft smile tugged at his mouth and triggered the dimples in his cheeks. He thought about their life together. It was strong, honest, and completely satisfying. Trin was CEO of Morton and Farber, a well-respected and successful financial investment firm. Dominique was riding her own wave of career success as a TV reporter for a local news channel. They enjoyed the perks of their exciting careers, and home life was just as exciting.

Everyone who knew the stunning couple always marvelled at how much in love the two of them seemed. It was no act. Dominque Carver Salem, with her natural curls and wide, light hazel eyes, was deeply in love with her husband. And she meant more to him than his life.

Trin's smile widened when he imagined his wife's reaction to the news that Hal Lymon would be keeping his newsstand.

Trin parked his black 4Runner in the detached garage behind the breathtaking Bedford home. Crossing the patio, he entered the house through the back entrance. He found the house filled with mouthwatering aromas and knew his wife had prepared one of her spectacular meals. He took the stairs two at a time and found Dominique in their bedroom. She was fresh from the shower, judging from the droplets of water on her skin and the wet mass of her dark ringlets.

Trin leaned against the doorjamb and watched her smooth lotion into her skin. He waited until she started on her back, then decided to make his presence known.

Dom gasped when she felt his hands on her skin. "Trindy." She whispered his nickname and happily relinquished her hold on the lotion bottle.

"What's for dinner?" he asked, rubbing the lotion into her flawless dark skin.

"Three-cheese manicotti with parmesean sauce, Caesar salad, rolls, and for dessert, I . . ."

As Dom rattled off the evening's menu, Trin lost interest in the lotion and treated himself to fondling her lovely physical attributes. He smiled when she gasped amid her talking. Her head fell back against his shoulder and he pulled her to sit astride his lap.

"That sounds good," he murmured into her neck. "I got a raging appetite."

"Mmm, I bet," Dom said, tugging the loosened tie from his neck before going to work on his shirt and his belt.

"Will dinner burn?" he asked, once he was as naked as Dom.

"It'll keep until we take a break," she assured him, her arms encircling his neck as he lowered her to the bed.

"I like the way you think, lady."

Dom giggled. "That's why you married me," she whispered, as they began to make love.

"I wrapped up your story," Trin proudly announced later when he set the table while Dom took the meal from the oven.

"Say what?" she called, inspecting the perfect dish of cheesy manicotti. At first, she only listened absently as Trin relayed the events of his meeting earlier that day. By the time he finished, she was watching him with amazement in her eyes.

"You're a hero. You know that, right?" she informed him, her thumbs hooked into the belt of the blue terry robe she wore. ". . . A golden soul in a kingdom full of black hearts," she said, already brainstorming intros for her story. "And Hal already told me that he's got almost two thousand signatures from people who frequent his stand, and that doesn't even include the people who work for Morton and Farber."

Trin tugged on the hem of his gray T-shirt and watched Dom uneasily. "Baby, if you don't mind, could you let the people of the city be the only 'hero' in this thing? I'd rather keep a low profile in this, if you get where I'm coming from."

"I understand. I may have to take a backseat on this as well, since you're involved." Dom sighed, sauntering over to pull him into a hug. Her hands disappeared into the pockets of his saggy blue jeans as she looked up into his gorgeous honey-toned face. "I'm content knowing who the *real* hero is, and I get to see him every day."

"And night," Trin added.

Dom pressed a kiss to the pulse point at his neck. "I could never forget the nights."

"I love you, Domino."

"I love you more."

The two of them swayed to music only they could hear.

After a couple of minutes, the ring of the phone pierced the serenity.

"Don't answer it," Dominique pleaded, arching into Trin's tall, hard frame.

Trin kept her close and didn't appear concerned with the sound. The machine picked up after five rings and the caller began to speak.

". . . Trinidad, this is Gordon Samuels. I apologize for bothering you at home. We tried to catch you before you left. Uh, we need you back here tonight. There's something . . ."

"Damn," Trin growled, as the man continued to speak. "Baby, lemme see what these jokers want." He left the kitchen while she finished setting out the food.

"Now?" Trin barked into the phone after he'd listened to Gordon Samuels repeat himself. "Can't this wait until tomorrow?"

"Sorry Trinidad, we need to handle this tonight."

"Handle what?"

"The sooner you get here, the sooner you'll know. I assure you, it's important."

Trin uttered a savage curse, choosing to speak the expletive right into the receiver. He told Gordon he would be there shortly and slammed down the phone. He massaged his eyes before going back to Dom and slipping his arms around her waist.

"Put mine back in the oven, girl."

Dom rested her head on his chest and sighed. "Can't you eat before you go?"

"I'd love to," Trin said, pressing his face into her curls, "but the sooner I go, the sooner I get back. And you know what happens when I get back?"

Dominque pretended to be confused. "We eat?" she replied.

"And then . . ."

"Hurry back," she ordered, turning in his arms. The soft kiss Trin pressed to her forehead brought a smile to her lips.

"Mmm . . ." he groaned, squeezing Dom closer before he made himself release her.

Dominique blew him a kiss when he turned to wink at her.

The alarm clock buzzed and Dom awoke with a jerk. The dream she'd had was fuzzy, but disturbing. She reached for Trin and realized he wasn't there. From the looks of the bed, he hadn't slept there at all. Concerned, she whipped back the covers and went downstairs to investigate.

Her expression softened when she found him in the kitchen dressed and pouring coffee. By the time his mug was filled, she was right next to him, taking the cup from his hand.

"Yuck. Black," she complained after sipping a bit of the brew. She set the mug back on the counter and stepped behind Trin to ease her arms around his waist and press her cheek against his back.

"What time'd you get back?" she asked, her eyes closed as she enjoyed the scent of his cologne.

"Late," he answered before walking away from the counter to take a seat at the table.

"Everything work out at the office?" Dom asked, selecting her own mug from an overhead cabinet. When Trin offered no response, she turned. "Trindy?"

"What?"

The sharp reply caused Dom to frown and she strolled over to the table. "Did something happen at work?"

"Why?"

Dom uttered a short laugh. "Because it's obvious something's wrong. You were in a great mood when you left here last night."

Instead of responding, Trin pushed his chair away from the table and went to dash the remainder of his coffee into the sink. When he brushed past Dominique, she caught his hand and tugged until he turned.

"Can I have my kiss?" she asked in a tiny voice.

"I need to go." Trin answered. He seemed to stiffen as he spoke.

Dom dropped his hand and watched as he walked out of the kitchen. Alone there, she leaned against the counter, her striking eyes focused on the doorway.

Trin's mood worsened as the day progressed. It took only a few hours for word to spread around the office. No one bothered the CEO unless it was by e-mail. By lunch time, the office blinds were drawn and Trin was lounging back on his sofa. He was far from relaxed, though. His pitch-black eyes stared unseeingly into the dim office as he recalled the events of the night before. His entire life had been turned inside out after the conversation that had taken place in the COO's office.

What James Hamrick had revealed shocked him to his soul. As the words replayed in his mind, Trin's hand clenched and he slammed the fist against his palm. The sound vibrated throughout the room.

"Good afternoon, Mary. Is it okay for me to disturb Trin?"

Trin's executive assistant, Mary Hills, managed a weary smile for her boss's wife. "Your husband is in one evil mood," the lovely woman announced, appearing to shudder as she spoke. "I have seen him brooding many times, but never anything like this."

Dom scratched her brow and grimaced. "Yeah, I know. Um, do you know what happened? He was fine when he left home last night."

Mary shook her head. "I have no idea, but he hasn't set foot outside that office since he got here. Anyone who's gone in there has left looking like they just had a meeting with the devil himself."

"Lord," Dom breathed, "after his meeting here last night, he seems like a completely changed man."

"A meeting?" Mary inquired, already scanning her appointment calendar.

"It sounded like something sudden," Dom shared.

"Hmm . . ." Mary calmly noted, though her expression appeared a bit troubled.

"Well, I guess I'll try to get through to him again." Dom sighed, pulling a turquoise linen wrap from her shoulders.

"Be careful," Mary teased.

Dom whispered a quick thank-you and headed toward the office. She knocked softly before pressing against the silver lever.

"Trindy?" she called, receiving no answer. She frowned at the darkness. Once her eyes adjusted she saw Trin sprawled on the sofa.

"Baby, what in the world is going on with you?" She tossed her purse and wrap onto one of the coordinating armchairs and turned on one of the lamps next to the sofa.

Trin frowned at the sudden intrusion of light. Eventually his dark gaze softened as it followed the outline of Dom's bottom against the snug-fitting turquoise pants she sported.

Dominique took a seat on the edge of the sofa and cupped his face in her hands. "Baby, what is it?" she whispered.

Trin's mood returned full force. "Get out of here," he grumbled, and jerked away from her touch.

Dominique gasped and watched him leave the sofa. "Look Trin, I'm sorry if you had a bad meeting or something, but that's no reason to take it out on me."

"You don't want to be around me right now, Dominique," he warned, his back toward her.

"What did I do?" she asked, knowing his anger was directed at her. Trin never used her full name unless he was upset with her. "I mean, yesterday was incredible," she recalled when he offered no reply to her question, "we made love several times—"

"Dominique—"

"We were going to have a great dinner and probably make love again," she continued, walking closer to him. "Sweetie, what happened?" She smoothed her hands against his light gray shirt.

"Dammit, why didn't you tell me?" Trin roared as he whirled around and caught her arms in a vicelike hold.

"Tell you what?" Dom asked, her voice a frantic whisper as she viewed the unmasked anger in his black eyes.

Trin's fingers massaged the soft white cotton sleeves of Dom's top before he released her and bolted from the office.

Dom pulled a shaking hand through her thick curls as she took a seat on the edge of Trin's desk. Soon, her entire body was shaking.

TWO

Dominique was inspecting herself in the full length mirror that evening. She was only in her underthings and didn't like the twist of one of her coffee-colored hose. She bent to fix it and when she looked into the mirror again, she saw Trin standing in the doorway. She hadn't seen or talked to him since the scene in his office earlier that day. She couldn't tell whether the set look on his face was one of anger, desire, or a mixture of both.

After a moment, Trin pushed himself from the doorjamb and stepped into the room with both hands hidden in his pockets. His dark eyes left her to slide over the bed where a gorgeous chocolate strapless evening gown lay. Without breaking his stride, he went to the closet and selected a black tux, which he placed next to her dress. His gaze swept Dom's half-clothed body. It lingered on the portion of her breasts that seemed to spill from the cups of the strapless, lacy, cocoa-colored bra.

"I'm goin' to take a quick shower before we leave."

Dom glanced at the stylish tux and turned back to Trin. "You're going?" she blurted.

"Didn't you ask me to?" he replied, sending her a scathing look.

Dom was so flustered, she grew hot all over. "I—I just thought . . ."

Trin offered no response and headed for the bathroom. He let the door slam behind him.

* * *

The rented banquet room at the Waldorf was filled with WQTZ personnel and their guests. The station was celebrating an excellence award received by the sports team. Everyone was having an incredible time. Everyone except Dominique, who was still trying to make some sense of the sudden change in her husband's mood. Trin appeared to be having a fine time as he mingled and joked with members of the sports crew whom he knew through his wife.

Dom blinked and finally tuned into Marshall Greene's voice. The news manager had apparently been calling her for a while and eventually had resorted to snapping his fingers in front of her face.

"I'm sorry, Marshall. What were you saying?"

"I want you on this story."

"Right."

"I really think these guys will open up to you. They're a bunch of chauvinists, but surprisingly, they'll talk business with a woman. Especially one who looks like you. That doesn't offend you, does it? Dom?"

"Huh?" she absently replied, her dazzling champagne gaze focused on Trin. He hadn't looked her way or spoken to her once since they'd left the house.

"Baby, are you okay?"

"What? Oh, Marshall, I'm sorry. Yes, I'm fine." She assured him, patting her hand against his dark, bearded face. "I think I need to get some fresh air, though. Could we talk about this tomorrow?"

Marshall pressed a kiss to her cheek. "No problem."

As Dom left the party to retreat to a quiet balcony, Trin's dark eyes followed her every move.

Much later, Dom's spirits seemed greatly improved. A few of her male colleagues found her out on the balcony and decided to keep her company. Soon, they had her talking and

laughing hysterically. Trin ventured outside around that time
and his expression softened at the sound of her laughter. Then
the anger returned and the hard expression with it. When the
guys left, he stepped out onto the balcony.

"Let's go."

Dom looked up to see her husband a few feet away.
"Now?" she replied, laughter still tingeing her voice.

Trin reached into his pocket for the keys to his SUV. "Stay
as long as you want, but I'm leaving."

"Why are you doing this?" she blurted, her uneasiness
returning.

"There a problem with me wanting to leave?"

"You know what I'm talkin' about."

"Don't start, Dominique."

"Start what? This whole thing is because of you, and I'm
sick of it!"

"You—" Trin began, but cut off his words. Instead, he
threw up one hand. He muttered a nasty expletive and walked
off.

Dominique followed. It killed her, walking through the
party and forcing herself to look happy. Trin, on the other
hand, didn't appear to have a problem at all. They both
laughed at a suggestive comment someone made about their
early departure. Once the banquet room's door closed behind
them the laughter died.

Trinidad Maxwell Salem had always been a gentleman in
the truest sense of the word. He opened doors, pulled out
chairs, and was the most attentive man Dom had ever met.
Now that persona had vanished. When they arrived in the
parking lot, he walked on ahead and settled behind the wheel
of the rugged sport utility. The moment Dom shut the door,
he sped out into the street with the music blasting.

As the CD changed, the silence gave Trin the chance to
hear soft sobs coming from the passenger side of the
4Runner. His onyx stare narrowed and he glanced at Dom,
who kept her face turned toward the window. His heart
slammed against his chest and he winced, knowing she was

hurt and confused. He just couldn't bring himself to talk about what he had learned. Whenever he entertained the thought, a murderous rage welled up inside him.

When Trin parked the car in the front driveway, Dom quickly got out. He still arrived at the front door before she did, keys in hand. He unlocked the door and even held it for her. Dom stepped in slowly and Trin followed. The sound of his keys hitting the dish just inside the foyer seemed to vibrate in the silent house.

Trin strolled into the den while Dom headed toward the stairway. Before she took the first step, she stopped and decided to try once more. She found Trin in the den, standing behind the polished pine bar. He downed three shots of liquor as she walked closer to the bar and waited for him to acknowledge her. He only slammed the glass to the counter and walked away.

"Trin—"

"Don't."

Dom pressed one hand to the bodice of her shimmery cocoa-colored gown. "Trin, what in the world have I done? Why are you treating me like this?"

"I can't talk about it."

"You can't talk about it? Is it that bad?" she asked, almost jumping at the hateful look he sent her. Despite that, she went to stand right before him. "If you want to act this way, that's fine. But, at least tell me why. At least show me that much respect."

"Respect?" Trin snapped. If possible, he looked even more murderous. "Is it respectful to keep secrets from your husband, Dominique?"

"What secrets? What are you talking about?"

"You have no idea?"

"Would I be asking you if I did?"

Trin stepped closer, using his height advantage to glare down at her. "In the four years we've been married, you've told me everything?" he asked, sounding as though he already had the answer. "You've never kept any secrets from me? Nothing?"

"No, Trin. I've always been honest with you," Dominique whispered fiercely, her bright gaze sparkling with tears.

Trin only shook his head, his dark eyes appearing to smolder with hate. "Lyin' bitch," he muttered.

Dom landed a quick, loud slap to his face. A split second later, Trin's fist rose. It loomed in the air, but he did not strike her. Dominique's eyes widened and she looked at him as though he were a stranger. A moment later, she ran from the den.

Over the next few weeks, things between the Salems grew worse. There were nights when Trin didn't bother to come home. When they did share the same bed, Dom was so on edge, she had to go to the guest room in order to get to sleep. Things became so tense, she began talking with Trin's first cousin, Arthur Cule. The two men were as close as brothers and Dominique hoped he would be able to tell her something.

Unfortunately, Arthur had no idea anything was wrong between the strongest couple he knew. Still, he offered Dom a sympathetic ear and it was greatly appreciated.

"Where'd you have lunch yesterday?" Trin asked one morning when they were both in the kitchen.

Dom almost dropped her coffee mug, since her husband had said nothing to her in weeks. "Lunch?" she whispered.

"Yes. Yesterday. You *did* have lunch yesterday?"

"Yeah."

"Where?"

"Trin—"

"Is it something you feel you need to hide?"

"No," Dom snapped, setting her mug on the counter with more force than necessary. "But it sounds like you already have the answers to these questions. I think you know where I had lunch and who I had it with."

"Don't go behind my back, Dominique. You keep Arthur out of this," he ordered, slicing the air with his index finger.

"Who the hell do you think you are, ordering me around like this? I'm trying to get answers about why you've changed. God, Trin, it's like I don't even know you any—"

"I said keep him out of this," Trin whispered, his hand loosely cupping her elbow. His slanting gaze filled with sinister intent.

Dominique tried not to react. Trin released her, his hard expression fading when she turned away. He reached out to console her, but clenched a fist before he could touch her.

"Don't forget dinner tonight," he told her instead, checking for his cell phone inside his jacket pocket.

"I'm not going," Dom replied in a hollow voice. Her back was still turned toward him.

"We need to be there by seven," Trin went on, ignoring her decline of an evening out with the executive staff of Morton and Farber.

"Are you deaf, Trin? I said I won't be there."

Trin slipped his arm around her waist and pulled her back against his chest. "If I have to suffer through evenings with your cackling colleagues, I damn well expect you to return the favor."

"I'll have to met you there," Dom said after he let her go.

"Fine," was his last word before he left the kitchen.

When the front door slammed behind him, Dom allowed herself to cry.

"Hey. You got a minute?"

"I'll make time for you," Marshall replied when he saw Dom leaning against the doorjamb. "What's up?" he asked, when she closed his office door.

"I need to take a leave of absence."

Marshall's heavy brows rose. "A leave? What's wrong?"

Dom raised her hands and walked farther into the room. "Nothing, nothing—I just need some time, that's all."

"For what? Honey, I know you haven't been yourself for a while now, and you're not making any sense here. I can tell something's upsetting you."

"Yes! All these damn questions are upsetting me!" Dom snapped, raking her fingers through her curly locks. "Listen, Marshall, I need this time. I haven't been feeling that well lately. I think it might be fatigue or something. Look, I'm begging you for this. If you won't approve, then I'll just turn in my resignation."

"Whoa, whoa," Marshall soothed, rushing across the room to take her hands in his. "Baby, don't even joke about that. I couldn't stand to lose you. You take all the time you need."

"Thank you," she whispered, closing her eyes resignedly.

"Honey, is everything alright with you and Trin?" he asked, the tone of his voice signifying that he already knew the answer.

Dom tried to nod, but broke into tears. She accepted Marshall's hug when he pulled her close.

"You okay, Dominique?" Jessica Rogers, Dom's assistant, asked, frowning as she handed Dom a pink message slip.

"If one more person asks me that, I think I'll scream," Dom told her, heading into her office to return the call.

"Arthur Cule," said a deep voice.

"Hey, it's me."

"Are you alright?"

"Nothing's changed." Dominique sighed, resting her head back against her white leather desk chair, "But your cousin has forbidden me to talk to you."

"Why?"

"Apparently he saw us having lunch together and he correctly assumed that we were discussing him."

"Damn." Arthur groaned. "Why the hell is he actin' so foolish?"

"Your guess is as good as mine. I mean, he keeps accusing me of keeping something from him and I've never—"

"Dom? What is it?" Arthur asked, when she suddenly stopped talking.

"Can't be . . ." Dom whispered.

"What? . . . Dom?"

"Arthur, listen, um . . . I've gotta go . . . see Spry," she said, sounding as though she were speaking to herself.

"Spry? What do you need to see my brother for? Dom, what—"

"Arthur, I have to go. But please don't tell Trin we talked. I'll call you," she promised, then hung up the phone. She braced her elbows on the polished oak desk and pressed her hands to her hot cheeks. "Lord, please, please, let me be wrong about this."

Despite her terrible day, Dom arrived at the dinner looking beautiful as usual. She wore a cream-colored dress with a flaring hemline that flattered her long, shapely legs. The sleeves fit her wrists tightly and the front dipped into a low V cut. She spent several minutes mingling and managed to appear confident and happy. She saw Trin and headed over to greet the group he was speaking with. When Trin pulled her close to kiss her cheek, he could feel her trembling. He lingered close to her longer than he had intended.

Dom managed to carry on the farce through the end of dinner. Just before coffee and drinks were served, she excused herself. When she didn't return, Trin said his good-nights and headed home. Sure enough, he found his wife's car in the driveway. Upstairs, he received a shock when he found her packing.

"Where are you going?"

"I have to get out of here," she answered, haphazardly tossing articles of clothing into a huge Louis Vuiton case. "It's a story. Marshall needs me on it right away."

Despite the cold way he had treated her, Trin could not handle Dom leaving, even if it was business related. He walked over to the bed and snatched a blouse from her hand.

"You think I'll just let you walk out?" he asked, his black eyes practically spewing daggers.

"Let me walk out? I'd expect you to be flipping cartwheels over the fact that I'm going. Over the last two months, you've treated me like I don't even matter to you! You have been mean, nasty, and hurtful. My God, can you blame me for leaving?!"

Trin pushed the heavy case to the floor with little more than a flick of his wrist. "So is it business or not?"

"I said it was, didn't I? Besides, I think we both need some time apart. Maybe you'll be off your period by the time I get back!" she spat, her bright eyes flashing with anger.

Trin shook his head, the muscle in his jaw twitching frantically. "You can't begin to know how angry I am."

"I'm angry too. So what?"

"Don't push me, Dominique."

"Why not? Why don't you just say it? Why don't you just stop this childish crap and tell me why you're acting like such a jackass!"

"You shut your mouth!"

"Or what?" she bellowed, unmindful of the evil glare from her husband.

"Tell me about Spry," he finally replied, waiting for her reaction.

Dom blinked. "You *do* know," she whispered.

"You lied to me."

"I didn't—"

"And you deny it still?" Trin snapped, pulling her even closer. "You little—"

"Trin, wait—"

"Shut up!" he roared.

Dom wrenched herself from his grasp and began to back away. Trin looked half crazed with anger as he stalked her.

"Four years . . ." Trin whispered, his steps slowing when he took notice of the fear in her eyes. "You kept quiet for four years," he repeated, his raspy voice gaining volume.

Dom blinked away the tears that were beginning to moisten her lashes. "Trin, if you just let me tell you why—"

"Why?" He snapped, his dark gaze hate-filled as he glared toward her. "I already know why," he decided, turning away to rub the back of his hand across his own tearing eyes. "You didn't tell me, because you enjoyed playin' me for a fool."

"Trin, no, no I never—"

"Didn't you, Dominique?" He raged.

Dom's breathing was shuddery and she felt dizzy as her blood pressure spiraled upward. "Will you please just calm down so we can discuss this?"

"Discuss what? Discuss what a lyin' bitch you are?"

"Trin—"

"Or maybe we can discuss how good you must feel knowing you've had two men from the same family?"

Dom was crying heavily now. She balled a fist to her mouth, but that did nothing to calm her.

Trin rolled his eyes, muttering something profane as he stormed over to where he had thrown the suitcase. "I think you had the right idea all along."

"What?" She whispered, swallowing down a sob as she watched him sling the case on top of the bed. "What are you doing?"

"Helping you pack so you can get the hell out." He grumbled, tossing everything back into the huge suitcase.

"Trin . . ." she called, when he went to her bureau and took out an armload of clothes which he also threw into the case.

"I want you to go enjoy my cousin or handle your station business or whatever the hell you're goin' to do." He softly commanded, shoving clothes into the case like a madman. "Don't worry, you'll get the house." He said, when he finally turned to look at her.

Dominique went still. "What do you mean? Trin?"

"This shit is a lie," he grated, heading towards Dom's closet. "Our marriage is a lie—"

"No, Trin."

"No? You've been lying to me since the day you discovered that jackass was my cousin."

"But I love you. I've always loved you."

The simple, softly spoken admission seemed to double Trin's anger.

"Mmm hmm," he grunted, pushing against the top of the suitcase in an attempt to close it. "I want a divorce," he said, as though it were an ordinary request.

"Trin, just let me talk to you." Dom pleaded, desperate to stop what was happening. She hugged his arm, closing her eyes as she squeezed.

"Get off me." He ordered, still trying to close the case. "Dominique." He urged, wrenching his arm from her grasp.

Dom had no intentions of listening and moved towards him again.

"I said, get off!" he blasted, pulling his arm away just as her fingers brushed his shirt sleeve.

The sudden movement caught Dom off guard and she lost her footing. She stumbled and landed against the nearby oak message table. Trin turned, his eyes wide with concern. He quickly masked the emotion, when Dom stood straight and appeared unharmed. He turned back to the case, his fists pounding against the top, until it closed over the protruding clothes.

"You're all set," he announced, taking the case and hurtling it toward the bedroom door.

Dom tried to speak, but the simple act was impossible. Her sobs now resembled loud wails and she could barely see her husband through the water pooling her hazel eyes.

"Get out."

"Tr-Trin, please, please wait—"

"Get out of here. Please, Domino," he whispered, his tone sounding less angry and more advisory. "You have a plane to catch," he said, turning to fix her with a weary stare, "I'm asking you to go, Domino. Now, please. Before I do something I know I'll surely regret."

Dominique stifled her crying, taking heed to his warning. Sniffling madly, she collected her things and left her home.

Three

The elegantly furnished cream-and-gold room was maddeningly quiet except for an ocassional sniffle or soft sob. The large group of people who had gathered watched the tall, handsome young man who began to rise from his place at the front of the room.

For a moment, Trinidad Salem braced himself against the plush, high-backed chair, then he stood. The short walk from his seat to the imposing mahogany stand seemed to take forever. Briefly, Trin let his long black lashes close over his slanting dark eyes. He willed himself not to faint. Clearing his throat, he looked across the sea of people who filled the lovely room in the Adams Funeral Home.

"Um . . . Uh, I wanna . . . want to thank you all for bein' here today," he managed. It was impossible to mistake the pain filling his deep, raspy voice.

"It would've meant a lot to . . ." He tried to say more, but words failed him. They were replaced by the sob rising in his throat. Trin balled a huge fist to his mouth and leaned over the podium.

Martika Salem moved from her seat and hurried to her son's side. Concern was clear in her lovely brown eyes as she watched Trin struggle to maintain his stoic demeanor.

"Dominique would've appreciated you all being here today," Martika said, finishing the statement her only child was unable to complete. "I'm sure I can speak for everyone when I say we'll miss her very much."

Trin wasn't sure how much longer he could hold his emotions in check. It wasn't long before he rushed from behind the podium, leaving through a side door near the back of the room.

Berta Millings approached Martika a few moments later and patted the woman's shoulder. "Sweetie, it was a lovely service," she said as people began to file out of the room.

"Thank you, Bertie," Martika replied, offering a weary smile to her fellow choir member. "I tell you, though, I never thought I'd outlive my daughter-in-law."

Berta simply nodded and pulled her friend into a close hug. When she left, Hamp and Phyllis Carver, Trin's in-laws, walked over.

"How are *you* holding up?" Phyllis asked as she pressed a tissue to the corner of her eye.

Martika shrugged. "No better than you, honey. Hamp?"

"I still can't believe we just had a memorial service for my baby," Hamp whispered, pressing strong fingers to the bridge of his nose.

Phyllis walked over to her husband and stroked the side of his smooth, dark face. In minutes, the three friends were embracing one another. More than a few people approached them to express sympathy for their loss. Martika, Phyllis, and Hamp all managed to hold it together, though a part of them had died with Dominique.

"Is Trin going to be okay?" Delores Fairing asked when she approached the threesome with her daughter and mother-in-law.

Martika closed her eyes briefly, then nodded. "He'll be fine. He just needs a little time."

Fanny Fairing leaned forward and patted Martika's hand. "Well, tell him we're praying for him," she said, then squeezed Hamp and Phyllis's arms before walking away with her daughter-in-law.

The Carvers and Marika Salem wanted to assure everyone that Trinidad would be fine. Unfortunately, even they were quite uncertain.

"We're gonna have to keep that boy from fallin' apart," Hamp said, rubbing a hand across his balding head.

Martika looked toward the door Trin had exited almost twenty minutes earlier. "I don't think my boy will ever be the same," she admitted with a quiet sigh.

Trin shut off the water faucet and took a few more deep breaths. He wanted to put in another appearance at the service, even if it was only for a few minutes. Sadly, that small feat was proving difficult to accomplish. Slowly, he raised his head to stare at himself in the lighted mirror that overlooked the gray and black marble sinks in the men's washroom. With a grimace, he shook his head at his own image. The flawless honey-toned complexion was complimented by pitch-black wavy hair, long sleek brows, slanting onyx eyes, and a wide sensual mouth graced by a pair of deep dimples. At the moment, however, Trin wasn't at all impressed by what he saw in the mirror.

"Damn!" he whispered, squeezing his eyes closed and cursing himself when tears streamed down his cheeks. He knew crying could not be avoided, though. Not that day, maybe not for a long time. He turned and leaned his tall, lean frame against the sink. He didn't know if he would ever get used to the idea of not seeing Dominique again. After almost four years of marriage . . . she was gone forever. That reality left him with a painful, raw feeling inside. That feeling was intensified when he remembered the way he had treated her. He had treated her so horribly . . .

Trin ran one hand over his face as he conjured up the image of his wife. There was a familiar tightening in his chest when he thought about his "Domino." Her long legs, her sexy, voluptuous body and enchanting dark face had captured him from the moment they met. Now, he would never see her again. After their awful fight, Dom had rushed out of the house, determined to get away from her husband. Unfortunately, the plane she boarded crashed halfway to its destination. From all reports, over half the lives on board had been lost. The news rendered Trin emotionally paralyzed for weeks and he wouldn't accept that it was true. He prayed she would be found among the survivors, but that hadn't happened.

Trin knew he would curse himself for the rest of his life. He would curse himself for letting anger and jealousy ruin the best thing he had ever known. He would curse himself for not having the chance to tell Dom how very sorry he was for the way he had treated her.

With a quick shake of his head, Trin dried his eyes and ordered himself out of the washroom. Out front, where the service was held, it seemed everyone had made their way out. Trin relished the solitude, pushing his hands into his black trouser pockets and pacing the room with his head bowed.

Trin's friend Terrance Adams had been locking up after the memorial service and found Trin in the empty room. Concerned, he headed over.

"Hey, man," Terrance called, clapping Trin softly on the back. "You gonna be okay?"

Trin wiped the back of his hand across his eyes. "No," he admitted. "But I'll make it . . . thanks for the service."

Terrance shook Trin's hand. "Save it, man. I loved Dom like a sister. I just hate that she needed me for this."

Trin bowed his head and ran one hand across the back of his neck. "I don't know if I can do this, Terry."

Terrance waved his hand lightly in the air. "Now, Dom wouldn't want you mournin' forever. It's gonna take a while, man, but you'll make it."

A skeptical look rose in the midnight depths of Trin's eyes, but he appreciated Terrance's optimism. The two friends talked a few minutes longer, then Terrance left Trin alone in the room with his memories.

Walking slowly back across the room, Trin stopped at the altar and picked up the picture of Dom. His gaze was intense as he studied the picture. He ran his strong fingers across the glass, tracing Dom's lovely dark face and imagining he was actually touching her.

"We're gonna really miss her," a low voice spoke up behind him.

Trin turned quickly upon hearing Marshall Greene's voice. Dominique's news manager at WQTZ was one of the many people from the station who had attended the service. A hard look fell across Trin's face as he watched the short, dark-complected man walk closer. Trin's hand tightened around the picture frame and his long dark lashes actually fluttered slightly as he struggled to control his temper. Since Dom had taken her trip for business reasons, he held Marshall and everyone at the station responsible for her death.

"I still can't believe she's gone," Marshall was saying, not noticing the drawn look on Trin's face. "If Peaches or I can do anything, man, just let us know."

At the thoughtful offer, Trin lost his temper. He dropped Dominique's picture on the stone steps of the altar and grabbed the lapels of Marshall's suit coat.

"Anything you can do? *Anything?*" Trin practically snarled, bringing his face close to Marshall's. "How 'bout bringing my wife back to me? What about that. Can you give Domino back to me?"

Marshall's eyes widened at Trin's outburst. Still, he tried a calm approach. "I understand how you feel, man, but—"

"You understand? Forget you, Marshall! If it hadn't been for you sendin' her off on the damn trip, we wouldn't be standin' in this funeral home havin' a memorial service for her!"

Marshall visibly cringed at the raspy baritone sound of Trin's voice. "Trin, listen—"

"Forget it! You and that stupid-ass television station. I hold personally responsible for all this shit."

Marshall sent Trin a rueful smile. "I wasn't the one operating the plane, man."

Trin jerked Marshall even closer and prepared to throw him across the room.

"Trin, hold it!" Marshall called, his hands raised defensively. "Now, I know you're in a lot of pain right now, but you're forgettin' something," he said, his small black eyes growing wider.

Trin's heavy dark brows drew close. "Forgetting what?"

"Didn't you know I gave Dom time off? I never knew anything about this trip of hers. I gave her the time because she said she wasn't feeling well."

As the words sank in, Trin slowly loosened his grip on Marshall's jacket. Yes, Dom had been given time off because of illness. At least that was the excuse she had given Marshall. Trin, of course, knew what the real problem had been.

Shaking away the disturbing thoughts, Trin took several steps away from Marshall. "Sorry, man," he said.

Marshall held up one trembling hand and shook his head. "I understand. Just know that the trip Dominique took had nothing to do with any station business."

Trin nodded slowly while turning his back toward Marshall. After a moment, his slanting onyx gaze shifted to the floor. His heart pounded harshly as he stared at Dominique's framed picture lying broken on the altar steps.

Martika Salem lived in a large beautiful brick home in a quiet Long Island neighborhood. After the memorial service, she asked family and a few friends to the house for lunch.

Trin wasn't in any mood to attend anything remotely social. He attended anyway to keep his mother from worrying. After speaking to Martika and talking with Dom's parents, he grabbed a bottle of liquor from the dining room bar and retreated to the upstairs den.

The warmly furnished den was decorated in mocha and beige. The place had a cozy aura that was immediately relaxing. Trin had no complaints about his surroundings, though he knew that loneliness, a bottle of Hennessy, and Sade playing on the CD player could do nothing to improve his mood. Still, that was the least important thing in the world to him just then—he had lost everything.

Ever since Trin left Adams Funeral Home, he had felt more

dazed than he had before he arrived. Marshall Greene's words replayed themselves over and over again in his mind. *Dom's trip had nothing to do with any station business.* Then where was she going, and why?

Much later, there was a knock on the den door. When Trin didn't answer, Arthur Cule opened the door and stuck his head inside. He saw his cousin sprawled across the long chocolate sofa in the corner and a smile crossed his handsome face. Arthur and Trin had been extremely close since childhood. The two were often mistaken for brothers in light of their striking resemblance. The only real difference was their the color of their eyes. Arthur's were a deep warm brown, while Trin's were a more penetrating black. Arthur shared Trin's sorrow over Dominique's death and was determined to be there for him. Whether Trin wanted him there or not.

Arthur stared down at Trin for a moment, then shook his head. He pulled the half-empty liquor bottle from the crook of his cousin's arm.

"What the hell are you doin'?" Trin slurred, his eyes opening to narrow slits.

"You don't need this crap, man," Arthur told him, setting the bottle on the mahogany desk across the room.

Trin sighed and pushed himself up on the sofa. "I don't need you tellin' me that."

Arthur turned and leaned against the desk. "Aunt Tika sent me to get you for dinner."

"Not hungry."

"She told me not to come back without you."

Trin toyed with the wavy swirls of hair atop his head. "I'm fine," he insisted.

"Yeah, you look fine," Arthur sarcastically retorted.

"Forget you, Arthur," Trin grated, his raspy voice filling the room.

"Look, man, I won't stand here and act like I know what you're goin' through."

"Good."

Arthur sighed and walked closer to Trin. "But I know how I'd feel if I lost someone I loved as much as you loved Dom. Now, I wanna be here for you and so does everybody downstairs."

Trin rested his head back against the couch and stared up at the ceiling. "I want to blame somebody for this. Somebody besides myself."

Arthur took a seat in a cushioned armchair next to the sofa. "We all do. And there's no reason for you to blame yourself, either."

Trin shook his head, silently telling his cousin how wrong he was about that. "Hmph, I thought I had somebody to blame," he finally admitted.

"'Scuse me?"

Trin propped his elbow on the back of the sofa and traced the long line of his eyebrow. "I thought Domino was leaving for a business trip for the station."

Arthur nodded slowly. "I see."

"No, you don't. I saw Marshall, her station manager, at the funeral home and he told me that he had given her time off. The trip had nothing to do with business."

A confused frown crept over Arthur's handsome face as he listened. "Uh, man, didn't she . . ."

Trin looked toward his cousin. "Didn't she what?"

Arthur realized his mistake and thought it was best that he not get involved in the situation. Unfortunately, he had already peaked his cousin's interest.

"Didn't she what, Arthur?" Trin asked again.

"Nothin'," Arthur said, leaving his chair and heading for the den door. Before he could touch the knob, Trin caught him and jerked him around.

"Didn't she what?" Trin insisted, his voice sounding rough as sandpaper.

"Man, I don't think I need to be gettin' into this."

Trin trained his onyx gaze on the plush gray carpet.

"Arthur, man, if you know somethin' I want you to tell me. Whatever it is."

"What difference will it make at this point?" Arthur reasoned.

"Exactly," Trin replied. "She's gone, so spill it."

Arthur sent a pointed look toward Trin's hands, which were clasped around the lapels of Arthur's suit jacket. Trin removed his hands and waited.

"Dom told me that she was going to see Spry. She also told me you had forbidden her to speak to me, but I assumed she had told you about taking the trip. It sounded like something heavy."

If possible, the murderous frown on Trin's face grew even deadlier. "What the hell do you mean she went to see Spry?"

"Just what I said."

"What the hell for?"

Arthur shrugged and walked away from the door. "She was very close-mouthed about it, almost as though she were speaking to herself about the whole thing. She was talking about your attitude, when all of a sudden she stopped, and the next thing I knew she's saying she needed to go see Spry."

Trin ran both hands over his head, then clenched them into huge fists. *Lord, as if I need another reason for hating that man,* he thought. Spencer Cule, or Spry as he was called, had always been thought of as the black sheep of the family. Trin and his cousin had never gotten along and it seemed they never would. Recently, Trin had discovered he had yet another reason to hate the man. That, compounded with the fact that Dom had gotten on a plane to see him, only increased Trin's bitter hatred of his first cousin.

"I don't believe this," he breathed, his black gaze narrowing sharply.

"Now you see why I didn't want to tell you?" Arthur asked from his spot across the room.

"Damn him."

"Trin—"

"Arthur, why did she have to get on that plane to see him? She could be here now," Trin lamented.

Arthur gave a short laugh. "Man, I'm sure she didn't know the plane was going to crash."

Trin shook his head. "It doesn't make sense. Hell, she could've called him! Why'd she have to leave like that," he cried, trying to ignore the panic and guilt in his voice.

Arthur shook his head, the look in his brown eyes revealing that he knew a lot more than he was saying. Now, however, was not the time to reveal it. There would probably never be a time.

Chicago, Illinois

Dr. Aaron Tirelli's coffee mug made a quiet click when he set it on the bedside table. He leaned back in his chair, his light brown gaze softening even more as he looked toward the bed in the center of the room. The woman lying there was undeniably beautiful. Her features, relaxed in sleep, and the curly hair that framed her stunning dark face gave her the look of an angel.

She was a mystery to him. A complete mystery. Two weeks earlier, she had been brought in by dockworkers tending a recently arrived ship. It seemed they had found the unconscious woman on the dock, with no idea of how she got there.

At first, Aaron and his colleagues speculated she may have been one of the passengers from the recent plane crash. Everyone, with the exception of Aaron, thought that theory was too far-fetched, given the fact that she had been found on the docks—far away from any wreckage. Since she had no identification, they decided she had probably been the victim of a mugging.

The lovely mystery lady had been unconscious for weeks, but besides that, she had no visible cuts or abrasions. That also served to negate the theory that she had been involved in the crash. There was one small thing that had caught Aaron's attention, though. The woman's otherwise flawless dark skin was slightly marred by a fading bruise toward the small of her back. It could have been the result of being thrown with great force during a crash.

A soft knock on the bedroom door interrupted Aaron's thoughts. He looked up and saw another beautiful woman enter the room. The caramel-complexioned lady stood there waving a finger at him.

Dr. Belinda Tirelli took a few steps inside the room until she was standing next to her husband's chair. She leaned down and pressed a kiss to the top of his head.

"Word is that you're caught up over another woman," she whispered in his ear.

Aaron smiled and pulled his wife into his lap. He tugged one of her long braids and pulled her into a deep kiss. "If the other woman is you, then I happily confess," he whispered.

Belinda tweaked Aaron's nose and hugged him. "I missed you."

"How was the trip?" Aaron asked, loving the feel of being held in her arms.

"It was unbelievable, baby. Though that may've had something to do with where it was held." Belinda had attended a two-week medical conference in Montego Bay.

Aaron pulled away from his wife and let his cocoa eyes travel over the front of her close-fitting T-shirt. "I'll bet every man there enjoyed all those bikinis you bought."

Belinda pretended to be shocked and poked her husband's wide shoulder. "Shame on you," she scolded.

"Shame, hell." Aaron quietly responded. "I'll bet their eyes and a few other things got a real workout."

Belinda simply shook her head. "You Italians," she complained. "Always got sex on the brain," she complained, though she beamed at the fact that her gorgeous husband found her so sexy.

"Of course," Aaron conceded.

Belinda shook her head again, then her wide black gaze drifted across the room. "So, who is she?"

Aaron's sigh was long and deep. "I have no idea, Bel. All we know is she was found near the Northside docks with no ID and she's been unconscious ever since. I guess I'm so involved because I feel like . . . I know her from somewhere, like I've seen her before."

Belinda leaned back against Aaron's wide chest and frowned. "I heard about some crash a few weeks back. Have y'all looked into that?"

Aaron was already nodding. "It didn't pan out, though I feel we should've probably delved deeper. She does have an ugly bruise on the small of her back, but . . ."

"But what?" Belinda prodded.

"She could've sustained that during a mugging."

"You think she was mugged?"

Aaron shrugged. "Well, she didn't have any ID and they found her on the docks—nowhere near the vicinity of the crash. How else would she have gotten there?"

Belinda gave a weary smile. "I guess we won't know until she wakes up."

After a moment, Belinda eased off Aaron's lap and decided to take a look at the mysterious Jane Doe. After she had gazed into the woman's face for a moment, a look of disbelief crept over her own face.

"Oh my God," she gasped.

Four

The tall, spotless windows in the chic corner office offered a magnificent view of downtown Manhattan. The paneled walls of the room were decorated with paintings by African-American artists as well as classic pictures depicting several events in the civil rights movement. The cream suede sofa in the corner of the room faced a long glass coffee table, and was flanked by two matching armchairs. The huge mahogany desk in front of the windows was cluttered, and the computer screen was blinking that there was e-mail to be opened.

Trin was slumped down in the large chair which was turned to face the windows, but the impressive view was lost on him. His dark gaze appeared blank as he stared out the window. A firm knock sounded on the door, but he was too embedded in his own thoughts to pay any attention to it.

Henry Thornton knocked again, then twisted the polished brass doorknob. He stuck his head inside the door and looked around the office. "Trinidad? You in here?" he called.

"What can I do for you, Henry" Trin called from his chair. His raspy voice sounded low and hollow.

Henry walked farther inside the office and around the desk. When he saw Trin slumped down in the chair, he shook his head. Ever since Henry met the intense young man, he'd known he would go far. Though his colleagues and a few board members wondered if Trin was the best choice for the position of CEO in an old-fashioned firm like Morton and Farber, Henry had never had a doubt. Trin was confident in his abilities and proud of his heritage. He never gave in if it went against his principles, and as a result he had won the respect of those who had doubted him most at the start.

Now, however, Trin had lost one of the things that gave him most, if not all, of his strength. Henry grimaced as he thought back to when Trin heard about the crash. It was like throwing a wrecking ball against a huge brick building. The man seemed to crumble.

"What are you doing here?" he questioned, since it was obvious that Trin was in no mood to be at the office so soon after his loss.

Trin kept his elbow propped on the arm of his chair and leaned his chin on his fist. "I'm working, Henry. Why else would I be here?"

Henry ran one hand through his graying hair. "I figured you wanted to cry over Dominique at work instead of at home."

Trin's dark, slanting gaze was murderous when he turned it on Henry. Still, deep down he knew that the older man was only trying to get him to snap out of his trancelike state. Unfortunately, nothing short of Dom coming back to him would do that.

"Trinidad?" Henry called, still watching Trin with concern in his blue eyes.

Trin pushed himself out of his chair. "Henry, I don't need this right now."

"Then why don't you go home? The office is the last place you need to be."

"No Henry, *home* is the last place I need to be," Trin corrected, heading over to the impressive well-stocked bar.

"Trin—"

"Henry, *please,*" Trin whispered, silently emphasizing his need to be alone.

Henry watched Trin pull a bottle of cognac from the bar. No glass, he noted. It was clear that nothing could be said to encourage Trin to take some time off, which was the reason he'd come. After a moment, he left the office.

Meanwhile, Trin had taken a seat on the back of one of the armchairs and tilted the bottle to his mouth. Though the liquor burned like crazy, he relished the taste. Moving to the suede sofa, he proceeded to finish the entire bottle.

Much later, Mary Hills, Trin's executive assistant, went into his office. She found her young boss passed out on the couch and walked over to retrieve the empty bottle from the floor. After depositing the bottle in the wastebasket, she reached beneath the desk and pressed the button which closed the long cream drapes. She knew Trin would be in no state for a bright office when he woke.

"Trin?" Mary called, clapping her hands like a school mistress. "Trin." She busied herself tidying the huge desk.

Mary's loud calling finally succeeded in pulling Trin from his unconscious state. A smile brightened her lovely face when she heard a deep groan.

"Mary, please," Trin begged. "Stop."

Mary didn't veer from her task of straightening the desk. "Not until you go clean yourself up . . . and brush your teeth."

"Yes, ma'am," Trin replied, sounding every bit like a little boy as he headed into the plush washroom located inside the office.

A short while later, Trin emerged, wiping a damp cloth over his face.

"Thanks, Mary," he said, his deep voice sounding muffled beneath the washcloth.

Mary nodded, though Trin could tell from the look in her green eyes that she wanted to say something. "I already know," he said, walking back to his desk.

Mary's reddish brown brows pulled together. "You already know what?" she asked.

"What you want to say."

"And that is?"

Trin sighed and leaned back in his chair. "You wanna tell me to get outta here and go home."

Mary shrugged and looked down at her hands clasped together in her lap. "Well . . . yes, I was going to say something to that effect."

Trin bowed his head and trailed his thumbs along the sleek line of his eyebrows. "Well, save it. I already heard that from Henry."

"Well, that's not all I was going to say," Mary haughtily informed him.

Trin looked up and spread his hands to urge her to continue.

Mary cleared her throat. "I think you should get away for a while. Take some time off."

"Hmph." Trin tossed the cloth back across his eyes. "Are you forgetting I haven't had this job all that long? I don't think it'll look good for me to go on vacation with so many people still hovering around to see me fail."

"Sweetie," Mary sighed, leaving her seat on the sofa, "you've just lost your wife. A woman you loved more than anything."

The distant, depressed look reappeared in Trin's onyx gaze. "I thought I'd be fine if I came to work . . . maybe I could forget."

"Honey, no one around here expects you to forget. Not even your biggest doubters."

"Mary—"

"I assure you that everyone will understand," Mary smoothly interrupted.

Trin considered the situation for a moment, then shuddered. "I can't spend all my time at home."

Mary frowned. "Who says you have to? Take a trip. Get out of town. Hell, out of the state."

Trin laughed, his first chuckle in what seemed an eternity. "You tryin' to get rid of me?"

"Never," Mary told him, leaning across the desk to pat his hand. "I just think you need some time away from this."

Trin ran his hand over the back of his neck. "You know Mary, I think you're right."

* * *

Hours away, in another time zone, Dr. Belinda Tirelli was seated at the bedside of the mysterious Jane Doe.

Jane Doe, hell. Belinda thought. This woman had to be Dominique Salem. She just had to be. Still, as many times as Belinda tried to convince herself, she wasn't sure. It had been so long since they had seen each other. . . .

Belinda found it funny, but she'd always felt she and Dominique could have become great friends. Dom had a quiet, observant quality that relaxed a person instead of putting them on edge. Although she was a woman who made her living asking tough questions and dealing with even tougher issues, she was as gentle and graceful as a queen.

Yes, Belinda thought, she and Dom had been well on their way to becoming great friends. If only Trinidad hadn't made things so unbearable. In fact, Belinda's entire family had made remaining in New York unbearable. She had married Aaron Tirelli when they were both attending medical school. Belinda's parents had made it abundantly clear that they did not approve of the marriage. Her own father wouldn't even attend the wedding. They all seemed to want to forget she had ever existed.

Still, no one had been as cold to her as Trin. Her cousin, older by two years, had always been loud and outspoken. His opinion was going to be heard no matter how harsh it was or who it hurt. Belinda shuddered when she remembered the hateful arguments they had had about her relationship with Aaron. Over the years, the intensity of the arguments never dwindled, and Belinda doubted they ever would. When she and her husband received their respective degrees, they headed out of New York and never looked back.

Belinda felt strong hands settle to her shoulders just then. She looked up as Aaron leaned down to press a kiss to her forehead. "You ready?" he asked.

* * *

"Bel, are you positive about this?" Aaron asked, once they were heading home in his Benz.

Belinda fiddled with one of her braids and nodded. "Almost, but I just don't know yet."

"So, what are you goin' to do in the meantime?"

"Hell, Doc, I don't know. I think I'll be sure if I can just see her eyes."

Aaron frowned. "Her eyes?"

"Mmm hmm," Belinda confirmed. "You weren't around Dom as much as I was, so you probably don't remember. But she has or . . . had the most beautiful hazel eyes. I mean, it was like she could see right through you with them. If I could see her eyes, I'd know for sure."

After a moment of silence, Aaron sighed. "If you do become sure it's her, what will you do?"

The innocent question set Belinda on edge. "I—I have to tell him. But Dom might be unconscious for a long time. I couldn't keep her away from him that long."

Aaron could tell by the hushed quality of his wife's voice that she was struggling with the decision of whether to involve Trin. Aaron knew how badly the man had hurt his cousin by turning his back on her when they had once been so close. Aaron finally decided to give Belinda time to think the situation over.

After his heart-to-heart with Mary, Trin finally decided to go home and plan his next move. Surprisingly, the talk with his experienced assistant had really done him some good . . . while he was at the office. As soon as he changed clothes and got himself settled at home, the depression set in once again.

"The hell with this," Trin grumbled, as he stormed through the house and into the study where his liquor was stored. He grabbed a bottle of vodka and succeeded in becoming drunk for the second time that day. Trin could admit to himself that he was already headed downwards and that alcohol was the last thing he needed. Still, it was the strongest medicine for the hurt . . . and the guilt.

Sometime later, the phone rang. In his drunken state, his thoughts were muddled and it took a while for him to recognize the sound.

Belinda had decided to follow her heart instead of her mind and tell Trin about the woman who she suspected was Dominique. Her doctor's instinct cautioned her to wait, but Belinda knew that she would want to know if anything ever happened to Aaron.

The phone's constant ringing, however, relieved her by the second. *Maybe he isn't home,* she thought. After so many years of no contact, it would be strange to hear his voice again.

Finally, the brief crackling tones, which indicated the phone was ringing on the other end, stopped. "Hello," said a deep, rough voice.

Belinda was struck speechless for a moment. *Can I do this?* She asked herself. *Can I—*

"Hello?" the deep voice bellowed, sounding somewhat slurred.

Belinda cleared her throat. "Hey—hey, Trin."

"Who the hell is this?" Trin asked, frowning slightly at the strangely familiar voice.

Again, the sound of a throat being cleared came through the receiver. "It's me, Trin. Belinda."

"Belinda?" Trin slowly replied, recognition dawning.

"Mmm hmm," she confirmed, comforted by the way he spoke her name. "I—I know it's been a—a long time . . . but I . . . uh, how are you?"

Trin was not in the mood for small talk. "What do you want?" he asked.

"I was just calling to—to—"

"To what, Belinda? Did the good doctor dump you?"

Belinda blinked at the harsh statement and gripped the receiver a bit more tightly. "Trin, I've got somethin' I need to tell you."

"What? Did Aaron dump you for a blonde? Or maybe he decided to get with one of his own kind?" Trin slurred. "Italian bastard."

Belinda could tell that Trin had obviously been drinking. Still, she knew that words much more cruel had been said when he was dead sober. Finally, she became so aggravated that she simply hung up without getting to the point of the call.

When Trin heard the click of the connection breaking, he jerked the phone from the socket and proceeded to trash his study. When his anger had somewhat spent itself, he decided to take Mary Hills's advice and made reservations to leave town.

The dull, gray blanket that covered the hospital bed rose higher on the mattress. The woman lying there was moving for the first time in weeks.

It took some effort, but Dominique managed to open her eyes and glance around at her surroundings. Her exquisite hazel gaze was blank at first, then began to shine with recognition. She realized she was in a hospital room and tried to sit up by bracing on her elbows. Unfortunately, weakness prohibited her and she fell back to the bed.

"God . . ." she moaned, pressing her hand over her eyes.

Myra Larson, one of the on-duty nurses, passed the room just in time to see Dom lie back on the bed. Myra frowned and walked into the room. Dominique seemed to sense another presence, for she turned toward the nurse and gave her a weak smile.

"Hello," Myra said in greeting, and checked the IV and heart monitors next to the bed.

Dom tried to speak, but her voice seemed to have left her. She cleared her throat and tried again. "Hi," she managed.

Myra turned away from the monitors and began to straighten the bedclothes. "You've got a lot of people talkin', young lady," she said.

Dom's hazel gaze narrowed. "Talking? About what?"

Myra continued fussing with the covers. "Ohhh . . . about what a beautiful mystery-lady you are."

Dom's laugh was weak, but it was there.

"So, do you know what happened?" Myra asked.

Dom's perfectly arched brows drew close as she considered the question. "I remember an airport, a plane ride that was . . . I remember bein' on a wooden bench or—or . . . something. That's all I know," she finally said, pain and aggravation evident in her voice.

The nurse patted her hand. "It's alright, you're still very weak, but I'm gonna get the doctors so they can take a look at you. . . . Sweetie, can you tell me your name?"

Again, Dom's brows met as she frowned. Her eyes shifted away from Myra and out across the room. Then they quickly darted back to the nurse's concerned expression.

"Kyla," Dom said, her voice surprisingly firm. "My name is Kyla."

"Are you absolutely sure, Myra?"

"That's what she said."

Aaron sighed and looked over at Belinda. Myra Larson had rushed right to Belinda's office to tell them the news. The Tirellis had hurried to Dom's room and were standing just outside the door.

"And she didn't remember any of the details of the plane ride?" Belinda asked.

Myra shook her head. "Just what I told you."

Aaron slapped his hands to his sides. "Well, now you'll get to see if it's really her."

Belinda sighed. "It's got to be."

"Myra, did she seem to remember anything else?" Aaron asked, a slight frown marring his bronze features.

Myra shook her head and squeezed her hands. "No, the poor thing. She did appear to be trying, though, but I didn't think she should be straining herself."

Aaron patted her hand. "You did good, Myra. Thanks."

Myra simply nodded and watched the two doctors head into the room. Inside, the woman was lying there with one arm thrown across her eyes.

Belinda turned and whispered to Aaron. "When I see her eyes, I'll know for sure."

The slight whispering caught Dom's attention and she turned. Belinda gasped and grasped her doctor's robe a bit tighter. It was Dominique. There was no doubt about it. The wide hazel eyes were still as clear and striking as they had always been.

Dom smiled weakly. "Hello," she whispered.

Aaron was first to step forward. "Well, hello. You gave us quite a scare there," he said, beginning to check the monitors.

"How long have I been here?" Dom asked.

Aaron prepared to take her blood pressure. "Oh, about eight weeks."

Dom's eyes widened. "Two months? I've been here that long?"

"Almost two months," Aaron replied, his stress on the word causing Dom to smile.

Belinda, who had held back at first, slowly inched forward. "Myra tells us you've remembered your name."

Dom frowned. "Myra?" she asked, gazing up at Aaron.

"The nurse who was in here earlier," he clarified.

"Oh," she said, smiling at Belinda. "Yeah, she was very nice."

"Glad to hear it . . . Well, I'm Doctor Belinda Tirelli and this is Doctor Aaron Tirelli."

"What a coincidence," Dom was saying, though she didn't really believe it was.

"It's not," Belinda confirmed. "We're married."

Dom didn't appear to express disapproval. In fact, she seemed comforted by them both. *Same old Dominique,* Belinda thought.

"So . . . Doctor Tirelli," Dom sighed, smiling up at the man, "Aaron, is it?"

He shrugged. "Weird first name for an Italian, huh? Named after my father's best friend. An Irishman ironically, if you can believe that." He jibed, smirking when his wife fixed him with a warning glare.

Dom looked over at Aaron when he finished taking her blood pressure. "How am I?" she asked.

"Well," Aaron began, placing his stethoscope back around his neck. "Internally, you're in perfect health."

"Are you experiencing any pain?" Belinda asked, bracing her hands on the rail at the foot of the bed.

Dom sighed and ran her fingers through the riot of thick curls on her head. "Uh-uh, I just can't seem to remember how I got here."

Belinda looked at Aaron and they decided to explain things. Aaron took a seat on the edge of the bed.

"Well, sweetie, a plane crashed several weeks ago. Over half the people on board were presumed dead."

"Oh, God," Dom breathed.

Aaron patted her hand. "We still aren't sure, but dock-workers found you unconscious on the pier. You had no kind of ID, so we assumed you'd been mugged."

"A wooden bench . . ." Dom whispered.

"What was that?" Aaron asked.

Dom shook her head. "I remember layin' on a wooden bench. It must've been the dock."

Belinda's hand rose to Aaron's shoulder. "Myra told us you remember the plane."

"Yeah, I remember the plane ride, a bumpy ride. I guess it was bumpier than I thought," she said.

"You don't remember anything before the airport?" Belinda asked.

"I have tried and tried and . . . I can't. I just can't."

Aaron patted her hand again. "Well don't worry about it now. You need to take your time with this. If you don't, you may never remember."

Dom nodded. "Thanks, I'll . . . remember that," she said, and Aaron laughed at her choice of words.

The three of them talked for only a few moments longer. Dom began to get sleepy after a while and Belinda and Aaron let her get her rest.

"I knew it was her! I knew it!" Belinda cried the moment they were outside the room.

Aaron leaned against the wall and pushed his large hands into the pockets of his slacks. "You gonna call Trin again?" he asked.

Belinda leaned against the wall as well. "After I talked to him the first time, I said hell no," she admitted. "But now, I have a different reason for not wanting to call back."

"And that is?"

"Well, it's obvious she doesn't remember anything about her life in New York. Not even Trin."

"I don't follow you."

"Well, she may not be able to handle all that so soon and I'm not saying that because of Trin's attitude on the phone. I just think it'd be better for us to wait."

Aaron could tell by the strained tone in Belinda's voice that she felt uneasy about the decision. He pushed himself away from the wall and pulled his wife close.

"Then it's settled," he whispered, kissing her forehead. "We'll wait."

The decision to wait seemed to be the right thing to do. Dom had been diagnosed with amnesia and it seemed that a full recovery would be a long time coming. Still, she was making progress. Dom's unbelievable energy and analytical mind were returning. As a result, she found herself looking forward to her release from the hospital.

Even though Belinda and Aaron felt positive about Dom's recovery, they decided not to inform her of too much too soon. Belinda knew that when the time did come to tell Trin, there would be hell to pay. Still, she was confident that she was doing the right thing. When the time arrived, she would deal with Trin's attitude.

* * *

As soon as Aaron and Belinda walked into Dom's room, she clasped her hands together in a pleading gesture.

"Would you two please tell me when I can get out of here?" she asked, her exquisite gaze wide and expectant.

Aaron's rich, deep laughter filled the room. "Funny you should ask, since we've decided to kick you out tomorrow afternoon."

"Yes!" Dom whispered, clenching her hand into a small fist. "I mean, this place is great, but I know y'all have plenty of other patients to look out for besides me."

"Well, you're our favorite," Belinda told her, taking a seat on the edge of the bed.

"Thanks. I don't know if I would've made it if you guys hadn't been so sweet."

"Well, don't tell too many people how sweet we are. We like our monstrous images!" Aaron proclaimed.

Dom gave a small laugh at the comment, but it didn't quite reach her eyes.

"What's wrong?" Belinda asked, placing one hand across Dom's.

"I'm glad to be getting out, but I just realized that I don't have anywhere to go."

Belinda grasped Aaron's hand and nodded.

Aaron knelt by Belinda and stared at Dom. "What would you say if we asked you to come stay with us for a while?"

Dom's mouth dropped open as her eyes shifted between Aaron and Belinda. "Live at your home? Are you serious?"

"As a heart attack," Aaron confirmed. "What do you say?"

"I don't know I—I don't think I should."

Neither Aaron or Belinda had any intentions of letting her say no. Belinda knew Dom was her responsibility until the situation took a turn for the better. Aaron, on the other hand, had become very protective of Dom and thought of of her as a little sister.

"If you're worried about room, don't be," Belinda informed her. "We're doctors, our house is huge."

Dom joined Aaron in laughter, and after a moment she nodded. "Alright . . . I'll stay for a while, but I don't know how I'll repay the two of you."

"You can clean our pool," Aaron suggested as he stood.

The new roommates were rolling with laughter when a knock sounded on the door a while later. A short, plump man with red cheeks and stark white hair was standing just inside the doorway.

"Am I interrupting anything?" he asked.

Belinda wiped a tear from her eye. "No, Wink, we're just laughin' at something crazy Aaron said."

The little man snapped his fingers. "I hate that I missed it. I decided it was about time I met our mystery patient."

Belinda and Aaron smiled at one of the hospital's top surgeons. Dr. Winkle Broderick was world-reknowned but was loved by his co-workers because he was so down-to-earth. Belinda had informed Wink of Dominique's situation and why they should wait to inform anyone. Wink had agreed with her, but advised her to inform Dom's family as soon as possible.

"So, this is the lady who has all my doctors buzzing," Wink said as he stepped closer to Dom's bed.

Dom shrugged. "I don't know what they're buzzing about."

"My dear, you're lovely. Some of my doctors never see the light of day and when they do, they're too tired to keep their eyes open for beautiful things."

"Thank you," Dom said, nodding slightly.

"I call it as I see it," Wink replied.

"Thank him anyway," Aaron advised, grinning broadly. "He hardly ever gives compliments."

"That's true," Wink admitted, and they all laughed. "So, uh, Kyla—Aaron and Belinda tell me you'll be leaving us tomorrow afternoon."

Dom sighed. "Yes, finally."

"Do you have any plans?"

Dom glanced toward Belinda and Aaron. "Well, these guys

have invited me to stay with them for a while. Beyond that, I have no other plans."

Wink massaged the gray beard covering his chin and frowned. "I see. Well, considering the size of their house, I'm sure you'll find plenty to do."

"I told her she was welcome to clean our pool," Aaron chimed in.

Dom laughed. "I'll settle for kitchen duty, Aaron."

"You like to cook?" Belinda asked hopefully, thinking a small breakthrough could be in progress.

Dom frowned. "I don't know . . . I just have a feeling that I could do it, you know?"

Wink chuckled. "That's the way I thought when I decided to open my restaurant."

Dom's hazel eyes widened. "You own a restaurant?"

"A little place," Wink humbly replied.

"Little?" Aaron cried, "The place is as big as a warehouse!"

"A restaurant." Dom breathed, settling back against the huge pillow on the bed. "I've always dreamed of owning one myself."

At once, the three doctors in the room turned to face her.

"Do you remember anything else?" Aaron immediately asked.

Dom was just as surprised by her admission as the doctors. "I—I don't know why I said that. I have no idea where the thought came from."

Belinda, Aaron, and Wink were pleased. Dominique was unknowingly taking the first steps toward a full recovery.

Smiling, Wink took a seat on the edge of her bed. "Well, dear, it's true. I *do* own a restaurant. Unfortunately, I may be forced to sell it."

Dom's mouth formed a perfect O as she stared at him. "Why?" she asked.

"Well, I don't have time to manage the place and I can't find anyone I feel comfortable with to do it. Most of my staff are college students, musicians, and actors. They certainly don't have time."

"I'm so sorry," Dom softly replied.

"Would you like the job?"

"'Scuse me?" Dom asked, knowing she had misheard Wink.

"Would you like to manage my restaurant?" he asked again.

"Wink, I—"

"Wink." Aaron interrupted. "The girl's not even out of the hospital yet. She can't think about working now."

"I think it'll be good for her," Wink argued.

"Wink, I may've lost my memory, but I don't think I've ever managed a restaurant before," Dom intervened.

"I'm sure you haven't, my dear, but I believe you could do it."

"Wink may have a point." Belinda chimed in, her brown eyes gazing at Aaron.

Aaron ran a hand through his wavy dark hair. "I don't think it's a good idea."

Wink turned toward his younger colleague. "Hell, boy, she can't stay cooped up in that house indefinitely."

"I know that, Wink."

The bantering between the three doctors went on for a while. Watching them soon wore Dom out. When everyone realized she was asleep, they left her alone.

"Aaron, this could really be good for Dominique," Wink cautioned once they were out in the corridor.

"Baby, she already feels some connection with wanting to own a restaurant. Though she never has, being in that atmosphere just may trigger deeper memories," Belinda reasoned.

Aaron's brown eyes shifted from his wife to Wink and finally he nodded. "I can't argue with that one."

"So you approve?" Wink asked.

"I'll *think* about it."

Belinda was ecstatic. "Oh, thank you, honey!" she cried, hugging Aaron tightly, knowing he was sold on the idea.

"Didn't I say I'd *think* about it?" Aaron said, holding his wife close.

Dom jumped out of bed early the next morning. Knowing that it was the day she would be released from the hospital had made it difficult to get a restful night's sleep. After showering, Dom stood in front of the bathroom mirror. At first, she simply stood there, staring at her reflection.

Who are you? she asked the image facing her. Though she was looking forward to what was in store, a new home and a possible job, there was her past. A past she had no clue about. Where did she come from? Were there children? A husband? The questions, none of which she had answers to, only frustrated her. Not wanting anything to ruin what promised to be a wonderful day, Dom shook away her disturbing thoughts.

Five

Several months had passed since Dominique's release from the hospital. While there had been small spurts of memories, they were largely related to the plane crash. During that time, however, Dom prospered in her role as manager of Wink Broderick's restaurant, the Terrace. There, everyone simply knew her as Kyla. Although Aaron and Belinda constantly questioned her about the name, Dom still had no clue about where the name came from. Though they were concerned that working at the Terrace hadn't sparked any memories beyond the crash, they were pleased that she had something to occupy her time. Still, for all the good in her life, Dominique was more worried than anyone that she would never remember. Aside from the quick flashes she'd had in relation to the scar on her back, there had been nothing.

"Listen, I need to tell you something," Dom said one afternoon while she and Belinda were folding clothes in the laundry room.

"Spill it," Belinda ordered, as she pulled a fluffy red towel from the dryer.

Dom hoisted herself on top of the washer. "Well, when I got out of the hospital that day, I had some kind of . . . flash. A quick one."

Belinda forgot about the wash and turned to face Dom. "Was anything familiar?"

Dom shook her head. "No, it was so fast. I've been seeing the same thing ever since that day and I can't understand it."

After a moment, Belinda shrugged. "It's probably something else from the crash."

"That's what I thought." Dom sighed. "But I just don't think that's it."

During the last several months, Trin had become somewhat settled with his life. He was far more secure in his role as CEO of Morton and Farber. He had returned from his trip to an upstate hunting resort, to focus all his attention on work. There had even been talk of a possible partnership in the near future.

As a result, Trin was never at a loss for work. Business became his life, and he relished it. He was respected by outside business associates as well as by his own co-workers. As far as his personal life was concerned, there were plenty of women ready to make it as fulfilling as his business life was. Most of them were aware of how much Trin adored his late wife. Dominique Salem's life could have been compared with that of a queen's, for that was the way they all had seen the man treat her. As a result, women who knew him, not to mention those who met him for the first time, were eager to become the love interest of such a gorgeous, powerful man.

Trin wasn't at all interested. He missed Dominique more every day, but knew he would have to move on eventually. For the time being, though, he was content spending his nights alone . . . remembering Dom.

Trin sat alone in his office with the drapes drawn. It would have been their fourth anniversary. Every year they'd taken off on some kind of exotic, erotic trip. The plan was to get away and see the sights of someplace they had never been. However, most if not all of their time was spent in the hotel room with a DO NOT DISTURB sign on the door. As sweet memories filled his mind, Trin's depression reasserted itself. In an effort to escape the feeling, he left his office.

* * *

"Thanks for squeezing me in, Doc."

Doctor Calvin Starks waved one hand toward his patient. "We were very lucky my earlier patient had to cancel," he remarked while attempting to situate his short, stout frame in the cushioned tweed armchair. "I had a feeling you might want a session today."

Trin propped his elbow along the arm of the matching tweed sofa. He rested his chin on his fist and regarded his therapist with a strange look. "What made you think that?"

"Well," Doctor Starks drawled, peering through his gold-rimmed spectacles at the pad he held, "my earlier notes indicate you mentioning that today is your fourth wedding anniversary."

Trin's long lashes fluttered and a deep shiver surged upward along his spine. "I always took her on a trip to celebrate," he recalled, returning in memory to the various romantic trips they had taken.

"Are the happier memories helping you to cope?" Doctor Starks asked.

Trin flashed the man a look of disbelief. "Cope? Doc, I don't even know the meaning of the word anymore. Those happy memories you're talkin' about make me feel even worse. If that's possible," he added in a low voice as he got up from the sofa.

Dr. Starks chewed on the cap of his black ballpoint and leaned forward in his chair. "Trinidad, I understand how your actions toward Dominique are affecting your ability to handle this. Unfortunately, you'll never progress if you don't allow yourself some leeway."

"Leeway?" Trin whispered, his pitch-black gaze turning sinister. "What the hell are you talking about?"

"Trinidad, the way you handled this situation with Dominique was wrong. Terribly so. But that doesn't mean that you can never conquer the demons that drove you to those actions and forgive yourself."

"Forgive myself?" Trin exploded, his chest heaving rapidly out of sheer frustration. "Doctor, she is dead. She's never coming back to me. I'll never have a chance to beg her forgiveness and you expect me to forgive *myself?*"

"If you ever hope to come out of this situation as anything other than a sorrowful, guilt-ridden person, yes I do expect you to forgive yourself . . . in time."

"Bullshit."

"Trinidad, you know, there may come a day when you'll become interested in someone else and—"

"Never. I don't want anyone else," Trin quickly assured his psychologist. "Domino was everything I ever wanted, Doc. She was everything to me. I would have given my life for her. Now, that may sound corny or overly dramatic, but it's true. You have no idea how much I loved her. How much I *still* love her. She was the most beautiful person I ever knew, inside and out. I treated her like she was nothing over something that happened years before she ever met me. I flushed away six years of love and respect because my ego couldn't handle it."

"Would you like to have been able to handle it?"

"What kind of question is that? Of course, I would have. If I'd been able to, none of this would've happened."

"Then don't you think you should get past this guilt and work on dealing with your anger over the situation?"

"What the hell for, Doc?" Trin raged, slamming his fists against the back of the sofa. "She's gone. There's no reason."

"There's your sanity," Dr. Starks interjected. "You are still alive, you know."

The mention of that fact forced Trin to close his eyes against a sudden onslaught of tears. He covered his face with his hands as the water began to stream down his face.

"Man, I got that new *Luscious* magazine. One look at those honeys will pull you right out of that depression!"

Trin shook his head and smiled at Hal Lymon, whose newsstand had been converted into a combination food and magazine stand. "Thanks, man, but I'll just settle for a burger," Trin said, reaching for his wallet.

Hal shook his head and called out the order to his assistant. "You wouldn't say that if you took a look at these girls," he teased.

"So I take it you know what's inside all these magazines?"

"Hell, man, it's one of the fringe benefits of owning this thing!" Hal boasted.

Trin rubbed his fingers against the silky black hair that feathered his temple. "Mmm hmm . . . well, maybe you can tell me what *Money* is saying about our stock?"

Hal sighed. "Not yet. I always read the smut first."

Trin burst out into deep, rich laughter.

"I can tell you what it said last month," Hal continued, before he too began to laugh.

The two men stood there conversing about everything and anything. Trin had yet to take a bite of the delicious-looking burger. He was about to indulge in the fattening lunch when he heard a desperate cry.

"Somebody! Oh God, please help! Help us!"

Trin frowned, turning to see a small dark-complected woman waving her hands and running around frantically. She was pointing toward the huge fountain that was constructed outside Morton and Farber. Though he still had no idea what the problem was, Trin's dark eyes narrowed at the scene. The look of desperation on the woman's face forced him to take action.

It appeared that no one except Trin had heard the woman's terrified screams. It took her a moment before she even realized that someone had rushed over to help. Suddenly, she grabbed the lapels of Trin's olive-green suit coat and pulled him close. "Oh God, thank you! Please, please help my son!" she cried.

Trin pulled off his suit jacket and ran over to the fountain. When he saw the child splashing in the seven-foot-deep water, he was surprised. The child was a small boy with curly blond hair. The surprise passed quickly as Trin focused on the situation at hand. The boy had disappeared under water for what appeared to be the last time. Trin waded around for a moment or two, searching for him. He found the child near the waterfall. The harsh force of the waves appeared to be plummeting the little boy deeper into the fountain. Trin arrived, hoisted the child out of the water, and started CPR. It took a few moments, but the little boy finally came around amid a bout of coughing and sneezing. Luckily, someone had called the paramedics and they were already approaching the scene.

"Thank you! Thanks so much!" the boy's mother cried. She hugged Trin and pressed dozens of kisses to his cheek.

Trin smiled and patted the woman's hand, then helped her into the ambulance where her son had been placed.

"Hey, there he is!"

Trin had just stepped off the elevator and it appeared that everyone on the floor was there to meet him. All he heard were well wishes and congratulations for saving the little boy. Trin enjoyed the praise, but found himself wishing he could have done the same thing for his wife when she needed him most.

Inside the quiet dark confines of his office, Trin thought about how surprised he'd been by the woman and her son. The last thing he'd expected to find when he rushed over to the fountain was a blond-haired boy struggling in the water. Still, the only thing that really mattered was saving the child's life. Neither his color nor his mother's had been of any consequence.

Trin sighed and thought about his cousin Belinda and her husband. True, he had not approved of her marrying a white man, but now, for the first time, he was realizing that Aaron's color was not important. As long as he was making Belinda happy, nothing else should have mattered.

Trin closed his eyes and tried to remember his last conversation with Belinda. The most he could recall was hearing her name. Of course, he didn't need to have perfect recollection of the conversation to know he'd probably said some pretty awful things to her. She deserved to hear him apologize. Especially when he had so much to apologize for. Trin decided to contact his cousin later that evening.

"Belinda, girl, hurry up!"

"Wait . . . oh hell, I can't find my keys!"

"Oh Lord . . ."

"Wait! Alright, alright!"

Belinda and Dom hurried in out of the downpour they had been caught in. Their girls' night out had been needed and very much deserved. They'd been strolling to the parking lot from the jazz club they'd visited when the rain began. It hadn't let up and they'd made a mad dash when they got home. Because, the four-car garage was at the back of the house and detached, it was no help against the rain.

Once inside the house, the women stripped out of their water-soaked clothing.

"Whew, lemme go put this stuff in the dryer," Belinda said as she grabbed their things and headed for the laundry room. The phone in her office began to ring just then. "Can you get that for me, girl?" she called.

Dom rubbed her arms to get warm and rushed to the office. "Hello?" she said.

"Um . . . Is Belinda Tirelli there?" a voice finally asked.

"Mmm hmm," Dom said. She had no clue who the man was and went in search of Belinda.

"Who is it?"

Dom shrugged. "I don't know, but he's got a great voice."

"Oh, shush," Belinda said, with a wave of her hand.

Dom laughed and headed upstairs for one of Belinda's robes.

"Hello, this is Belinda."

"Hey . . . it's Trin."

Belinda clutched the edge of her desk as her knees threatened to buckle beneath her. "Trin?" she croaked.

"Yeah, um . . . who answered the phone?" he asked, trying to keep his voice light.

Belinda's heart pounded hard in her chest. "Oh, just one of my girlfriends."

"Oh . . . you alright?" he asked, sounding skeptical.

"I'm . . . just surprised to hear your voice."

"Yeah, well, I need to talk to you."

"Oh? What about?"

Trin sighed. "Well, somethin' happened today that sorta brought me to my senses."

Belinda ran one hand through her braids. "I don't understand."

"Let's just say that I have a lot to apologize for. I'll start with the way I talked to you when you called me before."

"Trin, I—"

"No, let me finish. I was drunk and that whole episode is a blur to me, but I believe I went off on you pretty bad. I don't think you even got to the point of your call."

"Well . . . you'd just lost Dom. I'm sure you weren't in the mood to hear anything anyone had to say."

"Now, Belinda, you know I would have said what I did whether I'd just lost Dom or not."

Belinda was silent, unable to argue that point. "So, what brought about this change of heart?" she finally asked.

Trin's deep chuckle came through the line. "This little kid I know."

"I won't ask."

"Good . . . So why *did* you call me after all this time?" Trin asked.

"We need to see each other," Belinda immediately replied. She didn't want to waste any more time.

"We can't talk about this over the phone?"

"Uh-uh. And you'll have to come to Chicago," she added.

"What's goin' on? Are you okay?" Trin asked, trying to mask his concern.

"I'm fine. Never better."

Trin finally realized that he wasn't going to be able to get Belinda to reveal anything more to him over the phone. "Alright . . . alright, I'll try to get away sometime next week. I'll call you."

"I'll be waiting," she quietly replied, then hung up before anything more could be said.

A satisfied smile crossed Belinda's lovely face when she felt the most delicious kisses rain down her back. Large persuasive hands were added to the caress. They pushed away the thick comforter and massaged the luscious swell of her buttocks before circling her hips and teasing the extra sensitive area of her womanhood.

"Mmm, are you sure you just worked a double?" Belinda purred.

Aaron smiled. His coffee-colored gaze twinkled with mischief as his eyes glided over his wife's body. "Quite sure, but I got the feeling you could use my professional touch."

Belinda turned over and sank her fingers into Aaron's wavy hair. "So, this visit is strictly business, huh, Doc?"

Aaron lowered his lean yet powerful form over his wife and pressed her arms above her head. "Well, if you promise not to tell anybody, I'll let a little pleasure slip in." Belinda couldn't stop laughter from bubbling up inside her. Soon she and Aaron were giggling uncontrollably.

"Stop. I've got somethin' to tell you." Belinda gasped.

Aaron left the bed and started taking off his clothes. "Sounds serious," he commented.

"Trin called."

Aaron's eyes narrowed as he turned around to face her. The silent question they relayed was unmistakable.

Belinda shook her head. "No, he doesn't know about Dom. I did ask him to come to Chicago as soon as he could."

Aaron nodded. "I think it's time, don't you?"

"Hell, yeah. He's gonna kill us when he finds out we've known this long."

"Well, we had our reasons, but it's been several months. Maybe Dom needs a bigger push."

"That's what I think." Belinda agreed.

"It couldn't make things any worse," Aaron figured, but both he and his wife were still full of doubt.

Belinda twiddled her fingers as she stood in the crowded airport lobby. Trin had called two days after their phone conversation to inform her that he would be arriving in Chicago that Friday around nine. Until then, Belinda hadn't felt too nervous. Now, with each passing second, she thought she would collapse in a dead faint. Still, it had been a long time and she couldn't wait to see her cousin.

Countless women turned their heads when Trin made his way into the lobby. They couldn't tear their eyes away from the tall, gorgeous, intense-looking male. Trin, however, kept his midnight gaze straight ahead. He paused momentarily, checking the time on his wristwatch. His stance was unconsciously yet undeniably sexy and he looked like every woman's idea of the perfect man.

But Trin was in no mood to be admired. The plane ride had been terrible. The food had tasted awful, and all he could think of was Dominique.

He caught sight of a petite dark-skinned beauty who looked exactly like his cousin. When he raised his hand in a tentative wave and the woman waved back, a happy smile crossed his handsome face.

All the hurt and anger from the past appeared to have been forgotten. The two cousins rushed toward each other and hugged. Belinda hadn't realized how much she had missed Trin until she felt his strong arms around her tiny frame. For Trin, the feeling was mutual.

"Girl, what are these?" he asked, pushing his fingers against Belinda's braids.

"Don't you like 'em?"

"Hell, yeah. I just never thought I'd see the day when you'd wear a style you couldn't brush and curl and fuss with every day."

Belinda sucked her teeth and pushed against Trin's massive shoulder. "Hush. So, how was your flight?" she asked.

Trin rolled his eyes and shook his head. "Not so good." he admitted.

"Well, did you get any sleep?"

"I *had* to sleep to keep my mind off how bad the trip was. I'm hungry as a dog."

Belinda laughed at the pained expression on her cousin's gorgeous face. "Come on, I know a place that serves great food," she said, placing her hand around Trin's arm.

"Lead the way," he ordered.

"So, I know you have access to the company jet. Why didn't you use it?" Belinda asked once they got Trin's luggage and settled into her Benz.

"How'd you know that?" he asked, a smirk teasing the curve of his mouth.

"Well, you being named CEO of—what is it?—Morton and Farber, was national news. I was tellin' everybody you were my cousin."

"For real?" Trin asked, very surprised.

Belinda didn't think anything of it. "Mmm hmm, I was so proud."

Trin shook his head. "You're somethin' else. You know that, right?"

"I know, but why are you sayin' it?" Belinda asked.

"Hell, Belinda, I treated you and Aaron like crap. So did everybody else in the family, but I was probably the worst."

"Amen," she muttered.

Trin heard and bowed his head in acknowledgement. "And you still had time to brag about me."

"Well, I didn't *brag,*" Belinda denied.

Trin chuckled for a moment before a serious expression clouded his features. "Belinda?"

"Huh?"

"You did say you heard about Dominique, didn't you?"

Belinda's long lashes fluttered briefly. "I heard," she finally said.

"How? Have you been keeping in touch with someone from the family?"

Belinda gripped the steering wheel a bit more tightly. "Well, she *was* in the public eye and news of her death was broadcasted."

Trin expelled a heavy sigh and Belinda realized how devastated he still was at having to think of Dom as being dead.

"Sweetie, I'm sorry," she whispered, patting his hand.

Trin shook his head. "Don't worry about it. I should probably get over this. I loved Domino a lot, but I guess it's way past time for me to move on."

Belinda nodded but offered no reply. "So, why didn't you take your jet?" she teased.

"The *company* jet," Trin clarified, though he was pleased by his cousin's awe over the benefits of his job. "I guess I had the urge to take a commercial flight and I didn't want them knowing how to find me."

Belinda sighed. "Hmph, it must be nice to have a choice."

"Yeah, well, I made a poor choice. I've never tasted food so bad," he said, making a face. "I hope this restaurant is better."

Belinda looked in her rearview mirror and took the exit off the freeway. "Oh, it is. The Terrace has some of the best food in town." She knew Dom wasn't working that night, and figured it would be harmless to stop there for a bite before heading home.

"So, how's the family?" she finally asked.

"Everybody's good, but I know they all miss you."

"Oh? How do you know that?"

"Hell, girl, family parties and crap like that, you're missed. Believe me. Aunt Lilly and Uncle Sam are sick with worry and guilt," Trin shared, referring to Belinda's parents.

Her mouth dropped open and she looked over at Trin. "How do you know this?"

"That's what they tell Ma. I guess somebody just needs to make the first move."

"Hmph, well, it ain't gonna be me."

"Belinda—"

"Uh-uh Trin. I'm tired of gettin' my feelings hurt," she stubbornly replied.

"It's not good to hang onto that mess, Bel. Believe me, I know."

"Mmm hmm," Belinda replied, clearly unconvinced. "So, I guess you and Spry have made up?"

A hard look pulled Trin's magnificent features into a tight mask. "That's different."

"How?"

"Belinda, I couldn't work it out with him even if I wanted to."

"I don't get it."

Trin pounded his fist on the arm rest, then turned his midnight gaze toward the passenger window. "Domino was goin' to see him when her plane went down."

Belinda's hands loosened slightly on the steering wheel and the car swerved a little. "How do you know that?"

"Arthur told me."

"How'd he know?"

"They were talking and she let it slip that she needed to see Spry . . . about something. Arthur assumed I knew when he told me."

Belinda considered the new information for a long moment. "Sweetie, I know how hearing that must've upset you, but Spry's not to blame."

"From where I sit, he is."

"But she didn't even see him."

"I don't care."

Belinda shook her head. "Now, Trin, I know better than anyone how easy it is for you to hold onto a grudge. But even you must know this is unfair."

Trin refused to respond. Still, it was obvious that Belinda's words had hit home.

"There's gotta be another reason why you're so angry," She prodded.

"I don't want to talk about this, Belinda." Trin's voice grated.

Belinda could tell by his tone that he was deadly serious.

As usual, the Terrace was packed. Finding a parking space proved to be as difficult as getting inside and being seated. Since Belinda wanted Trin to be in a good mood when she told him about Dominique, she hoped the easy intimate atmosphere would keep him in mellow spirits.

When the two cousins walked arm in arm through the front door of the restaurant, they were greeted by the hostess.

Carol Pines's green eyes stretched in surprise when she saw Belinda on the arm of such an extremely gorgeous man. "Doctor T," she breathed.

Belinda sighed. "Don't even try it. Carol Pine, this is my cousin, Trinidad Salem," she explained. "Trin, this is Carol. She's the hostess here."

Trin leaned forward and took the woman's small hand in his much larger one. "Nice to meet you," he said.

Carol's lashes almost fluttered closed at the raspy, deep quality of Trin's voice. "Nice to meet you too," she whispered. "Um . . . Doctor T, are you here to see Kyla?"

Belinda frowned. "I thought she was off tonight."

Carol leaned against the wooden podium and tapped her fingers against the reservation book. "She was, but we got so busy we had to give her a call."

"Oh . . ." Belinda sighed, trying to ward off the sinking feeling in her stomach. "Um, Trin, maybe we should go somewhere else."

"Oh Doctor T, you don't have to do that," Carol cut in.

Belinda was becoming more edgy by the second. "Well, you just said y'all are real busy."

"Yeah, but you know we always have a table reserved for Doctor Wink's favorite customers."

"And as hungry as I am, you couldn't drag me outta here," Trin said.

Belinda knew a meeting between Trin and Dom would be inevitable. Since there was no reason to avoid it any longer, she slapped her hands to her sides and shrugged.

Carol had just ushered Trin and Belinda into the restaurant's dining area, when someone called her. "Doctor T, you guys just wait here and I'll be right back," she said before she rushed off.

"Mmm, this is a nice place, Belinda," Trin noted as he took in the cozy dark atmosphere. The Terrace was well named. Baskets of fresh pink roses and vines hung over every table and covered all the railings and columns. The foliage gave people the impression they were dining in the moonlight on a lovely, quiet terrace.

Belinda, however, didn't feel quite so calmed. Her large, lovely eyes searched the room for any sign of Dom, but she was nowhere in sight.

"Belinda?"

"Huh?"

Trin frowned and stared at his cousin. "You alright?" he asked.

"Yeah . . . why?"

Trin pushed his hand into the deep pockets of his Maurice Malone trousers. "Did you hear what I said?"

Belinda was completely lost. "No, um . . . what?"

"I was sayin' this is a nice restaurant."

"Oh! Yeah, yeah it is nice. The uh . . . new manager made a lot of changes."

Belinda closed her eyes in defeat the moment she felt a tapping against her shoulder. When she looked up, there was Dom, looking radiant and happy.

"Girl, what are you doing here?" she asked, the moment Belinda turned.

"Um . . ." Belinda's smile was watery as she struggled to catch her breath.

Trin's dark eyes narrowed when he heard the voice. It was

the same one he'd heard when he called Belinda a week earlier. He realized that what he'd been thinking had not been crazy and he began to struggle with a sudden shortness of breath. After a moment, he turned.

Six

The woman Trinidad thought he'd lost forever was standing there smiling and talking with his cousin. His mouth fell open and his midnight gaze widened as he watched the incredible scene. God, was he dreaming? Trin asked himself, his eyes closing momentarily. No, Dom was still there and standing less than ten feet away.

"I didn't expect to see you in here tonight," Dom was saying as she pushed her hands into the deep pockets of her peach bell-bottom pants.

Belinda gave a weak laugh and finally gathered the nerve to turn around. Trin stood there as though he had been struck by lightning. He finally squeezed his eyes shut tightly and prayed for an end to the cruel joke. When he opened them, he saw that the tall, dark beauty was still there. She was lovely, cool, and watching him with concern in her exquisite light eyes.

Trin pressed one hand to his chest and Belinda was sure he was about to tumble to the floor. She curled her hand around his arm and made the introductions.

"Um, Kyla, this is my cousin, Trinidad Salem," Belinda nervously announced.

Dominique extended her hand toward the devastatingly gorgeous man and smiled.

Slowly, Trin took her hand. He held it as though he'd just come in contact with a priceless jewel. "Domino?" he whispered.

Dom blinked and tilted her head slightly. "Excuse me?" she said.

Trin bowed his head, grinding his teeth so hard the muscles in his jaw danced wickedly. "I'm sorry," he told her, his dark gaze rising again. "I didn't hear what Belinda said your name was."

"Oh," Dom breathed, smiling at his words. "Kyla. My name is Kyla."

At her words, Trin appeared to be on the verge of fainting. Dom quickly stepped closer and squeezed both his hands in hers. "Are you okay?" she hurriedly inquired.

Trin could only stare at her with his intense gaze. The sexy onyx eyes travelled over every inch of her face and body. For a split second, Dominique thought he could see right through her clothes.

Belinda chose that moment to intervene. "Um, he's probably jet lagged. He just got off an unpleasant plane ride," she explained.

Dom's lovely hazel stare slid back to Trin, and she nodded. "Well, that explains it. I had a bad experience on a plane myself and lost my memory as a result. So, consider yourself lucky."

The lightly delivered comment was Trin's undoing. He would have surely crashed to the floor had it not been for Belinda and Dom's combined strength and quick reflexes.

"Let's get him to a table," Dom whispered, unaware of the deep concern flowing in her voice.

There was a nice secluded booth in the back of the dining room. Dom decided it would be best for Trin to relax there. She couldn't explain the strong tug of concern she felt toward the gorgeous, reserved stranger, but she knew she couldn't help what she felt.

"Goodness, that must've been *some* trip," Dom teased, and smiled across the table at Belinda. Dom had slid into the booth next to Trin and was absently massaging his shoulder as she spoke. When she looked over and saw that his eyes were closed as he enjoyed the innocent caress, she reluctantly removed her hand and set it against the back of the booth.

"I'm gonna go get you a drink, alright?" she quietly informed him, smiling when Trin opened his eyes. She patted his hand and left.

Trin's slanting pitch-black gaze followed Dom until she disappeared from view. Then he slowly turned to stare at Belinda. The question in his eyes was unmistakable.

"I went over this a thousand times and now my mind's a total blank," Belinda whispered as though she were speaking to herself.

"This?" Trin repeated, his voice sounding hollow and distant.

"Trin, we—I know we should've . . ."

"Just tell me this, I'm not crazy, am I? That's really Domino, isn't it?" Trin asked, his gaze wide and expectant.

Belinda nodded. "It is."

Trin let out the breath he'd been holding. "Thank you, God," he whispered.

"Trin—"

"What's she doin' here? Why didn't you tell me? Do you know what I've been through, thinking she was dead?"

Belinda felt dizzy at the calm yet quick way Trin delivered his questions. Still, she knew he deserved answers to all of them.

"Sweetie, when I got back from a medical trip I took, Dom was already here. Unconscious. Some dockworkers found her on the pier. She was found nowhere near the vicinity of the plane crash and because she had no ID and no massive bruises or abrasions, it was concluded that she'd been the victim of a mugging."

"A mugging?" Trin repeated. His dark brows drew close and he swallowed. "She wasn't um . . . hurt, was she?"

Belinda shook her head, knowing what he meant. "No honey, there was no evidence of rape."

Trin nodded, massaging his scalp as he consumed all the new information. "What about fingerprints? I mean, surely they would've told you who she was and y'all would've known she had been on that plane?"

Belinda nodded and raised her hand. "Well, baby, if she

isn't in the system, then running fingerprints wouldn't have done any good. And because the crash had ocurred so very far away, the conclusion that she'd been mugged seemed solid. When I walked into the hospital room, I was certain it was Dom. By the time we discovered she *had* been on that plane, she'd regained consciousness and we realized she had amnesia."

"Amnesia? That's why she doesn't know me?"

"Mmm hmm. She's had small breakthroughs, but they've only been related to the crash."

"Jesus, why didn't you tell me?"

"Well, if you recall, I tried to tell you. Unfortunately, you were in no mood to hear what I had to say."

"You should've made me listen."

Belinda shrugged. "I guess you're right."

"So, why is she working here? Have you and Aaron just let her settle into a new life and forget about the one she has in New York?"

Before Belinda could answer, she felt hands at her shoulders. Looking up, she saw her husband. "Hey, baby," she greeted him, meeting his kiss.

"Trin," Aaron said, shaking hands with him over the table.

"Aaron." Trin returned the greeting. "Look, man, thanks for takin' care of Domino. But can one of you please tell me what she's doin' workin' in this place?"

"Well, hello, Aaron. Lord, everybody's just poppin' in tonight."

Everyone turned to see Dominique at the table. A waiter stood behind her, carrying a tray filled with drinks.

"Sorry I took so long, Trinidad," she apologized, setting a glass of brandy in front of him. "I hope this is okay?"

Again, Trin was stunned speechless. God, she was more beautiful than he remembered. "It's fine," he finally replied.

"Belinda, I brought you a white wine and Aaron, if you tell Jerry what you want, he'll get it for you."

Aaron set his briefcase down and smiled. "Thanks Curly, um . . . Jerry, I'll have a Corona."

Dom smiled at Trin, who was still watching her, and resumed her place next to him in the booth. "Is your drink alright?" she softly inquired, her lovely eyes lingering on his handsome face.

"It's fine," Trin assured her.

Dom smiled at the tiny sound of his voice. "Um, I went on and ordered for everybody. The special tonight is broiled lobster tail with this thick cream sauce. It's really good."

"So, how long have you worked here?" Trin asked after a moment.

Dom leaned back against the dark-cushioned booth and rolled her eyes toward the ceiling. "Hmmm, lemme see . . . about seven months."

"It looks like they can't get along without you," Trin noted, his sexy slanting gaze travelling across the crowded room.

Dom's smile radiated happiness. "Thanks, that's what I like to think. For the first job I can remember having, I'd say I'm doing pretty good."

Trin ground his perfect, white teeth and hoped she couldn't see the muscle jumping in his jaw. The foursome engaged in light conversation until the food arrived. Dom decided to join them for a bowl of salad, though she wasn't very hungry. Still, being next to Belinda's tall, gorgeous cousin was a treat. Several times, Dom lifted her extraordinary gaze to find Trin watching her with the strangest look in his slanting black eyes. She tried to not to make too much of it, figuring he was simply still shaken from his flight.

Trin was struggling to maintain his composure. He had already squeezed the fork he held so hard that he'd dented the handle. It was taking every ounce of his strong will not to reach over and pull Dominique to him. Lord, he'd missed her so. Now she was right here. Close, but still so far away.

Dom's eyes widened when she saw the condition of the heavy metal fork in Trin's hand. The set look of his gorgeous profile as he stared off into space made him appear as though he'd seen a ghost. She was concerned and reached over to pat his hand.

Trin's fork fell to his plate with a clatter. Dom's simple touch pushed him right over the edge, and soon he rushed away from the booth. He didn't know where he was headed, but he kept walking until he found the men's washroom. Inside the clean, well-kept, deserted area, Trin spent the next ten minutes splashing water over his face. He let the water continue to run and braced his hands on the counter.

Sweet Lord, he thought, *this is unbelievable.* Never in a million years did he think he would have another chance with Dominique. Still, she was alive. As beautiful and vibrant as she had ever been. If only she knew him, that would make things alright . . . maybe . . .

Trin felt a hand on his arm the moment he left the rest room. There was Dominique, watching him with concern in her fantastic light eyes.

"Are you okay?" she whispered, a small frown pulling at the natural arch of her brows.

Trin looked at her small hand resting lightly on his bicep and willed himself not to pull her into his arms. Tentatively, he placed his own hand over hers. "I'm sorry, I didn't mean to scare you. You just . . ."

Dom leaned forward. "I just what?"

Trin took a deep breath and traced her delicate hand with his strong fingers. "You just remind me of someone."

"Oh . . ." Dom breathed, then smiled deviously. "The love of your life, I take it?" she teased.

Trin was dead serious. "You're right."

Dom pressed her full lips together and nodded. "What happened?"

"I lost her."

Dom's mouth fell open. "She's . . . dead?"

Trin didn't answer and Dom took that as confirmation to her question. "I'm so sorry," she whispered.

"Thanks," Trin told her, patting Dom's hand this time. "I feel a lot better now. I just needed to splash some water over my face."

Dom's bright smile returned. "Good, but you still need to eat, so come on."

Trin was happy to let her lead him back to the table.

If possible, Dom felt even more concern for Trin now that she knew he had lost someone he loved so much. She would have given anything to remember a love like that, but assured herself that it would come in time.

"Trin, are you alright?" Belinda asked, the moment they returned to the table.

"Yeah," Trin weakly replied, easing back into the booth.

"Um, Kyla, Jerry left your piña colada while you were gone," Aaron said as he concentrated on the delicious broiled lobster.

"Is that your favorite?" Trin asked, already knowing how much Dom adored the drink.

"Mmm, I love 'em. It's the only mixed drink I've wanted since I started working here," she explained.

Trin nodded, then leaned back against the booth and raised his sleek, dark brows toward Belinda and Aaron. The couple looked on with interest.

"Kyla, we got a problem!"

Dominique had barely tasted her drink when one of the waitresses rushed to the table.

"What's wrong now?" Dom asked in an uneasy voice.

The woman shook her head. "That same old stove is on the fritz again. The chefs are holdin' heavyweight bouts to see who gets to use the two stoves that are working."

"Oh no. Alright Sheila, I'll be right in. Tell Frank, Maurice and Harold to cool it," Dom ordered, and Sheila sprinted away. Sighing her regret, she smiled at her dinner partners. "Well guys, looks like that's the only break I'll get for the night. I'll see y'all when I get home," she told Belinda and Aaron. Then, turning to Trin, she tapped one perfectly manicured nail on his shoulder. "I enjoyed meeting you, Trinidad."

"Same here," he replied, his onyx stare intent as he watched her. *And you'll never know how much,* he silently added.

The moment Dom left the table, Trin's dark gaze grew

murderous and he turned to his cousin and her husband. "Why the hell did y'all keep her from me this long?" he asked in a fierce whisper.

Belinda spread her small hands across the table in a defensive gesture. "Trin, it wouldn't have done a bit of good to tell you. She still wouldn't have known who you were."

"We didn't want to take a chance on hittin' her with too much too soon," Aaron said.

Trin slid his dark gaze toward Aaron. "So, I guess if Belinda were laid up in a hospital, practically out of her mind, you wouldn't want to know?"

Aaron and Belinda were silent.

"I'm takin' her back with me," Trin finally informed them.

"You can't do that!" Belinda whispered, leaning forward in her seat.

"Man, that's not a good idea," Aaron agreed.

"Forget y'all."

"Trin, honey, listen, you're right. Maybe this could've been handled better—"

"You damn right it could've been."

Belinda rolled her eyes. "But taking Dom with you is the last thing you should do."

Trin slammed one huge fist to the table. "She's my wife. I miss her. I love her, for goodness' sake!"

"Man, we know that," insisted Aaron, "but if you take Dom away from all she knows right now, she could be so devastated that she may never remember. And you won't ever get your wife back."

"Trin, just let her stay with us for a while longer until she's more settled," Belinda pleaded.

Trin uttered a sigh of disgust and ran one hand over his curly hair. "It's been almost a year, and you and Aaron are sadly mistaken if you think I'm gonna leave her here."

Aaron cast his warm gaze to his wife and shrugged. Belinda cleared her throat and nodded.

"Trin," Aaron began, "we want you to stay with us while you're here."

The look on Trin's face made it obvious that he was quite stunned by the offer. "I can't believe y'all would even offer somethin' like that considering . . ."

"Man, this is a helluva lot more important than all that mess that went down seven years ago. Don't you agree?"

Trin sighed. "You're right, but—"

"Trin, if you can forget all that mess and accept Aaron and me and respect us, then it's over. Forgotten."

"Are you sure?" Trin asked his cousin.

"We are," Belinda assured him. "Are you?"

Trin nodded and held his hand out to Aaron. They shook and then Belinda placed her hand over theirs.

"We're gonna have to be very careful around her, Trin. I know it'll be tough, but you have to remember that she doesn't remember."

"I will," Trin promised as he and Aaron let go of each other's hand.

The threesome sat in silence for a moment, then Aaron leaned forward.

"Man, do you know where Dom got the name Kyla from?"

Trin took a sip of water and nodded. "Mmm hmm, it was her great-grandmother's name and Domino's middle name."

Belinda sighed as she and Aaron nodded their satisfaction.

"What?" Trin asked, frowning.

"Well, it's a good sign," Belinda explained. "She may not remember where it came from, but perhaps she will in time."

"Hell, how much time? It's almost been a year."

"But it hasn't been a totally unproductive year," Belinda reminded him.

Trin wasn't satisfied. "What about specialists? There's gotta be more we can do to push her along."

"They'll all tell you that the best thing we can do is give her time," Aaron said.

"Besides, Trin, she already feels some kind of connection to you. That was very obvious. We'll just work from there."

Trin shook his head at Belinda's reasoning, but he decided

to give their advice a shot. The only thing he cared about wa~
getting Dominique back.

"Trin, you ready?" Belinda asked as the waiter cleared
away their dinner plates. It was almost time for the restauran
to close and they had been there for more than three hours.
Belinda knew she was wasting her breath, asking Trin if he
was ready. He wouldn't leave as long as Dom was there.

"Does she have a car here?" Trin was asking.

"We've offered to have a car shuttle her back and forth,"
Belinda explained, "but she prefers to either take a cab or
get a ride from someone here at the restaurant."

"I'll give Domino a ride home in your car," Trin decided,
meaning Belinda should ride with her husband.

"Come on Doc, we can get Trin's luggage out of the trunk
before we go," she decided.

"Mmm hmm," Aaron replied. "All right, Trin."

"All right, man." Trin said, as he and Aaron slapped hands
again.

"Sweetie, *try* and remember what we said," Belinda cautioned, before she kissed his temple and left with her
husband.

The restaurant was clearing out slowly but surely. Trin didn't
mind, since it gave him the opportunity to watch Dominique
more easily. His dark gaze followed her every move. It was easy
to see that she was extremely comfortable in her role as manager of the establishment. She was obviously very confident
with her work, for she knew the inner workings of the kitchen
and dining room as well as the bar and music sections.

Dom was reviewing the last of the evening's receipts. She
nodded and handed them to the waitress who was waiting to
deposit them in the safe. She then walked by the bar and
tapped lightly on the polished mahogany counter to get the attention of the man standing there.

"Whit, I called Cory about fixing that stove. He was pissed
but I got him to promise he'd be in tomorrow morning."

"What time? 'Cause we might have to call and remind him," Whit sarcastically replied.

Dom laughed. "I know. I'll call here in the morning and if he hasn't shown up by nine-thirty, I'll call him."

"Deal," Whit said, winking at Dom before he walked away.

Dom sighed and massaged the tired muscles in her back. Turning, she noticed Trin still sitting in the booth at the back of the dining room.

"Are you waiting to complain about the food?" she teased, sliding into the opposite side of the booth when she walked over.

"Negative," Trin assured her. "The food was great. You have good taste."

"Thank you," Dom said, her curly hair bouncing as she nodded. "So, what are you still doing here? I take it Belinda and Aaron left already."

Trin's nod was slow. "I stayed to offer you a ride home," he explained.

Dom's full lips parted slightly in surprise and she felt uneasy for the first time that evening. "Trin . . . I don't know."

"Why not?" he asked, his voice soft and nonthreatening.

She sighed. "I just . . . I . . ." She trailed off, wanting desperately to accept but not knowing if she should.

Trin smiled, thinking that she looked as uneasy as she'd been the first time he'd asked her for a date. "Look, if you turn me down, I'll be stranded."

Dom appeared skeptical. "How come?"

"Belinda left me her car, but I don't know where the hell I'm goin'."

Dom laughed at his reasoning. "You have a point. . . . Alright, just gimme a few minutes to get my stuff."

Trin expelled a sigh of relief as he watched her walk away. *Take it easy man,* he ordered himself.

After locking up, Dominique and a few other people were the last to leave. Trin was already outside waiting for her next to Belinda's red Benz. All the waitresses complimented Dom on snagging a ride with the handsome, sexy stranger.

"You got everything?" Trin asked, as soon as Dom stepped next to the car.

For a moment, she frowned. She knew it was crazy, but she couldn't help but think she'd heard the man ask her that before. With a quick shake of her head, she decided that was impossible. "Yeah, I'm all set," she finally told him.

"So, where are we headed?" Trin asked once they were settled inside and he had started the car.

Dom flipped a thick curl out of her eye and cleared her throat. "After you leave the parking lot, make a right and head that way until I tell you to turn."

"Yes, ma'am."

They rode in comfortable silence for a while, but Trin couldn't remain passive for long. Not with Dominique seated next to him.

"So, what do you usually do after work?" he asked.

"This," she simply replied.

"Stop lyin'."

Dom laughed. "I'm not. I go right home after work. Every night."

"And you've been workin' here for about seven months?" Trin asked, tapping his strong fingers to the steering wheel, while he waited for the light to change.

"That's right."

"Hmph. I'm sorry, I just don't believe you."

Dominique turned in her seat to stare at him. "Why not?" she asked, her hazel stare lingering on his perfect profile. "Turn here," she told him, pointing before resting against the seat. "Why not?" she asked again.

Trin groaned. "Out of all the men that work at that restaurant and all the ones who must come there to eat, you mean not one of 'em has asked you out?" he probed lightly, though his interest was peaked.

"Well, I've had my offers," Dom admitted.

"But you've turned them down?" he guessed.

"Mmm hmm."

"Why?"

"I don't know. This amnesia thing, it's . . ."

"What?"

"I keep thinking that maybe I've got a real life somewhere else. I mean, I don't want to get too caught up in all this only to find out I have a husband somewhere," she explained.

Trin's hold on the steering wheel tightened to a death grip. "Do you think there is a husband?"

"I don't know. Listening to you talk about the woman you lost, all I could think about was a man out there missing me that way."

Trin groaned and the car swerved just slightly. Luckily, Dom didn't notice and he regained control of himself. He tried to remember all the warnings Belinda and Aaron had given him. Finally, he decided it was best to cut off all conversation.

Fortunately, the ride didn't last much longer. Dom's perfectly delivered directions soon led them to Aaron and Belinda's home in one of Chicago's most exclusive neighborhoods.

"Trin, you can take the car around back since I live in the guest house," Dom instructed.

A dark frown clouded Trin's gorgeous face. "The guest house? You shouldn't be livin' so far away."

Dom giggled. "You sound just like Aaron. I 'bout had to beg him to let me have the place. It's not all that far, though. I love it."

One side of Trin's mouth tilted upward, but he wasn't smiling. "Mmm hmm." Once the car was parked, he helped her out and escorted her to the front door of the lovely, spacious cottage.

"Do you want to come in for a little while?" Dom innocently offered once she'd opened the door.

Trin stared into his wife's captivating hazel eyes and ordered himself to turn her down. He knew that once he accepted her sweetly delivered offer, "a little while" would turn into the entire night.

Softly, he ran the back of his hand down her satiny smooth cheek. "As lovely as you are, I'd never want to leave. So, I better say good night right now."

Dominique was obviously disappointed, judging from the downturn of her soft mouth. Still, she managed to smile.

"Good night, Trin," she said, before disappearing into the house.

Hearing her shorten his name made Trin smile. He pressed his fist against the door for a moment, then headed to the main house across the yard.

Seven

"Aaron! Hand me another bowl, you put too much popcorn in this thing!"

Aaron sprinted across the kitchen and did as he was told. He and Belinda were preparing to watch a movie scheduled to begin in less than ten minutes and were getting their last-minute snacks.

"Why don't we just buy microwave popcorn?" he asked, handing his wife another bowl.

Belinda smiled up at her gorgeous husband. "Because *you* said it was bad for us."

"Yeah, that may be true, but it's a helluva lot less messy."

Belinda just shook her head and focused on the popcorn. While she was bent over the counter, Aaron helped himself to the heavenly view of her derriere encased in tight-fitting black shorts. His brown gaze slid away from Belinda, and he noticed Trin walk in. He watched his cousin-in-law drop to an armchair in the corridor.

Belinda looked up when Aaron tapped her shoulder. She followed the direction of his finger and saw Trin sitting with one arm slung over the back of the chair and his head bowed. She frowned, forgetting about the popcorn as she walked over to him. Aaron followed closely behind. When Belinda reached the side of the chair, she realized that Trin was crying. Her eyes widened at the totally unfamiliar sound and she dropped to her knees and patted his hand.

"Honey, don't do this to yourself," she whispered, her large dark eyes filled with worry.

"I can't believe she doesn't know who I am," Trin whispered back, through his soft weeping.

"Sweetie, it won't be this way forever." Belinda tried to reassure him.

"Is that a promise?" he asked, watching Belinda rest her head on his knee. "I'm sorry," he said, a tiny sniffle following his words. "I'll kill you both if you tell anybody you saw me cryin'." He rubbed the back of his hand across his eyes.

Aaron grinned and clapped Trin on the back. "The strongest man would cry in your position," he bellowed, joining Trin when he began to laugh.

"Why don't you come watch the movies with us?" Belinda offered. "They're all action-packed," she added, hoping to take his mind off the situation at hand.

Trin pulled one of Belinda's braids and stood from the chair. "No thanks, girl. If you tell me where I sleep, I'm goin' straight to bed."

Belinda nodded and stood as well. "Go up the right stairwell and your room is fourth on the left. We took your bags out of the car and you'll find them in there."

"Thanks," Trin whispered, kissing his cousin's cheek before he disappeared upstairs.

"Hmmm . . . this one fits better than I thought it would," Dom was telling herself as she twisted and turned. As she admired her attire in front of the full-length mirror, a satisfied smile crossed her lovely, dark face. The black bikini was skimpy yet classy and very flattering. It more than complimented her natural attributes and, as she stood there, she wondered if Trin would be visiting the pool that morning.

With a shake of her head, Dom silently chastised herself for even hoping for that. Behind the closed doors of her home the night before, she had gone over her actions. She couldn't believe she had fawned over him the way she had. Her behavior was quite out of the ordinary, but she finally chalked it up to the simple fact that Trinidad Salem was sexy and very gorgeous.

Still, Dominique had to admit that her actions may not have been as outrageous as she wanted to believe. Sure, she was flirting, but there was just something about Trin. Something that went beyond the charming, handsome package—a subdued yet powerful aura that she found immensely appealing. Satisfied with the explanation, Dominique nodded, grabbed a towel, and headed out to the pool.

Trin was still in his room, standing before the window overlooking the backyard. He had been up at dawn, but waited until Belinda and Aaron left for work before he got up to loaf around. Now, back in the guest room, he had the chance to think about everything that had happened in the last twelve hours. Though he had become a little more used to the idea of Dominique being alive, it still had him a bit dazed. She was here though, and he was determined to have her back in his life . . . as his wife. He lived for the day when he could take her home and begin their lives again. Trin wanted Dom to know him and how things were between them. However, there were things he prayed she would never remember.

A few moments had passed when he saw Dom coming to the large, in-ground pool located in the backyard. His intriguing slanted gaze widened in surprise, and his mouth fell open at the sight of her in a sexy black bikini.

"My God," he breathed as he watched his wife settle into one of the many cushioned lounge chairs surrounding the deck. In the next second, he felt his long legs weaken beneath him and cursed at his reaction. Bracing his hands along the window sill, he willed himself to calm down. He thought his memories of Dom's spirit, her lovely face, and voluptuous body would suffice. But one look at her in that skimpy piece of material and he had to admit there was nothing like the real thing. After another brief look in the direction of the pool, he left the room.

* * *

"He's not makin' any excuses about not being able to fix it, is he?"

"No, but he did ask how we managed to break it this time."

Dom sighed and rolled her eyes toward the sky. "It broke down because he didn't *manage* to fix it the last time."

Sammy Charleston chuckled over the phone at Dom's comment. They were discussing the previous night's business and because Sammy handled the lunch crowd, he could only speak with Dom during the morning.

"Keep an eye on Cory, Sammy," Dom said, referring to their contracted repair man. "You may want to drop a few hints that if he screws up again, we'll be looking for a new repairman when his contract is up."

"Oooh, I can't wait to drop that bomb," Sammy happily replied.

While Dom was on the phone, Trin had arrived in the backyard. He smiled as he caught on to her conversation, admiring the authority in her voice. While Dom carried on her conversation, Trin allowed himself to take a closer look at her dark curvaceous body. The bikini revealed far more than it concealed, but he had no complaints. After so long with only his memories to get him through the night, she was a welcome sight.

Trin's midnight gaze narrowed even more when it landed on a round glass table covered with news magazines and papers. Every publication, from those dealing with local news to international information, was spread across the glass surface.

Dom finally finished her conversation and set the cordless phone aside. She leaned back against the lounge, eyes closed. She opened them after a moment and stared right at Trin as though she had known he was there all along.

"Hello," she said softly.

Trin ran one finger along the smooth line of his jaw and stepped around to face her. "What's goin' on?" he asked.

Dom sighed and rested her head back against the lounge. "Not much and I hope it stays that way," she said, loving the rich, deep sound of his laughter touching her ears.

"May I sit?" he asked, gesturing toward the vacant lounge chair.

"Mmm . . ." Dom replied, nodding. She wasn't about to refuse the request.

"Somethin's gotta be goin' on," Trin noted, pushing his fingers along the magazines and newspapers on the glass table.

Dom shrugged. "I'll admit that I can't get enough of the news."

Trin's sleek black brows drew close and he closed his eyes for a moment. "Maybe when you get your memory back, you'll discover that you're a big-shot reporter."

Dominique laughed. "I doubt it. I don't think I have the stomach for some of the stuff I've been reading."

"But you still read it?"

"I guess I'm a news junkie—I know it's not good for me, but I can't get enough."

Trin couldn't contain his laughter. He leaned his heavy frame back against the lounge and propped the side of his head in his hand. "So, what are you gonna get into today?" he asked.

Dom stretched lazily and sighed. "Not a thing," she purred, unaware of what an inviting picture she made. "At least, I hope not." She shot Trin a doubtful look.

His dark eyes narrowed when he smiled. "You think they'll call you in again?" he asked.

Dom pressed her hand to her forehead. "Well, yesterday was my day off and they called me, so I don't know what would stop 'em today." She sighed, running her hands over her thighs.

Trin's slanting gaze travelled over the luscious vision before him. He prayed he could keep the promise he'd made to himself not to touch her.

"I think I know a way we could avoid that," he finally told her.

"How?" Dom asked, toying with one of her thick curls as she watched him with mounting interest.

Reluctantly, Trin rose from his chair. "If you go get dressed and meet me in the kitchen, I'll tell you," he bargained.

Dom smiled, though a slight frown tugged at her brows. "Sounds mysterious."

Trin shrugged one broad shoulder. "You won't know 'til you meet me in the kitchen," he cautioned.

Dominique eased herself off the lounge chair with the grace of a queen. "What should I change into?"

Trin gaze a short laugh and turned his probing stare toward the ground. "It doesn't matter."

Dom brought her hand to his cheek and rubbed the slightly rough surface. "You okay?" she asked, smiling when he pulled her hand away and pressed it to his mouth.

After a moment Trin sighed and released her. "I'll see you in the kitchen," he promised, then left Dom watching his quickly departing figure.

"Oh, forget this," Estelle Wallace muttered as she slammed down the phone. She pushed her chair away from the desk and stood to look across the noisy, crowded office. "Mr Cule! Mr Cule!"

Arthur Cule was principal of one of New York's many elementary schools. He was in the process of getting the story on a fight that had occured during recess, his office filled with the eight students involved in the scuffle.

"No recess for a week," he told the children's teacher, Margret Lowery.

"Aw Mr. Cule!" the boys cried at once.

Arthur turned a hard stare toward the kids and raised his brows. "Y'all wanna go for suspension?"

The kids decided not to push him further.

Arthur nodded. "Good. Now, back to class." Standing from his desk, he followed the children and their teacher from his office. Leaning against the doorjamb, he sent his secretary an expectant look.

"You've got a call that seems pretty urgent," Estelle informed him.

"What now?" Arthur grumbled, reaching across his desk to pick up the receiver. "Arthur Cule."

"Hey, Arthur!" a cheery, female voice greeted him.

"Hello." Arthur slowly replied. His voice was polite in a reserved way, since he didn't recognize the woman on the line.

She laughed. "It's me, Belinda!"

Arthur laughed as well. "Girl, where the hell have you been?!"

"I could ask you that same thing, Mr. Principal," Belinda teased.

Arthur rolled his eyes. "Don't start," he warned.

"What? So when did you decide to do this? As I recall you always thought the principal was the enemy."

"I had a change of heart." Arthur said, coming around the desk to take a seat.

"Mmm hmm."

"So . . . how's Aaron?"

Belinda sighed. "He's fine. We're very happy. Thanks for asking."

"Well, you know I never approved of all the shit that happened before y'all left," he explained.

"I know, you were about the only one who didn't give us a hard time," Belinda remembered.

"So, what's goin' on in Chi Town?" Arthur asked.

Belinda gave a weak laugh and decided to get right to the point. "Well, Trin's here."

Arthur frowned. "He's in Chicago?"

"Mmm hmm, I'm surprised he didn't tell you."

"Well, he told me he was goin' out of town. He probably didn't tell me where because he knew I'd ask if he was going to start some trouble and try to talk him out of it."

"Well, he didn't come to start any problems."

"Come again?"

"It's true. I asked him to come."

"What for?"

"Are you sitting down, Arthur?" Belinda asked.

Arthur frowned. "Yeah, why?" he asked, uneasiness filling his voice.

"Dominique's alive."

The phone almost slipped from Arthur's hand, and he was glad he was sitting down. "Can you repeat that?"

"Dom survived that crash."

Arthur leaned forward in his chair and rested his elbows on the desk. "Well, how? . . . "

"How is something we'll probably never be clear on. She was found on a dock in Chicago and she remembers the crash, but not how she got on that dock," Belinda explained.

"Well, what's she still doing in Chicago? Why didn't she come home?" Arthur wanted to know.

"She doesn't remember anything beyond the crash."

"'Scuse me?"

"She's got amnesia. We're confident that she'll remember, but she hasn't had any serious breakthroughs yet."

"Belinda, it's been almost a year," Arthur reminded her.

"I know that, but she is making progress."

Arthur shook his head, still stunned by what he was hearing. "You said Trin's there. I take it she hasn't remembered him either?"

Belinda sighed and leaned back in the comfortable suede desk chair in her hospital office. "Uh-uh, she just thinks he's my cousin."

"Jesus." Arthur breathed. "How's he taking it?"

"Not well, but we've explained the situation to him and I think he's just shocked that she's alive more than anything."

"So, have you told her people?" he asked, still taking in the news.

"No, we wanted to wait a while. You know, give Trin and Dom some time alone."

Arthur nodded. "Yeah, I can understand that."

After a while, Belinda cleared her throat. "Um, Arthur, have you talked to Spry lately?"

"Spry? Where'd that come from?"

"Well, Trin told me Dom was on her way to see him, and I can understand why that would upset Trin, but . . ."

"But?"

"But it just seems like there's more to it than that. I still don't understand why they're such enemies."

"Well, you know they never got along from when we were all little," Arthur said.

"I know that, but that was a long time ago and Trin's dislike seems, I don't know . . . renewed for some reason."

"Well, like you said, Dom was on her way to see Spry when that plane went down."

"Yeah, there just seems to be more to it. I don't know what it is and Trin doesn't want to talk about it."

Arthur shifted in his seat and rubbed the back of his hand across his eyes. "You know Trin and Dom *were* havin' problems," he said.

"Get the hell out."

"It's true."

Belinda wasn't convinced. "Are we talking about the same people here? Trinidad and Dominique? The happiest couple we know?"

Arthur gave a rueful smile. "We are, but they were having some serious problems before that accident. Dom confided in me a little, but—"

"Wait a minute. Things were so bad, she couldn't talk to Trin?" Belinda asked in disbelief.

Arthur sighed. "I guess. But she never went into detail. All I knew was that she needed space from Trin. He'd changed for some reason, started acting real crazy, shutting her out . . ."

"Why?"

"She never found out."

"Damn."

Arthur didn't have answers. Belinda was sure there was a lot more to the story than either of them could begin to know.

* * *

As promised, Dom went to meet Trin forty-five minutes after they parted company at the pool. When she walked into the spacious, state-of-the-art kitchen, Trin was nowhere in sight. She tapped her fingers along the oak countertop and waited. She was a lovely thing, standing there in a short DKNY creation. The navy blue and white dress reached her mid-thigh and had a empire waist that showed off her very full breasts.

"Where is he?" she whispered, absently toying with a thick curl that had escaped her upswept hairstyle.

Suddenly her eyes were covered and she felt fingers curl around her upper arm in a firm, yet gentle hold.

"Walk," Trin ordered, his soothing, raspy voice whispering in her ear.

Dominique followed his instructions, breathless from the feel of his tall frame behind her. Once outside, her eyes were uncovered and she gasped at the sight of a long gray limo parked in the curving driveway.

"Trin . . ." she breathed.

"I figured the best way to avoid getting called in to work was not to be around to answer the phone."

His heavy Long Island accent sent chills down Dom's spine. She could only watch as he nodded toward the driver, before he turned to face her.

"Since I don't know Chicago, and I take it you're not all that familiar with it either, I figured we could use a guide."

"But a limo?" Dom asked, appearing slightly awed as she stared at the long, sleek vehicle.

Trin shrugged and opened the car door. "I rarely get the chance to impress women as lovely as you," he told her, a serious expression on his handsome face.

Dominique didn't believe him for a minute, but she was delighted by the gesture. She couldn't wait to settle into the luxurious ride. Once inside the cushioned dark interior of the car, however, she grew a bit uneasy. Being alone with such an intense stranger had its effects.

"Um," Dom began, then cleared her throat, "so where are we going?"

Trin could see the nervousness in her striking, clear eyes and he hid his smile. *Lord, she is so beautiful,* he thought. "Where would you like to go?" he asked, trailing one finger along her bare thigh.

Dom followed the trail of the caress and briefly closed her eyes. "Trin . . ." she whispered.

He halted his fingers' pursuit. The caress stopped right at the hem of Dom's dress. "We'll just ride around for a while and then stop wherever, alright?" he suggested, pulling his hand away from her thigh and resting it on his cream-colored Hilfiger trousers. He'd decided to use Dominique's obvious attraction, as well as her uneasiness, to his advantage. Of course, the last thing he wanted to do was scare her away.

The limo ride was a treat in itself. There was a well-stocked bar, old and new R&B and hip-hop CDs, and movies galore. Trin and Dom had a great time sightseeing and acting like kids.

After almost an hour of riding around the beautiful city, the limo stopped at the pier. Dominique was extremely curious.

"What are we doin' here?" she asked Trin, who simply shrugged and sent her an innocent dark stare.

He opened the door and Dom took his hand and stepped out behind him. The double dimples in his cheeks appeared when he saw the surprise brightening her face.

"Boy, what have you done?" she cried, staring at the huge impressive yacht docked at the pier.

"Well, I can't take you back home hungry or the doctors will have my ass," Trin argued. "Care for a tour?"

The yacht was just as impressive as the limo, if not more so. It appeared to be even more spacious on the inside than it looked on the outside. The color scheme consisted of gold, wine and navy tones. It was cozy, chic, and very intimate.

"What's in here?" Dom was asking when they bypassed a closed door. She went back to open it. When she peeked inside, her question was answered.

"The main cabin," Trin answered, standing close behind her as he looked into the gorgeous suite.

"Mmm hmm," Dom nodded, trying to ignore his hand where it rested around her waist.

A wolfish grin spread across Trin's devastatingly handsome face and he pressed his mouth against Dom's ear. "We can stay in here as long as you want."

Dom's laughter was short and shaky. "Yeah, I'll bet we can," she said, turning to face him. "But I'll pass." She patted her hand against his rock-solid bicep.

Trin's grin widened before he began to laugh. Dominique began to make her way back to the upper deck and he followed behind.

On the polished wooden deck, Dom got another surprise. Trin had obviously arranged for them to have lunch on the impressive boat, for there was a spectacular spread on a cozy table for two. While Trin was busy speaking to the cook, Dom took time to enjoy the beautiful view of the water.

Trin's smoldering onyx gaze caught and held onto Dom as her unforgettable hazel eyes focused out over the harbor. He seemed to be as captivated by her as she was by the rippling, blue water.

After a moment, he shook his head and ran one hand over his soft, curly hair. "Domino," he began, then silenced himself and bowed his head as he realized his blunder.

Though Dom had turned and was staring at him, Trin knew the name meant nothing to her. "It's time for lunch," he called as he moved to the table.

"Why'd you do all of this?" she asked, when they were seated and preparing to dig into the meal.

Trin shrugged and kept his eyes focused on the table. "We gotta eat," he murmured.

Dom smiled. "We could've stopped for a burger."

Trin's sexy smirk triggered a dimple. "Not my style," he said.

Dom nodded and popped a tiny, broiled shrimp into her mouth. "So, I guess every woman who has lunch with you has had the chance to eat on a luxury yacht?"

"No."

"Then, why me?"

"You should know why," Trin said, though his words meant more than Dom realized.

"Are you tryin' to tell me that I'm special?" she teased.

Trin finally looked up. "Very," he said, his dark gaze relaying the seriousness of his answer.

Dominique tugged her lower lip between her teeth and Trin's eyes were immediately drawn to the action.

"But you don't even know me," she argued.

Trin expelled a heavy sigh and closed his eyes for a moment. "You'd be surprised," he said, too low for Dominique to hear.

"I must admit, I hate to leave here, it's so nice," Dom said later, after they'd finished lunch and were preparing to leave the boat.

"Well, we can stay as long as you want," Trin assured her, his hand resting possessively against the small of her back.

Dom scratched her temple and smiled. "Hmm, why doesn't that surprise me?" She shook her head at Trin's train of thought.

They were rounding the corner of the deck that led to the side of the pier, where the boat had docked. The wind must have shifted, because the yacht tipped wildly and Dom fell back against Trin.

When she landed against his hard chest, the action brought on another quick flash. It was different this time, though, because Dom could have sworn she saw someone falling.

Meanwhile, Trin was relishing the chance to hold his wife so close. He clutched her tightly, breathing in the soft fragrant scent of her hair as his hands caress her bare arms.

"Are you okay?" he finally managed to inquire.

Dom could only nod in response. She was quiet as they exited the boat and barely participated in Trin's efforts to make conversation when they returned to the car.

The ride back to the house seemed surprisingly short. As the limo pulled into the curving driveway, Dominique averted her gaze, staring out the window. She had hoped something more would come of the quick flash, but there was nothing else.

Trin was clearing his throat and the sound brought Dom out of her trance.

"You with me?" he was asking, extending his hand.

Dom smiled, noticing that he was offering to help her out of the car. "I'm sorry," she whispered when she accepted his assistance.

"Don't be. I guess that thing with the boat shook you up, huh?" he asked as they walked to the guest house.

"A little, but that was no reason for me to be so quiet during the ride back. Not when you've been so sweet."

Trin chuckled. "I don't get called 'sweet' very often."

They'd reached her front door and Dom unlocked it. "Well, you should be," she said when she turned to face him. "Would you like to come inside?" She pushed the door open as she spoke.

Trin knew he should have turned her down again, but he couldn't. Instead of responding verbally, he just began to walk toward her, forcing her to retreat into the house.

"Do you want something to—to drink or . . . anything?" she asked, gasping when her back touched one of the beige walls in the cozy living room.

"Uh-uh," Trin responded, his pitch-black gaze intense and determined.

Dom knew there was no need for further conversation, so she gave up. Her fantastic stare settled on Trin's mouth, and her lashes fluttered closed over her eyes. Trin placed one hand on the wall near her head and the other next to her waist. His mouth settled firmly against hers and Dom moaned, allowing his tongue the entrance it craved.

A deep moan rumbled within Trin's throat the moment he stroked the dark cavern of Dom's mouth. Her lips were so sweet and supple, and Trin couldn't get enough.

An excited shriek escaped Dom when Trin's large hands cupped her bottom beneath her short dress. He lifted her against the wall in one smooth, effortless movement and settled her snugly against him. Dominique wrapped her shapely legs around his lean waist and locked them as she struggled to feel as much of his body as possible.

Trinidad couldn't believe how starved he was for her. His hands were everywhere. They cupped her full breasts, squeezing them mercilessly through the soft material of her dress. He finally broke the kiss and buried his face in the crook of her neck. He had dreamed of touching her that way for so long and now that he had the chance, he couldn't get enough of her.

"Trin . . ." she moaned.

His hands and body stilled and he prayed that she wasn't about to ask him to stop. "What?" he whispered.

"Don't stop," she moaned, not about to give up the pleasure she was experiencing.

Trin's long lashes closed briefly as he uttered a silent prayer of gratitude. He pushed Dom's legs down from around his waist and turned her around to face the wall.

She gasped when she felt his hands sliding down her thighs and legs as he dropped to his knees. She pressed her head against the wall and sighed his name as he trailed long wet kisses over the soft, sleek line of her calves and thighs. Trin's fingers curled around the drenched middle of her satin bikinis and caressed the outside of her womanhood.

Dom was in heaven, but she still couldn't believe she was giving this man such free reign over her body. She couldn't explain why it felt so right, she only knew that it was.

Trin's kisses paid homage to the fulness of Dom's derriere. Soon he'd moved around in front of her to replace his fingers with his tongue.

"God . . . Trin," Dom gasped as she caressed his soft hair.

Trin held her thighs in a vicelike grip and ripped the panties away. Then he spread her legs to his satisfaction. His handsome face was buried in the plush valley of her thighs as his tongue stroked her deeply and intimately.

After what seemed an eternity, Trin pushed Dominique away. She pressed her hands to her thighs and silently willed them to stop shaking. Slowly, her hazel stare met Trin's black one.

"Take off your clothes," he quietly ordered, resting his head against the wall.

Dominique undid the fastening at the nape of her neck and eased the dress away from her shoulders. Her chest heaved as a result of her heavy breathing and Trin's dark eyes were drawn to the erotic picture.

The dress pooled around her feet and Dom unsnapped the front fastening of her bra and pulled it away. Trin's lashes fluttered and he thought his breathing had stopped. Slowly, his eyes travelled over her incredibly beautiful dark body. He began at her feet, still encased in the strappy, navy blue heels, before moving upwards.

Dom held her hand out to Trin and pulled him from the floor when he placed his fingers against her palm. She wound her arms around his neck and kissed him deeply. That was Trin's undoing. His hands gripped her waist and he eagerly returned the kiss.

"Where's your room?" he whispered in her ear before kissing her cheek.

Dom pointed across his shoulder. "Down the hall on the right," she instructed in a voice weakened by desire.

Trin lifted her in his arms and headed in that direction. Though it was still daylight outside, the bedroom was slightly darkened due to the lovely burgundy drapes that covered the windows. Trin placed her on the bed before burying his head in the soft valley of her breasts. For a moment he simply rested there, breathing in the soft and very missed scent of her. Then he began to press kisses to the lush roundness, finally taking one tip between his lips.

"Trin," Dom moaned as her hands roamed the wide muscled expanse of his back. Her body responded intensely to him suckling one nipple while his fingers teased the other.

Trin wasn't in any hurry to remove his clothes. He wanted to pleasure Dominique for as long as possible. After a while, though, his body actually ached to feel her against him without any barriers.

Dom's eyes widened innocently and she opened her mouth to protest when Trin left the bed to remove his clothes. His huge frame shuddered when he felt her beneath him. For Trin, the only thing that could've made the moment truly perfect was if Dom knew who she was really making love with. He shook off the thought, choosing to be thankful for what he *did* have.

His fingers explored every part of her body, paying special attention to her most sensitive area. A knowing smile crossed his gorgeous face when Dominique cried out in response to the intimate caress. Her need was quite obvious, but Trin refused to take her until she asked.

He didn't have long to wait. At first, Dom tried to communicate her desire by tugging on his powerful shoulders. Trin satisfied himself by kissing every inch of her silky, dark body. When she pounded her small fists against his chest, Trin looked up.

"What?" he taunted.

Dom's full lips curved into a downwards pout. "Please . . ." she whispered.

"What?" he persisted.

"You know . . ." she purred.

Trin smiled but didn't give in. "What?"

Dominique sighed and trailed her fingers across his rippling abs. "Please make love to me," she whispered.

Trin kissed the base of her throat. "That's what I'm doing."

"I want everything." She sighed, her small hand closing around the long, rock solid length of his manhood.

Trin winced at the intense pleasure she was unknowingly giving him. His hands curved around her thighs and he pulled them farther apart.

Dom squeezed her eyes shut when she finally felt him inside her. Trin was still for a while as he allowed her to become comfortable with his size. Then he began to move and the pleasure forced moans from them both. Dom's cries grew louder and fever-pitched, while Trin's were deep and rumbling.

Dominique had forgotten such pleasure existed. Trin reveled in the fact that he was experiencing it again. The amnesia and problems of the past were irrelevant now. All that mattered was the incredible experience, which lasted well into the evening.

Eight

Dominique sighed, stretching her long legs against the crisp cotton sheets. She ran her fingers through her curly hair and snuggled deeper into the pillow. She couldn't remember when she'd felt so incredible, then gave a rueful smile at the thought.

When she turned over and saw Trin next to her in bed, she froze. Uneasiness washed over her as she thought about what she had done. Goodness, how many times had they made love that evening? she had lost count. This was a man she knew absolutely nothing about and she had tossed caution right out the window. *Lord, what he must think of me now?* Dominique shook her head at her actions, berating herself for not even protesting a little. The thought had never entered her mind. The moment they got to her front door, Dom had known what she wanted.

An insistent knocking pulled her from her trance, and she pushed the covers away. Careful not to wake Trin, who slept soundly, Dom left the bed and retrieved a robe from her closet. She turned again before leaving the room and cast another look toward the bed. God, he was so gorgeous, she thought. *Cool it, Kyla. His good looks are what got you in this situation in the first place.*

Shaking away the criticism, she hurried out to the living room. "Who is it?" she whispered through the door.

"It's Belinda. Are you okay?"

Dom leaned her head against the door. "Yeah, I was just in the back. I didn't hear you knocking."

"Well, can I come in?"

Dom knew it was foolish to keep talking through the door and slowly pulled it open.

Belinda frowned. "You sure you're okay?" she asked again.

"Why?" Dom snapped, immediately on the defensive.

Belinda toyed with one of her braids as she leaned against the doorjamb. "You look like you just woke up," watching Dom shrug. "Can I come in?"

Dom cleared her throat and pulled the lapels of the short, white cotton robe more closely together. "As soon as I get dressed, I'll be over to the house, alright?"

Belinda didn't press the issue, though a little smile played around her mouth. She started to turn away from the door, when she changed her mind. "Um, have you seen my cousin?" she asked.

"Trin?" Dom weakly inquired.

"Mmm hmm, who else?" Belinda replied, enjoying her friend's discomfort.

"Uh-uh. Listen, I'll be over later," Dom promised, then pushed the door shut.

Dom rested her head against the door and took a few deep breaths. When she turned, Trin was leaning against the wall. He was dressed and looked completely satisfied.

Dominique's nervousness went into overdrive again. She cut her eyes away from him and grimaced at her own tousled state. Trin was quite pleased as he admired her unintentionally inviting appearance.

Dom cleared her throat and began to wring her hands. "Trin . . . about what happened—"

"It was incredible."

The simple admission threw Dominique off balance, but she wouldn't allow herself to lose control. "Trin, look, I um, I want you to know that I don't do this kind of thing."

"I know."

"I mean, I don't *think* I do this kind of thing," she continued.

He smiled and pushed himself away from the wall. "You don't have to explain anything to me."

"But I don't want you to think I'm some kind of—of slut. Even if that is what I've been actin' like."

Trin wrapped his hands around Dom's upper arms and made her face him. "Now you listen to me. Don't ever think of yourself that way."

"But—"

"But nothin'. I don't want you talkin' about yourself that way. I don't have one negative thought about what just happened. You wouldn't either if . . ."

"If what?" Dom asked, frowning.

A sexy smile tugged at the sensuous curve of Trin's mouth. "If you could see yourself through my eyes."

Dominique shook her head and smiled. "Still trying to be sweet."

"Uh-uh, trying to be honest," he corrected, and pressed a soft kiss to the corner of her mouth.

Dom's lips parted in anticipation of more, but Trin pulled away. It was obvious that she was still uncertain, so he decided to leave her be . . . for a while.

Later that night, the table in Belinda's casual dining room was filled with enough food to feed a church choir. Belinda knew what a huge appetite her husband and her cousin had. Besides, she figured Trin's exciting day had probably fueled his hunger.

She was right. After a long, hot shower, Trin was more than ready for a good meal. He hadn't been in such a good mood in a long time. Knowing that Dominique was just as starved for closeness as he was almost made the entire ordeal worth the heartache.

"Can I help?" He asked, when he arrived in the kitchen.

Belinda rubbed her hand across the front of the white T-shirt he wore. "Nah, sweetie, just go have a seat. We're about done here. Aaron, can you handle the salad?" she called in a hasty tone.

"Yeah, forget about it!"

Trin leaned against the doorjamb and pushed his hands into the pockets of his sagging light blue jeans. "Y'all work well together in the kitchen," he teased.

Aaron waved off the comment. "Save it, man. That little lady is a beast in the kitchen."

"I understand. Me and Domino always took turns in the kitchen." Trin chuckled, remembering. "If we didn't, an argument was bound to happen."

Aaron joined Trin in laughter before a slightly serious look crossed his handsome bronzed face. "Don't worry, you guys will be arguing over kitchen duties again."

Trin smiled. "I hope so, man. I hope so." He smiled and left the kitchen so Aaron could finish his chores. He had just settled into his seat when Dominique rushed in.

She was dressed casually, wearing a pair of jeans and a peach-and-white striped halter top that showed off her belly-button and flat stomach.

"Girl, what'cha doin' with that phone?" Belinda asked as she poured iced tea.

Dom sighed and set the small cordless next to her plate. "The restaurant."

Belinda rolled her eyes toward the ceiling. "I hope you don't have to go out there tonight."

"I shouldn't, but we've been havin' problems with one of the stoves. I should be around in case something happens," Dom explained.

"I thought they were fixed this morning," Belinda said, propping one hand on her hip.

"Yeah, Cory Stevenson was out there to handle it," Dom answered, pushing a wayward curl from her forehead, "but this is the third time he's 'fixed' them. I seriously think his days at the Terrace are numbered."

Belinda laughed and Dom tried to join in, but couldn't. Her exquisite hazel eyes cast repeated glances toward Trin, who had one finger propped alongside his temple as he watched her intently.

The foursome was halfway through the delectable feast when the phone began to ring. Aaron sighed and tossed his napkin to the table.

"Lord, please don't let that be a telemarketer," he groaned, smiling when everyone else laughed. He was gone only a few minutes, then he reappeared in the diningroom. "Arthur's on the phone for you," he said, clapping his hand to Trin's shoulder.

"Thanks," Trin said, pushing his chair away from the table. He sent Dom a quick wink before he walked out of the room.

"Man, how'd you know I was here?" Trin asked, the moment he pressed the kitchen phone to his ear.

Arthur sighed. "Well, I miss you too, baby," he teased.

"I'm sorry, what's goin' on?" Trin asked, shaking his head at his cousin.

"Same ol' mess," Arthur replied. "Belinda told me you were there when she called me today."

"Oh."

"She told me about Dominique."

Trin ran one hand across the back of his head. "I almost fainted when I saw her."

"I can believe that."

Trin cleared his throat. "So, did she tell you everything?"

"About the amnesia? Yeah, she told me all that. So, what are you gonna do now?" he asked.

"I don't know," Trin wearily admitted. "I wanna take her home and tell her everything. *Make* her remember."

"Trin . . ." Arthur warned.

"I know, I know. Belinda and Aaron tell me that's just what she doesn't need. I guess I'll just have to play it by ear."

Arthur was quiet for a moment, then cleared his throat. "Well, I was callin' to ask you to get in touch with Aunt Tika. She's worrying about you."

Trin chuckled. "Hell, I ain't been gone but two days."

"You know how she is about you," Arthur reminded him.

"Yeah . . ." Trin said, loving his mother for her unending concern. "I'll call her tonight. Arthur?"

"Yeah?"

"Um . . . listen, don't tell anybody about all this yet, alright?"

"You got it," Arthur promised. "Just take care of yourself and Dom, okay?"

"Count on it . . . alright . . . yeah, peace." Trin ended the call, then went back to the diningroom. "I'll bet Arthur was surprised to hear from you today," he said to Belinda when he took his seat.

Belinda nodded as she feasted on a tender piece of chicken. "He was," she confirmed, "but I was just callin' to ask about Spry," she added, then closed her eyes and cursed her slip.

Trin's dark brows drew close and he leaned back in his chair. Belinda saw him watching her murderously and she held out her hand.

"I'm sorry," she squeaked.

"Why were you asking about Spry?" he wanted to know, tapping his fingers against the black tablecloth.

Belinda shrugged. "Actually, Trin, his name just came up."

"How?"

"Trin . . ."

"How?"

"None of your business!" she snapped. "Dammit, this was a conversation between Arthur and me. It had nothin' to do with you."

"Yeah, right."

"Look, Trin, if you wanna know that badly, then ask Arthur 'cause I'm not gonna get into this with you."

"Well, you can bet on that."

Belinda slammed her hand against the table. "Can you just let it go?"

Trin raised his finger and was about to issue a snappy comeback, when he noticed Dominique watching the argument. He focused on his plate and let the subject drop.

"Who's Spry?" Dom asked Belinda after a few seconds of silence.

Belinda's dark eyes widened as she glanced across the table at Trin. His head had snapped up and his midnight stare narrowed the moment he heard Dom utter Spry's name.

Belinda cleared her throat and looked back at Dom. "Spry?" she parroted.

"Mmm hmm," Dominique replied, wincing slightly. "The name sounds sort of familiar. I don't know why, but it does."

That was all Trin needed to hear. Knowing he was about to lose his temper, he threw down his fork and pushed his heavy chair back with so much force it almost teetered to the floor.

"Oh Lord," Belinda breathed as she watched him leave the dining room.

Dom watched as Belinda left after Trin, confusion evident on her lovely face. After a moment, Aaron slammed his hands to the table.

"How 'bout dessert?" he asked, smiling when Dom shrugged and nodded.

"What the hell is wrong with you?!" Belinda demanded, when she'd followed Trin outside.

He wrapped his hands around a banister and squeezed his eyes shut. "Leave me alone, Belinda," he softly warned.

"Not 'til you tell me what's got you in such a terrible mood."

"This is unbelievable. How the hell can *his* name be familiar, when she doesn't even know *me?*" he asked, turning to lean against the patio railing.

"Honey, that should make you happy," Belinda pointed out. "At least she's having some kind of connection to the past."

"Jesus . . ." Trin breathed, rolling his dark gaze toward the sky.

"What *is* it?" Belinda demanded. "Why are you so angry with Spry?"

"Leave it alone."

"Uh-uh," Belinda said, shaking her head. "I know you and Spry never got along, but now you seem to hate him more than you ever did."

Trin turned his back on his cousin and stood there with one hand across his forehead. "This shit would never have happened if she hadn't been goin' to see him," he muttered. Inside, he was thinking: It would never have happened if I hadn't—

"But that's not what all this is about, is it?" Belinda inquired, waiting for him to answer her. He never did and she finally stormed off the patio.

Trin never returned to the dinner table and Dom decided to bite the bullet and go look for him. She found him gazing out over the water as he lounged back on one of the chaise longues near the pool. From the set look on his handsome face, it was clear that he didn't want to be disturbed. But Dom had been concerned since he stormed out of the dining room, and she had to know what was bothering him.

Taking a deep breath, she walked over and ran her fingers through his soft, dark hair. "Hey, are you okay?" she whispered.

"Fine." Trin's reply was short, but his voice was soft.

"Why did you run out of dinner that way?" she asked, taking a seat next to him.

"I needed some air."

Dom nodded. "Did it have something to do with . . . Spry?"

Trin literally had to bite his tongue to keep from exploding over the innocent question. His gaze snapped from Dom's lovely face and he stared out into space.

"That's such a strange name," she continued, never realizing how tense Trin was. "I wonder where I've heard it before. You think I could know him from somewhere?"

Trin ran his hand across the back of his neck, then caught Dom's wrist and pulled her to him. The soft gasp she uttered was smothered when his tongue thrust past her lips. Her fingers

curled around the neckline of his T-shirt and she moaned. The
mastery and overt possessiveness of the kiss weakened her with
every stroke. Meanwhile, Trin's fingers slipped beneath the
hemline of Dom's top and he caressed the underside of her
breasts. They both moaned from the sheer pleasure. Dom shivered in delight, until something made her push Trin away.

The surprised look on his gorgeous face caused Dom to
avert her gaze toward the ground.

"I'm sorry," she whispered, pulling her hands away from
his chest and rushing from the pool.

"Alright, Melanie, I'll see you tomorrow."

Melanie Graves frowned at her boss and shook her head.
"Uh-uh."

Dom was about to step out of the Corolla. "Uh-uh, what?"

"You gave me the next three nights off, remember?"
Melanie explained.

"Oh damn, I forgot. Well, have fun."

"Whew!" Melanie sighed. "Don't scare me like that again,
girl."

Dom laughed. "Forgive me. I've had a lot on my mind. So,
where are you going, anyway?"

Melanie leaned back against the headrest and stared out the
windshield. "To the Island of Ecstasy. At least, that's what
Carl calls it," she said.

Dom shook her head and stepped out of the car. "Well, save
something for the honeymoon," she cautioned.

"Oh, we will!" Melanie promised with a laugh.

"Bye, girl, thanks for the ride."

"Anytime!"

The evening was surprisingly cool and Dom hadn't bothered to carry a blazer or anything to wear over the
capped-sleeved Calvin Klein design. The dress was powder
pink and form-fitting. The tight scoop bodice emphasized her
ample bosom, and the zipper stopped just below the cleft of
her breasts.

Dom always received tons of compliments on her attire at the restaurant, and that evening was no exception. That night, several men called her to their table for one reason or another. Dominique was so unaware of her sexuality that she thought nothing of it.

As she hurried to her door, Dom found a huge arrangement of pink roses on the top step. She gasped and lifted one of the flowers to her nose, inhaling the delicate scent. She couldn't get over how beautiful they were and felt sure that if she could remember, she would discover that pink roses had always been her favorite.

Juggling the huge basket of flowers in one hand and her keys in the other, she managed to make it inside the house. She figured Trin must have sent them, but still looked for a card. What she found instead was a square black velvet box nestled among the flurry of roses. A soft frown tugged at her brows and she gasped when she found an exquisite emerald choker inside the box.

"Oh . . . My God," she breathed, picking up the necklace and letting it dangle in the light. It was the most beautiful thing she had ever seen but . . .

Dominique shook her head and placed the choker back in its box. She tossed her purse aside and rushed out the front door.

Belinda and Aaron weren't home, and Dom was glad. She hadn't planned on staying long and headed straight to Trin's room, her intentions set on returning his sweet but unacceptable gift.

When he answered the door, Dominique's thoughts of returning the jewelry vanished. Trin had just left the shower, judging from his damp hair and the droplets of water clinging to his muscular honey-toned body.

Dominique blinked and glanced toward the floor. Gathering the nerve to look at him again, she held out the box. "I can't take this," she whispered.

It appeared that Trin was going to take the box, but instead, he grabbed her wrist and pulled her inside the room. He slammed the door and leaned against it with his arms folded across his chest.

"Why?" he asked.

Dom placed the box on the dresser. "It's not . . . I just can't."

"Why?" he persisted.

"Trin . . . you don't know me like that to be giving me something like this."

Trin bowed his head and took a deep breath. The choker was filled with emeralds—her birthstone. Other than simply wanting to give her something, he had hoped she would have some reaction to it.

"I'd like for you to keep it."

Dom wasn't convinced by the simplicity of it all. "Why? I couldn't have been *that* good in bed."

Trin chuckled and his dark brows rose slightly at the statement. *If you only knew, Domino.* "I tell ya," he began, "it's been a whole day since I've had you in bed, so why don't you refresh my memory." He pushed himself from the door and walked toward her.

"Huh?" Dom asked, sending him a blank look.

"Then I can answer your question better," he reasoned, reaching her before she could move away.

"Trin, don't," she weakly protested, trying to twist her arm out of his grasp.

He eased his arms around her small waist. "I won't unless you want me to and I think you do."

His voice sounded so wonderful in Dominique's ear that she reached up to grasp his wide shoulders. She moaned when his mouth settled to the base of her throat, where he kissed her.

"This isn't fair," she moaned.

Trin laughed. "I know," he whispered in her ear, before sliding his mouth across the smooth line of her jaw.

Dom couldn't resist when he kissed her. Resistance, in fact, was the last thing on her mind. She concentrated instead on the possessive mastery of his tongue smoothly thrusting inside her mouth. Her nails grazed his finely chiseled back, and she felt a surge of power when he moaned in response.

Trin pulled his hand from Dom's hip and focused his attention on the zippered front of her dress. He teased her on purpose, slowly tugging the zipper down and slipping one hand inside to cup her breast.

Dominique moaned softly into Trin's mouth. Her knees almost gave out beneath her as he caressed the soft skin that spilled over the top of her lacy, pink bra. His thumb circled her nipple, brushing it once or twice. Trin grunted when he felt the tip rise to a hard bud against his thumb.

"Baby . . ." he breathed weakly against her lips before kissing her with greater force. His hands circled around her back, unhooking her bra with experienced, persuasive fingers. He pulled the lacy piece of lingerie away and pushed the dress from her shoulders. As though she weighed nothing, he lifted her and carried her to his bed.

Soft cries escaped Dom's lips when she felt Trin's weight cover her. His large hands travelled the length of her voluptuous body until they met the waistband of her panties. Trin slipped his hand right inside and smiled when he found her very wet for him. He buried his head in the satiny crook of her neck and thrust his fingers inside her body just to hear her soft gasps fill his ears.

With each finger he added to the caress, Dom's responses grew louder. Her hips rose from the bed as she struggled to feel as much of his touch as possible. She finally pulled Trin's towel away from his hips and cupped his tight buttocks in her hands.

After a while, neither of them could hold out against the powerful arousal that had ignited. Trin pulled Dom's panties away and took her at once. He moaned, feeling the creamy heat surrounding the most sensitive part of his anatomy.

Dominique's lashes fluttered open and closed with each powerful thrust. She could barely catch her breath. Her long dark legs encircled Trin's wide back and the tips of her strappy powder pink heels grazed his massive thighs.

The pleasure of the erotic encounter engulfed them, and

their throaty cries could be heard outside. None of that mattered, though, as they drew closer to the inevitable peak of satisfaction.

Dom awakened early the next morning to find herself cradled in Trin's strong arms. A lazy smile crossed her mouth as she snuggled deeper into the embrace. She had never felt so incredible upon waking up. Rain beat against the windows, and the faint roll of thunder in the distance made her want to stay in bed forever.

She opened her eyes slowly and the smile faded from her lovely face. "Oh no." She breathed.

Gingerly, Dominique moved from the bed and took a sweatshirt she found lying across a chair. She looked down at Trin. Her stare lingered on his face for a moment before she left the room and ran down the long hallway.

Belinda and Aaron were in a deep sleep of their own. Belinda began to awaken when she heard the light but insistent knocking on the door. She tried to turn over, but one of Aaron's heavy thighs resting across both of hers made that impossible.

"Aaron," she whispered. "Wake up."

"Belinda? Aaron? I need to talk to you," Dom whispered, her voice sounding frantic as she called through the door.

"Aaron," Belinda called again, nudging her husband's tightly muscled abdomen.

"Mmm." Aaron grunted, aggravated by the intrusion on his sleep.

"Get off me and wake up," Belinda said, watching as he slowly responded. "Come in," she finally called.

Dom stepped inside and hurried over to their four-poster king-sized bed. She stood there like a child with her hands clasped together.

"I remember," she whispered, watching as the sleepiness in Aaron and Belinda's eyes was replaced by shock.

Nine

Belinda reached for Aaron's hand beneath the covers and waved her other hand toward Dom. "Come sit down," she whispered, tucking her legs beneath her.

Dom responded slowly, smiling at Belinda and Aaron as they watched her expectantly.

"Just take your time, Curly," Aaron encouraged.

Dom focused on the lovely gray-and-burgundy comforter as she spoke. "I'm married," she whispered.

The Tirellis' expelled relieved sighs when they glanced at each other.

"How do you feel?" Belinda finally asked.

"Good," Dom quickly responded with a curt nod. "I feel good. I just don't quite understand why I haven't seen my husband in so long."

A small frown pulled Aaron's long black brows together and he shook his head. "What did you just say?"

Dom shrugged. "I haven't seen him in years and I don't know why. All that's still sort of fuzzy."

Belinda glanced at Aaron again as she, too, became confused. "Sweetie, who's your husband?"

"Well, you know him," Dom said, raising her striking gaze. "Spry? Spry's my husband."

"Oh my God," Belinda breathed, covering her eyes with one hand.

"How did you happen to remember this?" Aaron whispered.

"Well, it happened a long time ago and . . ."

"Honey, are you sure it's Spry?" Belinda asked.

Dom nodded quickly. "I'm positive. It was a long time ago, but I'm sure."

Belinda and Aaron were completely devastated. Aaron leaned back against the headboard and folded his arms across his wide chest.

"When did all this happen, Curly?" he finally asked.

Dominique sighed. "It was a long time ago. We were . . . in college, I think. There was some trip to the islands or something. That's why I love piña coladas so much, mine were loaded with alcohol. That's probably why I accepted Spry's proposal so fast," she rambled, revealing information as though it were coming to her as she spoke.

Belinda rested her chin against her palm as she watched Dom in disbelief. "I never expected this," she whispered.

"Me either," Dom sighed. "I never thought I'd remember something like this. When I heard his name the other night, I couldn't forget it. His last name is Cule, isn't it?" she asked.

"Yeah," Aaron and Belinda both confirmed.

"Sweetie . . . what about Trin?" Belinda asked, raising her hand in a helpless gesture.

Dom closed her eyes tightly before looking directly at Belinda. "I can't . . . think about him now. I need to get this figured out between me and Spry before I can deal with anything else."

Belinda nodded.

"I need to find him," Dom was saying. "Can you do that for me?"

Belinda grimaced, knowing that she was about to open a family-sized can of worms. She knew that she couldn't disappoint Dom, though, and was soon agreeing to do as she'd asked.

Dom couldn't ignore her feelings for Trin, despite her determination to find Spry Cule and get some answers about her life. She didn't return to Trin's room after her talk with Belinda and Aaron, deciding to head back to her home instead. Cowardice won out and she went jogging to avoid seeing him.

* * *

Trin awoke and wasn't really surprised to find Dominique gone, but when she wasn't in the guest house, he began to worry. He searched the entire main house and there was no sign of her. Trin finally found Aaron and Belinda in the kitchen. From the looks of things, though, they weren't in the mood to be disturbed.

"What the hell is this mess all about, Bel?" Aaron was asking, as he leaned against the breakfast nook.

Belinda raised her hands. "Sweetie, you're askin' the wrong person."

"You're sayin' nobody knew about it?"

Belinda sighed. "That's exactly what I'm sayin', and if they did, I wasn't told."

There was a lull in the conversation and Trin decided to take advantage of the moment. He knocked on the wall and stuck his head just inside the doorway.

"I don't mean to interrupt, but have y'all seen Domino anywhere?" he asked.

Belinda's eyes were wide as she stared at Trin, before looking back at Aaron.

"What?" he said, not liking the looks he was receiving. "Where is she?"

Belinda turned her back on Trin and moved closer to her husband.

"Man, maybe you should sit down," Aaron advised.

Trin walked farther into the kitchen. His slanting dark gaze narrowed even more. "Where the hell is she?" he almost whispered.

Aaron shrugged. "She told me and Bel that she remembers. But um, what she remembers is being married to Spry."

"What?" Trin thundered, his expression growing murderous. "What the hell—"

"Man, we were as surprised as you are, but—"

"What else does she remember?"

"Huh?" Aaron was stumped.

"Does she remember me?"

"No . . . no she doesn't."

Trin turned to the burgundy tiled counter and slammed his palms against it. "Damn this," he grated.

"This doesn't make any sense," Belinda finally responded, her back still facing Trin. "She doesn't even know Spry."

Aaron walked over to Belinda and tugged on her braids. "Well, she did think his name sounded familiar the other night," he pointed out.

"Trin, why would Dom think Spry was her husband?" Belinda asked sighing.

"Belinda . . ." Trin warned.

She turned to look at him. "Well, she's wrong, isn't she?"

The back of Trin's hand connected with a glass on the edge of the sink and he smashed it against the stainless-steel interior. When he was gone from the room, Belinda rested her head against Aaron's chest and took several deep breaths.

"Talk about strangers in the night, what the hell possessed you to call me?"

Belinda chuckled as she listened to Spry Cule's boisterous voice on the other end of the phone. "Well, we need to talk," she told him.

"You got *that* right. How long has it been? 'Bout fifty years?" he mercilessly teased.

"You're killin' me, Spry." Belinda sighed, lounging back on her bed.

Spry stopped laughing after a moment. "I'm sorry, honey. It's just real good to be hearin' from you, that's all."

"I know, I feel the same way," Belinda assured him.

"So, what's goin' on?"

Belinda cleared her throat. "Well, I guess you heard about Dominique? Trin's wife?"

Spry was silent for a moment. "I heard. Ma told me, but I still can't believe it."

"Don't."

"Say what?"

"Dom didn't die in the crash."

"Well what—"

"She survived the crash."

"Thank you, Lord," Spry said, relief clearly evident in his voice.

"Um . . . Spry, Dom was on her way to see you," Belinda informed him.

"What? . . . Why?"

"Well, when I talked to Arthur, he mentioned something about her coming to see you. He didn't know why. Maybe she was going to try and get you and Trin to patch up your differences."

"You mean, she got on that plane for nothing."

"Spry—"

"What, Lind?" Spry cut in, whispering her nickname. "You know me and Trin never came close to patching up anything."

"Well, Dom obviously thought something was important enough to make that trip."

"Damn, what the hell was she thinking?"

"I don't know. Maybe we're on our way to finding out, though."

"What's that suppose to mean?"

"Well . . . after the crash, Dom wound up in Chicago at the same hospital where Aaron and I work. When she regained consciousness, we discovered she had amnesia."

"Jesus." Spry breathed. "You said *had*. Is she better now?"

"This morning she told us that she remembers being married."

Spry chuckled. "Hell, I guess no woman could forget being married to Trin's crazy ass."

"Hmph, Dom did."

"Well, anyway, I'll bet he's as happy as a clam. He knows everything, doesn't he?"

"Oh yeah. He knows everything but he's not too happy," Belinda revealed.

"Why the hell not?"

"Spry, Dom thinks she's married to you."

Silence controlled the conversation for the next few minutes. Belinda chose not to speak in order to give Spry a while to digest the information.

"So, she thinks she's still married to me?"

Belinda frowned. "Wait a minute, *still?* You mean she's not confused?"

Spry chuckled. "Well, her timing's a lot of years off, but no, she's not confused."

"Spry—"

"Now wait a minute," said Spry, using his deepest, most mellow tone of voice to calm his cousin. "Gimme a chance to explain."

"Please."

"It happened when we were at Howard. It was stupid to do, but we had a thing goin' and we thought we loved each other."

"I just can't imagine Dom doing something as serious as getting married on a whim," Belinda said.

"Well, we did spend the better part of the weekend drunk as hell. When I popped the question . . . well, you know."

"Yeah . . ." Belinda breathed. "So, how long did it last?"

"Three weeks," Spry replied, smiling when he heard Belinda gasp. "It took us that long to realize we'd made a mistake. We were gonna try and make it work, but I guess in the end we knew it wasn't meant to be."

"Hmph," Belinda grunted, shocked more than words could say. "Well, do you think you could share this with Dom? She wants to meet you and asked me to set it up."

"I'd be happy to. Maybe after this mess gets cleared up, she can move on to remembering her present husband."

Belinda breathed a sigh of relief. She had no cause to be worried, Spry was happy to help in any way he could. In truth, he had always been a very honest and forthright person. He hated disagreements that spiraled out of control. In fact, the tensions between him and Trin were what prompted him to leave home.

The two cousins spent another half hour on the phone.

They ended the conversation after arranging the details for the meeting.

"Watch it man, watch it now . . . you don't want none a this!" Trin shouted as he released a perfect three point shot to the basket overhead.

Aaron rolled his eyes as he caught the ball and dribbled it to the side of the court. "Forget you, what's the score? Thirty to twenty-two, my favor?"

Trin shrugged as he made a play for the ball. "Who won the last one?" he countered.

Aaron made a quick turn and released his shot. "Mmm," he grunted, adding three more points to his own score. "I think the question is, who won this one?"

It was a Saturday afternoon and the two men had opted for a game of one on one instead of going to the gym. Aaron's main reason for wanting to get out and do something was to keep Trin's mind off Dom. Since he and Trin had taken the time to get to know each other, they had become great friends.

They had been ribbing and taunting each other for almost two hours. After a while, Trin owned up to the fact that Aaron would win their second game.

"Thank you for admitting that I'm the betta playa, man," Aaron chided, clapping Trin's back. "I know how much it hurt you."

Trin leaned over and braced his hands on his knees as he caught his breath. "Anyway . . . it's tied one to one and I demand a rematch."

Aaron shot Trin a skeptical look. "Man, please, you are sorry. Dom gave me a better run for my money one Saturday afternoon and I know she'd whip the hell out of you."

The comment brought a smile to Trin's face, but it didn't reach his eyes. Aaron knew he'd made a mistake mentioning Dom and closed his eyes with regret.

"Sorry, man."

Trin raised his hand and shook his head. "Don't worry

about it," he said, pulling the gray and black bandana from his head and wiping it across his face.

Aaron dribbled the ball and leaned against the basketball goal. "Have you talked to her since . . ."

Trin shook his head. "Uh-uh. . . . I don't think she wants to talk to me."

"Man, this mess has got her all mixed up."

"I know that, but how long is this supposed to go on? When's she gonna remember bein' married to me?" Trin asked, trying to mask the hurt in his rough voice.

"It's hard to say. I doubt anybody could tell you that."

Aaron's bleak outlook on the situation only succeeded in making Trin angry. He knew Aaron was being honest with him, but that did little to soothe his temper.

Struggling to retain his calm, Trin massaged the back of his neck. "Aaron," he sighed, closing his eyes as he spoke, "you can pass this on to your wife. Y'all got two more weeks to pamper your patient and then I'm taking her home."

"So, how was the Shrimp Fettucine tonight, Mrs. Dumas?"

Elizabeth Dumas smiled at the striking young woman who stood next to her table. "Sweetie, it was heavenly. This more than made up for the dish I got last week."

Dom nodded in understanding. "Well, we were having some problems with our equipment but it's safe to say everything's back to normal."

Mrs. Dumas patted Dom's hand. "I'm glad to hear that, dearie, and you tell Maurice he's still my favorite chef."

Dom laughed. "I will," she promised.

"Excuse me, Kyla, can I see you for a minute?"

Dom turned and smiled at the waitress who called her. "What's up, Lisa?"

Lisa Jourman's long lashes fluttered madly. "Honey, there's someone to see you in your office."

"Who?"

"Girl, I don't know but he is so fine and sexy I had to make—you hear me?—*make* myself come get you."

Dom laughed and patted Lisa's shoulder. "Thanks, girl," she said, and headed upstairs to her office. When she got there, she found Trin lounging in one of the chairs facing her desk. She took a deep breath and stepped inside.

"Hey, Trin," she said in greeting, smoothing her hands across the form-fitting tan bell bottoms she wore. She had been avoiding him since her breakthrough about Spry, but silently admitted that she had missed him.

Trin's dark slanting eyes travelled up over Dom's long legs and he enjoyed the way the fabric of her pants stretched over her very full derriere. His appraisal stopped at the cleft of her breasts, visible above the low-cut tan top she wore. "What's up?" he finally replied.

Dom shrugged, slapping both hands to her sides. "Just work."

"Mmm hmm," Trin said, a slow nod following the response. "Busy, huh?" He asked, tapping his strong fingers along the arms of the chair he occupied.

Dom sighed. "Very."

Trin stood and stepped closer, causing Dom to move toward the desk until she was leaning against it. "Too busy to come see me?" he asked.

Dom's extraordinary gaze traced Trin's handsome features before she looked away. "I just haven't had time," she whispered.

Trin braced his hands on either side of her on the desk. "I don't stay that far away," he reminded her.

Dom closed her eyes and breathed in the clean, hypnotic scent of his Nautica cologne. "I know you don't live that . . . far away . . . I've just . . ."

"Been avoiding me?" He finished, smiling when her eyes snapped to his.

"No, Trin, I just haven't had time."

He placed one of his large hands against her hip and the other cupped her chin. "Baby, how much time does it take to speak? Unless you had something else in mind?" he teased, pressing his mouth to the sensitive area beneath her ear.

Dom curled her hands into tiny fists. "Trin . . ."

"Hmm?"

"Please don't . . . I can't."

Trin brought his hands to the front of Dom's snug-fitting top and cupped her breasts. "Yes, you can," he assured her, the kisses he planted below her ear growing wetter.

"Uh-uh," she insisted, squeezing her eyes more tightly closed.

"Why not?" he challenged.

Dom gathered all her strength and pushed him away. "Because I'm married!" she snapped.

Trin braced his hands on the desk and dropped his head. "I know."

Dom whirled around and stared at him. Trin cursed himself and turned to face her. "Belinda told me," he said, smoothly masking his slip-up.

"Well, then, you should know this can't happen."

Trin shrugged one of his massive shoulders and pushed his hands into his gray Maurice Malone trousers. "I don't know that," he told her.

Dom took a deep breath. "Trin, I can't think about anything . . . I can't think about us until I see my husband."

The innocent, yet hurtful remark sent Trin's temper spiraling. "You can't think about us until you see your husband," he repeated.

"That's what I said."

Trin scratched his temple. "You didn't think about him when you were sleepin' with me, did you?"

"Trin—"

"Twice, if I recall, and we won't talk about how many times we had sex."

"I didn't know about this then."

"You knew there was a possibility," Trin threw at her.

"So did you!"

Trin pointed one finger in the air. "I didn't force you to do anything."

Dom nodded. "Then you won't force me to continue this discussion, will you?" she asked, turning her back on him.

Trin's hands curled into fists, but he got control of himself. Completely losing his temper was the *last* thing he wanted to do. The last thing. Instead, he decided to leave, and closed the office door softly.

Outside, he leaned his head against the wall. "Two weeks," he promised himself.

"Girl, Trin fronts like he's this big tough guy, when he's really very sensitive."

Dom shook her head at Belinda's assessment of her cousin. "Sensitive" was not a word she would use when describing Trinidad Salem.

"He didn't seem too sensitive in my office when he came by."

Belinda rolled her eyes and leaned back in the recliner Dom had in her kitchen. "Well, I won't deny he's got a temper. A bad one. But I also know he cares a lot about you."

"I know that too, but I told him I have to clear this up with Spry before I do anything else."

"I can understand that."

"Um . . . Belinda?"

"Uh-huh?"

Dom held a dishtowel; now she tossed it across the counter. "How do you know Spry Cule?"

Belinda blinked at the question. Since she didn't want to make Dom anymore confused than she already was, not telling her Spry was a relative seemed best for the time being. "He's a family aquaintance," she said.

"It's kinda funny, don't you think?"

"Honey, this whole situation's kinda funny."

Dom nodded, agreeing wholeheartedly.

"So, what are you gonna do about Trin after you see Spry?" Belinda asked, hoping to change the subject somewhat.

"I don't know. I wanna be with Trin so much, but sometimes . . ."

"Sometimes what?"

Dom shrugged. "I don't know. I just . . . have this feeling."

Belinda frowned a bit. "You wanna talk about it?" she probed.

"I wouldn't know where to start, Belinda. I wouldn't know where to start."

Ten

Belinda felt a definite sense of déjà vu wash over her as she stood in the airport later that week. Spry had called and told her when his plane would arrive in Chicago from Minneapolis, where he lived. Never did she think she would be bringing two husbands for Dominique to meet!

Aaron pulled her back against him and pressed his handsome bronzed face into her neck. "Don't worry about this, alright?" he soothed.

"Hmph, you should've told me that a week ago." Belinda sighed, enjoying the security of Aaron's strong embrace.

"You couldn't have known Curly would remember something like this," he whispered.

"Yeah, but I could've told Trin that Spry was coming here tonight. When he finds out, he's gonna—"

"Shh . . . now stop this. We'll worry about that when the time comes."

"Hey! Hey Lind, Aaron!"

Aaron and Belinda looked up when they heard their names. Spry Cule was headed toward them, a huge grin on his dark handsome face.

"The time is here," Belinda mumbled and hurried forward to meet her cousin.

"Hey, boy," she whispered, enjoying the hug he gave her.

Spencer Cule was tall and well-built, like most of the men in his family. Unlike his brother Arthur, though, Spry was very dark. His eyes were pitch black and slanting, similar to

Trin's. The man was undeniably handsome. Spry never took himself too seriously, though. His huge sense of humor, along with the wide grin he always wore, put people at ease the moment they met him.

"Girl, you are lookin' good and I do mean good!" Spry complimented her as he held his hand out to Aaron. "What's goin' on, my man?"

Aaron grinned. "Hell, I need to be askin' you that, Counselor Cule."

Spry gave Aaron a mocking, suspicious look. "Now, are you referring to my prestigious law practice or—"

"I'm referring to your prestigious work at the Minneapolis Boys Club."

"Damn, y'all heard," Spry said, snapping his fingers. He had become so instrumental in the volunteer work he did that there had been many newspaper, magazine, and television stories done on him.

"You should be proud of yourself," Belinda said, punching Spry's shoulder.

"Oh I am . . . but there's a lot more to be done," Spry assured her as the three of them stood there nodding in agreement.

Finally, Belinda sighed. "Well, thanks for takin' the time to come out here."

Spry shook his head. "You don't have to thank me. This whole situation is messed up. Dom shouldn't have to go through this. She's a sweet one."

"Spry, how in the world did all of this happen?" Belinda asked as they went to get the luggage.

"Well, I told you, it happened in school."

"And y'all kept it a secret all these years?" Belinda asked in disbelief. "I mean, Trin hit the roof when we told him. He obviously didn't know."

Spry shrugged. "Well, it was a long time ago and it didn't last long. Hell, I was already in Minneapolis when Dom and Trin started seeing each other. She probably didn't dare tell him once she found out how much he hates me."

Aaron grabbed the gray suede duffel bag with Spry's name on it and pulled the strap across his shoulder. "Dominique doesn't know we're all related," he revealed.

Spry looked surprised and smiled at Belinda. "Damn, you're leavin' it all up to me, huh?"

Belinda gave an uneasy shrug. "I just didn't wanna confuse her anymore than she already was . . . I tell ya, this has been such a trial."

Spry grinned and pulled her close. "Well, trials are my specialty."

Dom was just getting in from work when she heard her phone ringing. She dropped her tiny black purse to a chair and rushed to answer it.

"Kyla? We're on our way from the airport."

"Belinda? Is that you? What's all that static?"

"I'm on the carphone. Listen, Spry's with us."

Dom reached for the chair behind her as she took a seat. "He is?"

"Yeah, don't leave. We'll be there soon."

Dom nodded, but said nothing. She hung up the phone and stared off into space. For just a moment she closed her eyes to gather her wits. When her eyes opened, it was as though a scene from a movie was flashing right before her eyes. This quick flash was much different from the one she'd had almost a year ago. Now she realized that there was a person falling— or being pushed—toward a desk or against a wall. Horrified, she realized that the person was herself.

"So, what are you gonna say to her?" Belinda asked on their way to the house.

"I don't know. I'll play it by ear, I guess," Spry decided, lounging in the back seat. "I won't pamper her, y'all," he warned them. "I'm gonna tell her like it is . . . or was. Whatever she asks I'll answer."

Aaron glanced at Spry in the rearview mirror. "Within reason?" he inquired.

"Within reason," Spry promised.

"Because she doesn't remember Trin." Belinda interjected.

Spry raised his hand. "And it's not my place to get into that with her. Don't worry."

Belinda nodded and turned in her seat. Aaron noticed her fingers tapping nervously against her thigh and he pulled his hand off the gear console and covered hers. Belinda gave him a grateful smile and squeezed his hand tightly.

"Sweetie, Aaron and I are gonna go out to dinner. Give you and Dom some time alone, alright?"

Spry nodded and opened the car door. "That's good. Say, does she remember her name?"

Belinda looked at Aaron and shrugged. "I don't think so. We've been callin' her by her middle name. I think that's all she remembers."

"Alright. Well, I'm gonna take my luggage. After I'm through here, I'll call a cab and get a hotel room."

"Spry—"

"Belinda, now you know I can't stay here while Trin's around, don't you?"

Belinda gave a reluctant nod and watched Spry as he got his bags and headed to the guest house.

Dom smoothed her hands over the gray and black Liz Claiborne pantsuit she wore. She heard a firm knock on the door and took a deep breath before going to answer it.

Her first thoughts when she looked up at the tall, handsome dark-complexioned man, was that he looked exactly like Trin. She cleared her throat and held onto the door.

"I don't know if I should kiss you or what," she said with a smile.

Spry shook his head. "You don't have to kiss me, just invite me in."

Dom gave a short, nervous laugh and stepped aside. "Sorry."

"Don't be," Spry said, setting his bag on the carpet. "Spencer Cule," he said, holding out his hand.

"Kyla," Dom said, shaking his outstretched hand.

Spry held onto her hand and tilted his head to the side. "No last name?"

Dom shrugged. "I don't know," she whispered.

Spry nodded and let go of Dom's hand. "My cousin tells me you have amnesia."

Dominique propped her hand on her hip. "Your cousin?"

"Belinda," Spry clarified, smiling at the shocked look on Dom's lovely face.

"Belinda Tirelli's your cousin?" she asked, watching Spry nod. "So that means Trinidad Salem's your cousin too, right?"

Spry tried to mask the tense look on his handsome face. "That's right."

"Oh no." Dom breathed, pressing one hand to her chest as she took a seat on the sofa.

"What's wrong?"

"Everything."

"I take it you've met Trin?"

"Oh yes . . . I've *met* him."

"Kyla?"

"Hmm?" Dom said, as she stared off into space.

"Look at me," Spry softly ordered, waiting until her extraordinary gaze met his dark one. "We're not married."

"We're not?"

"Uh-uh . . . not anymore."

Dom clasped her hands together and glanced up at the ceiling. "Thank you, Lord," she breathed, then looked over at Spry. "Oh, I'm sorry, it's just—"

"You don't need to explain. It was a long time ago. We were young."

"Very young."

Spry nodded and took a seat next to Dom on the sofa. "So you don't remember anything beyond that?"

Dom knocked her knuckles lightly against her chin and shook her head. "No, and I know there's more to my life than what I did in college."

"It'll come to you in time," Spry assured her.

Dom turned to stare at him. "I still can't believe all of you are cousins."

Spry shrugged. "That's us, one big family."

"Well, you do look a lot like Trin," Dom noted, laughing when Spry pretended to gag.

"He'd die if he ever heard anybody say that."

Spry and Dom talked for almost two hours. In that time, Dom learned a lot about herself as well as her parents. Spry managed to steer the conversation clear of Trin and his true relationship to Dom. He did a very good job and eventually the discussion became much lighter. In typical Spry Cule fashion, he had Dom laughing uncontrollably within minutes.

It was Dominique's boisterous laughter that caught Trin's ear when he returned home a long while later. At first, he thought she might be watching TV or laughing at something Belinda said. When he heard the deep laughter joining in, he frowned. He had a strange feeling about the situation, but chose not to overreact. Instead, he unzipped his white Boss jacket and took a seat in the shadows on a bench outside the guesthouse.

Trin didn't know how long he'd sat there on that bench before the front door opened. There was Dominique walking hand in hand with Spry Cule. Trin's temper hit such a fevered pitch that he had to grip the arm of the bench with both hands to remain rooted to the spot. That was when Trin noticed the taxi in the driveway. He watched Spry kiss Dom on the cheek and head down the walkway. When she closed her door and the taxi sped off, he went to his own room.

Fifteen minutes later, Dom burst into kitchen in the main house. She was very excited about the news that her marriage to Spry was a thing of the past. It meant she could continue to see Trin and that elated her beyond words.

Unable to find him anywhere downstairs, Dom ran upstairs to his room, hoping to catch him there. When she reached the top of the stairs, she found Trin's door ajar and went inside without knocking. Trin was nowhere in sight, but his suitcase was on the bed lying open and half-filled.

Dominique jumped when she heard Trin's raspy voice behind her.

"Through with your company?" Trin asked, the tone of his voice hard as steel.

Dom waved her hand toward the bed. "What are you doing?" she asked, unaware of the edge in his voice.

Trin shrugged and walked past her. "What does it look like?" he asked, dropping a sweatshirt into the case.

"It looks like you're packing, but I'd like to know why."

"Can't stay here forever."

Dom rolled her eyes. "Were you gonna tell me?"

Trin slammed the case shut with a thud. "Oh yeah, you would've been the first to know," he assured her.

The murderous look in Trin's pitch-black eyes left no doubt in Dom's mind that he was in a mood. A bad one. She started to back away from him, desperately trying to think of a way to lighten the scene.

"Are you okay?" she whispered.

The dark gaze narrowed. "I'm fine," he replied, in a voice that said just the opposite.

"I hoped you'd be in a better mood."

Trin pushed his hands into the deep pockets of his jeans. "Mmm hmm . . . so how was your visit with Spry?"

Dom's face brightened as she remembered the fruitful discussion she'd just had with Spencer Cule. "How'd you know?" she asked.

"I saw him."

"Oh," Dom said, nodding slightly. "Well, after I remembered the marriage, I told Belinda that I wanted to meet him."

"Uh-huh."

"I didn't think he'd get here so fast, but he was so sweet about the whole thing. . . ." Dom rambled on and on. She didn't tune into Trin's responses to her statements as they became shorter and harsher. ". . . He's so funny, I tell you, I never laughed so hard and I—"

"Will you please be quiet?"

Dom's smile disappeared and she frowned. "Excuse me?"

"You heard me."

Dom raised her hand in the air. "Wait a minute, didn't you just ask me about my visit with Spry?"

Trin could feel his vicious mood threatening to show through and feared he was about to snap. "Dammit, will you please?!" he roared.

Dom gasped, both confused and frightened.

As if he were snapping out of horrible dream, Trin realized how strange his actions must have appeared.

"What's wrong with you?!" Dom cried, her eyes filling with tears.

Trin massaged his head and took several deep breaths. "Baby . . . I'm—I'm sorry, I—"

"What?" Dom said, aggravated by his quiet stammering.

"I said I'm sorry!"

"You're damned right! I mean, who in hell do you think you are?"

Trin, finally having enough of protecting Dom, stormed over and clamped his large hands across her shoulders. "I'm your husband! *That's* who the hell I am. Your husband!"

At first Dom just stood there staring at him with her clear, hazel eyes. Then she shrugged off his hold and took several steps away from him. Meanwhile, Trin was silent and waited to see how the news would affect her.

"You're crazy," she said, her voice no more than a whisper.

Trin gave her a one-dimpled smile that was far from humorous and shook his head. "No, you just don't remember."

"Why are you doing this?"

"Domino, please listen to—"

"Who?"

"Your name is Dominique Carver. Carver before we got married," Trin explained, his dark gaze narrowed as he watched her.

Dom shook her head. "My name is Kyla Carver," she said, remembering the name Spry said when he referred to her parents.

"Kyla was your great-grandmother's name. It's your middle name. Spry should've told you that."

Dom ran one hand through her hair and walked across the room. "Why are you saying this?!"

"Because it's the truth," Trin said, remaining disturbingly calm. "Baby, why do you think I came here?"

"To visit your cousin, or that's the lie you told me."

"Belinda is my cousin. She and Aaron knew who you were, but kept it a secret hoping you'd remember on your own."

"Kept it a secret," Dom repeated, becoming frustrated by each new revelation. "So they knew about Spry and all that?"

Trin shook his head. "No. All they knew was that you were my wife. Nobody knew about the rest except you and Spry." *And me,* he silently added.

"You've been here all this time and you're just tellin' me this now? I slept with you and thought that I'd done something cheap and dirty and—"

"Domino—"

"And you never told me?!"

"Baby—"

Dom raised her hand. "No—no, it's not your fault, it's mine. I should've demanded to know everything there was to tell."

"Love, Belinda and Aaron thought it was for the best and after a while I thought so too."

"Mmm hmm . . . well, I'll tell you right now what's best is for me to get the hell out of here," Dom decided, rushing toward the door.

Trin caught her before she could make it that far. "I can't let you stay here, Domino."

"Forget you, you have no choice."

Trin began to grind his teeth. He didn't want to force Dom

into going back, but he knew he would if there was no other way. "Baby, don't you want to see your friends again? Your family in New York? Your father almost died when he heard about the crash."

Dom blinked and snapped her eyes away from Trin's. He had peaked her curiosity with the statement and she couldn't deny how badly she wanted, needed to see her family, to recall the life she'd left behind. Finally, she began to nod.

"Alright . . . alright, I'll go back."

"Trin, what the hell are you talking about?"

Trin sighed and reclined on the sofa. He was in Aaron's study later that evening. He had just told his cousins what had happened. "She knows everything," he was saying for the second time.

"How?" Belinda questioned, slapping her hands to her sides. "Trin?" she called, when he took too long to respond.

"She came over to see me after her visit with Spry."

"Wait a minute," Aaron whispered, "you knew?"

"Mmm hmm, y'all almost pulled it off, but I saw him leaving when I got back from dinner."

"So I take it you lost your temper?"

Trin looked at Belinda and nodded. "I did."

"Trin . . ."

"Belinda, it's over now and I can't change it."

Aaron was toying with a paperweight on his desk. "So how'd she take it?"

Trin shrugged. "She was upset, but not hysterical."

"I'm goin' to see her," Belinda decided, and left the room.

"Are you taking her back?" Aaron asked.

Trin nodded once. "Yeah, we leave day after tomorrow."

"She put up a fight?"

"At first . . . but she came around."

Aaron ran one hand through his wavy hair. Trin could tell that he was very concerned.

"Look Aaron, I know I wasn't thinking when I blurted this

out. Once I started talking, I couldn't shut up. Anyway, I'm glad it's done. We'll just have to wait and see what happens."

"It's open," Dom called, tossing a Nike windsuit into her suitcase.

Belinda entered the house slowly and found Dom in the bedroom. "Hey," she called, watching Dom walk back and forth filling her case on the bed.

Dom didn't answer, but continued to pack. Belinda knew she must have been devastated, but wanted to try and get her to open up.

"Kyla—"

"Maybe you should try callin' me by my first name instead."

"Sweetie, please—"

"Why didn't you tell me?" Dom snapped, turning to pin Belinda with an angry stare.

"Honey, we thought it was for the best."

"Maybe for the first month or two. Maybe. But it's been so long . . . I mean, were y'all ever gonna tell me?"

Belinda held out her hands in a defensive gesture. "We wanted you to come around on your own."

"But my name, Belinda. You could've at least told me my name."

"Okay . . . you're right. That's over with now, though, and you know everything. Still, I bet you're confused."

"Hmph, that's a bet you'd win," Dom admitted, trying to make light of the situation. It didn't work and she plopped to her bed covering her face with both hands. "Belinda, I'm so scared," she whispered.

Belinda rushed over and sat next to her. "Honey, I know. Are you sure you want to go back?"

"Uh-uh, but I know I have to. Trin's my husband. He's so gorgeous and sexy, I should be jumping with joy about it. I believe I would've fallen in love with him anyway."

"But?"

"Well, now it's different. I don't remember anything about us or our life together and I can't just act like I do."

"That's not what you're supposed to do, either." Belinda assured her. "I doubt you could, even if you tried. Trin'll understand and if he doesn't, call me and I'll handle him."

Belinda's words brought a smile to Dom's face. The small smile signified that her mood was slowly but surely improving.

"Wink, I'm sorry to do this to you."

"Nonsense, child, you've got more important things to take care of."

Dom smiled at the sweet tone of Dr. Wink Broderick's voice. She was really going to miss him, but as he'd said, she had more important things to take care of.

"Well, I'll be in later on today to answer everybody's questions about the business . . . or whatever."

"We'll miss you," Wink assured her.

"The feeling's mutual . . . Wink?"

"Yes, my darlin'?"

"Um . . . are you still gonna sell the place?" she weakly inquired.

Wink gave a hearty laugh. "My love, you've got that place running so smoothly, I wouldn't dream of it. It could probably run itself, but I have someone in mind who just may be interested."

Dom's silky arched brows rose slightly. "Oh? Who?"

"Well, Sammy's been hinting that he hates the lunch crowd. I'll talk to him about it."

Dom was very pleased. "I think he's a good choice. You're pretty smart, Doctor B."

Wink chuckled. "Hell, I surprise myself sometimes."

Trin entered the guest house amidst Dom's discussion with Wink. He knew it was tearing her apart to have to say goodbye to the only people she'd known since her accident. Still, he knew she'd agree it was for the best. Trin waited until she hung up the phone and then he knocked on her open door and stepped inside.

Dom blinked a couple of times when she saw Trin, but managed to keep calm. Clearing her throat, she ran a shaky hand through her hair. "Hey, Trin," she whispered.

"What's up?"

She shrugged. "I just got off the phone with Doctor Broderick at the restaurant."

"You told him you were leaving?"

"Mmm hmm."

Trin walked inside and closed the door. Dom was suddenly more uneasy and stood from her chair.

"How'd he take it?" he asked.

"Oh, he was fine. He knows how, um, important this is."

Trin pushed his hands deep into the pockets of his jeans and nodded. "Well, we leave tomorrow at three."

"Alright."

"Um . . . we'll be goin' back on the jet. Is that alright with you?"

Again, Dom shrugged. "It's fine. Maybe, it'll crash and I'll get my memory back."

The soft, yet sadistic remark shocked Trin, but he knew how frightened Dominique must be. He walked over to her and pulled her close.

"Domino," he sighed, "everything's gonna work out. We'll get through this."

Dom rested her head on his shoulder for a while, but her nervous state wouldn't allow her to remain there for long. "Trin, I got some stuff to take care of before we go, so I better get to it."

Trin didn't press to stay, deciding she needed the time alone. Instead, he went back to the main house, where he made two calls. The first was to Dominique's parents, Phyllis and Hamp Carver. The second was to his mother, Martika Salem. Shocked could only begin to describe their reaction to Trin's news. He answered their frantic questions and informed them that they would be home in two nights instead of the very next evening. Trin had already decided that he wanted to be alone with Dom on their first evening back.

"I don't want her to go."

Aaron pulled Belinda against him and smiled. They were lying across their bed, discussing everything that had happened.

"He's her husband, Bel."

Belinda pounded her small fist lightly against Aaron's massive chest. "I know and I know she has to go. I've just gotten used to havin' her here."

"I know. Me too."

"Aaron?"

"Hmm?"

Belinda propped herself up on Aaron's chest and looked into his deep, brown eyes. "When I talked to Arthur, he told me Trin and Dom were having problems."

"Get out."

Belinda nodded. "That's what I said, but Arthur told me Dom had been confiding in him and he thinks her trip was a lot more than a simple visit to Spry."

Aaron's heavy, dark brows drew closer. "You don't think she was leavin' him, do you?"

"Aaron, I don't know, I just wish she would remember before going back."

"Baby, Trin'll take care of her. He loves her."

Belinda rested her head against her husband's chest. "Sweetie, I know. But, if it was something so intense that she couldn't even talk to Trin about it, what's gonna happen when she goes to New York and it all comes flooding back?"

Eleven

At 1:45 the next afternoon, Trin and Dom were standing on the steps of Aaron and Belinda's home in the midst of saying their goodbyes.

"I want you to call as much as you need to," Belinda ordered, her dark eyes full of tears.

Dom nodded and hugged her tightly. "I will."

Belinda raised her eyes to Trin, who stood next to Aaron. "You take care of her."

Trin nodded, his expression somber. "I will," he promised, pressing a kiss to his cousin's cheek.

Dom sniffed and pulled away from Belinda. Then she hugged Aaron.

"Curly, now you can't be doin' all this crying or you'll get me started," he whispered, holding her close.

She nodded and buried her face in the crook of his neck. "I know," she sighed.

Trin hated to break up the moment, but he knew the longer they waited, the harder it would be to leave. "Baby, we better go," he told Dom softly, pressing a hand against her waist.

"Okay," she whispered, smiling back at him.

"Alright Trin," Aaron said, holding out his hand.

"Thanks, man," Trin said, shaking Aaron's hand before they shared a hug.

"Don't be a stranger," Aaron encouraged.

Trin chuckled. "You either," he warned, pulling away and

staring at Aaron and Belinda. "You have the number and the address. You've been away from New York too long."

Aaron and Belinda were surprised, yet touched by Trin's invitation. The three of them hugged before Belinda pushed Trin off the porch and told him and Dom to get going.

As the taxi pulled out of the driveway, Dom kept her eyes focused ahead. She knew if she looked back, she'd never leave.

The long ride to the executive airport was maddeningly silent. Once Trin and Dom boarded the posh jet courtesy of Morton and Farber, it appeared that the silence would continue. Trin knew Dom was upset about leaving Chicago and uneasy about returning to New York. Still, he couldn't bear the silence and thought it would help if she talked to him.

"I know it can't be doing you any good to be keeping all this inside, Domino."

Dom slid her gaze to Trin. "I think it's better like this."

Trin's sleek black brows drew close. "How so?"

"Trin, you don't want to hear what I have to say. I guarantee you that."

The snappish comment caught and held Trin's attention. "Why wouldn't I?"

Dom kept her mouth shut and tapped her long nails against the arm rest.

"Domino?"

"Why didn't you tell me all this before? When you first got to Chicago?"

Trin rolled his eyes and leaned back in the cushioned swivel chair. "Baby, I thought we already talked about this."

"Well, we're gonna talk about it again. You wanted me to let it out, so I'm letting it out!"

Trin propped the side of his handsome face against his palm. "Domino—"

"What?"

"Belinda and Aaron thought it would be better if we

waited. I agreed with them. I already told you that." His raspy voice was low and solemn, though his temper was becoming heated by Dom's hostility.

"You thought, Belinda thought, and Aaron thought! What about what Dominique thought?"

"You?" Trin blurted, slowly rising from his seat.

Dom's mouth fell open at his reaction. "Yeah, Trin, me—remember me?"

Trin shook his head. "Where's all this coming from, Domino? I thought you understood all this."

Dom kept her eyes downcast. "Why are you taking me back to New York, Trin?"

" 'Scuse me?"

"Why, all of a sudden did you decide it was time for us to go back?"

A short aggravated laugh escaped Trin's throat. "You know, I know you can't remember, but we have careers, a home, friends, all in New York! You're my wife, we have a life there!"

Dom kept her cool. "Well, that sounds real good, Trin. So all of a sudden, after weeks of keeping me in the dark, it was time for me to know the truth—why?"

Frustrated and angry, Trin ran one hand through his silky, close-cut hair. "I'd had enough of beating around the bush," he whispered.

Dom leaned forward and pinned him with a knowing glare. "No! I think you had enough when you saw Spry leavin' my house!"

The accusation was Trin's undoing. He stormed across the short distance to where Dom was seated and curled his large hands around the arms of her chair.

"Watch it, Dominique. Don't push me," he warned.

Dom swallowed and leaned back against her seat. The remainder of the trip passed without discussion.

Trin took Dom out for an early dinner when they arrived in Manhattan at around five-thirty that evening. The delicious meal at The Tavern soothed both their boiling tempers. Dinner passed in easy silence and they were having dessert, before Trin decided to test the waters.

"Um . . . Domino?" he called softly, waiting for Dom to meet his gaze. "About the way I acted before—"

"Don't worry about it. I shouldn't have mentioned Spry," she said.

"No, you had every right to mention him . . . since you were right."

Dom's hazel stare widened. "I was?" she croaked.

"Yeah, I know I scared you before and that's the last thing I want to do."

"I know," she assured him. "I didn't have to jump on your back about not telling me the whole story. I know you all were trying to protect me."

"Well, I should've followed my instinct and told you," Trin said, his smoldering black stare intense and unwavering.

Dom smacked her palm to the table. "Are you gonna let me apologize or not?"

Trin's double dimples appeared. "I'll accept your apology, if you accept mine."

Dominique sighed. "Deal."

Trin had everything planned from the moment they arrived in town. When they left the restaurant, a car was already waiting out front. The trip from the restaurant to the upscale neighborhood of Bedford seemed so short, Dom felt as though she were in a whirlwind.

"Are you ready?" Trin asked, once they were turning down the street that led to their home.

Dom smoothed her shaking hands over her stylish pearl jumper. The most she could manage was a nod. The car slowed and turned into a curving brick driveway. Her eyes widened to huge saucers as she stared at the magnificent house before her. She glanced over at Trin, knowing that a wrong turn had to have been made.

The first time she saw Aaron and Belinda's home, she was shocked. This one, however, had her stunned . . . devastated almost. To say it was beautiful would have been an understatement. On a perfectly manicured lawn sat the most magnificent brick house Dom had ever seen. There were two large bay windows next to wide double doors on the lower level of the house, and five smaller but equally impressive windows along the upper level. Each window was filled with a long box of pink roses—her favorite. Medium-sized baskets, filled with the same lovely flowers, were situated along the curves of the wide brick steps. There were large fir trees along the outskirts of the front lawn, shielding the house from view.

Dom cleared her throat and looked at Trin. "We live here?" she whispered.

A soft chuckle escaped him. "Yeah, this is it," he confirmed.

The car stopped right in front of the steps and Trin got out and held his hand toward Dom. She lingered behind for a moment, still in awe of the house.

"Domino? It's not gonna hurt you," he promised, his dazzling white grin as comforting as it was humorous.

Dom took a deep breath and accepted Trin's hand. For a moment, she stood there taking in her surroundings. If she was dreaming, she hoped she'd never wake up.

Trin's hand curled around her upper arm and he escorted her into the house. Of course, it was even more beautiful on the inside. The foyer was a small round area with just a brass coatrack to one side. The tiny space was encased in little glass windows that gave a view of the livingroom on one side and the den on the other.

"Trin . . ." Dom breathed, walking out of the foyer.

The livingroom was a large room with a cream-and-gold color scheme. Long, flowing drapes gave the room an even more elegant appearance. The thick cushiony sofas, arm chairs and recliners were offset by a gold chandelier, lamps, and gold-trimmed coffee- and endtables.

"Oh, this is so beautiful," she whispered just loud enough for Trin to hear.

He smiled and leaned against the doorjamb. "Well, you *should* like it. You decorated just about every room."

"I did?" she drawled, whirling around to face him.

"Mmm hmm, let's see . . ." Trin bowed his head as though he were in deep thought. "You let me do the den, my gym, and my study."

"Hmm, looks like I've got good taste."

"You do," Trin assured her, hoping the remark sounded suggestive enough.

Dominique cleared her throat. "Well, let's check out your work. Which way is the den?" she asked.

"Follow me," Trin ordered, leading the way to the room located on the other side of the foyer.

The den was as spacious as the living room. At first glance, the room appeared to be cluttered. A closer look, however, showed that it had a rather artistic feel. In one corner, there were black and gold bean bags surrounding a short card table. A large bar to one side held a high-tech stereo system and carried a stock of every beer, wine and liquor imaginable. The sofa and arm chairs were black and gold plaid. They faced a wide-screen TV complete with DVD and CD Changer.

The room made Dom want to kick off her shoes and lounge. Still, she didn't want to increase the size of Trin's head any further.

"Did you say I let you decorate this room?" she teased.

"Very funny," he replied, loving the sight of her touring the house. Never had he thought he would ever see that sight again.

Dom spent the next two hours becoming reaquainted with her lovely home. She had no complaints and couldn't wait to get settled. While Trin was downstairs on the phone in the study, she decided to unpack. She chose one of the cozy guest rooms and took her bags from the lovely master bedroom.

Trin finished the call he'd made to his office and sprinted upstairs. He passed the guest bedroom, then stopped in his tracks. Slowly, he walked back to the doorway and stood there.

"What are you doin'?"

"Unpacking," Dom answered, knowing he wasn't happy.

"The bedroom's farther down the hall," Trin instructed.

"Your bedroom."

"Our bedroom."

"Trin . . ."

"What?"

Dom sighed and ran her fingers through her curls. "Don't do this."

Trin stepped inside the room. His darkly handsome face carried a fierce expression. "Don't do what, Domino? Don't want my wife to sleep in my bed, in *our* bed?"

Dom stepped closer to him, pressing one hand against her chest in a pleading gesture.

"Trin, I'm still gonna be in this house. So what difference does it make? I won't be in your bed, but in a room three doors down. I'll be your wife no matter where I sleep."

Trin nodded slowly and Dominique could see that he was gnawing the inside of his jaw as he considered her statement. Suddenly, a purely wicked grin spread across his gorgeous face and he ran one finger down the side of her cheek.

"You'll be my wife no matter where you sleep?" he asked, repeating her words.

Dom nodded, though she didn't like the look in his eyes one bit. "That's right," she whispered.

"Well, in that case . . ." Trin let his words drift off and slipped his arm around her waist.

She gasped at the feel of his muscled form against her body. Her lips parted immediately beneath the force of his and Trin uttered a soft moan as his tongue slid into the dark cavern of her mouth. His hands lowered from her waist and cupped her derriere beneath her short jumper. He squeezed

the luscious, round area and lifted Dom closer so that she
could feel the extent of his arousal.

"Trin . . ." Dom whispered, feeling herself being carried
across the room. She had expected to be placed on the bed,
but her eyes snapped open when she felt the cool wood of the
door behind her.

Trin let her slide down the length of his body, before he
pulled down the zipper along the front of the jumper. He
placed the wettest kisses against every inch of dark chocolate
skin exposed to his view. Dom was in heaven and could tell
just how deeply Trin's actions were affecting her.

When her clothes had been removed, Trin let his midnight
eyes slide over her body. She still wore a lacy bra with matching panties, garters, and hose.

"Damn . . ." he breathed, lowering his mouth to one of her
breasts. Without removing the bra, he found the nipple and
teased it wickedly with his lips and tongue.

Dom moaned as she buried her hands in the soft curls on
top of Trin's head. Her legs shifted apart in silent invitation
and he didn't disappoint her. One of his large hands curved
over her bottom and squeezed it gently. Then, his fingers disappeared beneath the soaked middle of her panties. He
smiled, hearing Dom's gasp when his fingers were inside her.

Trin carried on his wicked persuasion just a little while
longer before he removed his fingers and rose to his full
height. Dominique's lovely eyes were downcast as she struggled to control her breathing. It was next to impossible since
Trin was towering over her and she could feel his hot, pitch-
black gaze on her.

He pressed his hand to the door and kissed the corner of
her mouth. "You know where I am if you change your mind
about sleeping in here."

Dom's eyes snapped to his and her gaze was immediately
accusing when she realized what he was doing. Trin's hand
slid past her waist to curve around the doorknob and she
slowly moved away from the door. He sent her a wicked

smirk, then opened the door and left her alone in the bedroom.

After such an exhausting day, Dom and Trin each made silent decisions to turn in early. Dom was sure she'd get a good night's sleep, since she was so tired, but the moment her head touched the soft down pillow, she was wide awake. Trin was at the center of her thoughts and sleep was a hopeless wish. She was tossing and turning for well over an hour, when she finally decided to give up.

A cup of tea sounds good, she said to herself, pulling up the strap of her silk gown.

The house was dark, with the exception of small brass electric candles that lined the long corridor. Not wanting to awaken Trin, Dom quietly made her way down the hall. When she approached the door to the master bedroom, her steps slowed, then stopped. She pressed her forehead against the door, debating. She wanted to go to him so much, but things were so complicated already . . . She hadn't pondered the issue long, when the oak door opened and she stumbled forward.

The smile on Trin's handsome face was as gorgeous as the look in his intense dark eyes. Without hesitation, he pulled Dom inside. He lifted her as though she were weightless and carried her to the majestic king-size bed in the center of the darkly furnished room.

Dominique woke early the next morning. When she discovered she'd slept in Trin's arms all night, she smiled and snuggled deeper into his powerful embrace. His lean muscular body was sprawled over hers. Their bodies were still intimately connected.

Dom's movement as she snuggled closer to Trin woke him as well. A smile crossed his face when he discovered he was still inside her.

"Hmm . . . what have we here?" he whispered, tugging her earlobe between his lips.

Dom raised her extraordinary gaze to his and gasped when she felt him stiffen inside her. "Are men always like this in the morning?" she wickedly inquired.

The double dimples instantly appeared in Trin's cheeks. "Always," he confirmed.

Dom's long lashes fluttered closed as he began to move inside her. The fact that she was already wet and ready for him only increased his arousal. The room was filled with the sounds of throaty cries and deep groans. Trin held Dom's thighs in an unbreakable hold as his thrusts grew more forceful.

"Dammit," he suddenly grumbled, and pulled away.

Dom frowned, watching him take deep breaths as he lay across her chest. "What?" She asked.

Trin raised his hand and tried to slow his breathing. "You could get pregnant this way," he finally told her.

A slow, guilty smile tugged at Dom's mouth. "I hadn't thought of that."

"Hmph, I had."

"Would that be so bad?"

Trin raised his head and gave her a heartmelting smile. "You can't know how happy I'd be if that happened. But I hope everything will be right when it happens. You know what I mean?"

Dom fiddled with the thick silver-gray comforter. "Yeah, I know."

Trin kissed her cheek and moved reluctantly from the bed. "I gotta go to work, but I'll be back early."

Dom watched him head into the spacious connecting bathroom and heard him start the shower. She lounged in bed thinking about what Trin had just said. *When things are right . . . will they ever be right?* she thought. There hadn't been any significant memories since her breakthrough about Spry. Besides seeing herself falling—or being pushed—there had been nothing more. Would things ever be right again?

* * *

"You feel like going to see Miss P and Mr. C tonight?"

"Who?" Dom asked from the bed as she watched Trin slip into a navy-blue dress shirt.

He smiled and shook his head. "Your parents." he clarified.

"Oh yeah. Yeah, that sounds good."

Trin turned away from the mirror to pin her with a concerned onyx stare. "Are you up for it?"

"Yes," Dom immediately assured him. "I think it'll help a lot to see them, and with everything they've been through, I think I've stayed away too long."

Trin nodded in agreement, pulling a matching jacket over the shirt, which required no tie. "Well, I'll be home around six-thirty and we can move from there."

Dom was silent as she watched Trin finish getting ready. Soon, he was giving her a soft, thorough kiss good-bye. When she heard the powerful bass from the sound system in Trin's Escalade, she made her way out of bed and headed for the shower. Parts of her body ached from her husband's ravenous sexual appetite. She welcomed it, though. She found it exciting to know that she was desired by such an intriguing, intense man.

The water coursing over her skin felt so invigorating that for a moment Dom just stood there enjoying it. When she finally decided to move, a bar of soap resting on the floor of the stall was her downfall.

"Dammit," she groaned as she fell back against the wall of the shower. Everything she had forgotten for almost a year came rushing back. She stood there staring off into space as though she were watching the events of her life on a screen. Slowly, she pulled open the sliding-glass shower door and went to sit on the edge of the tub. There, she began to cry.

"So, you think you did the right thing?" Arthur asked Trin when they spoke over the phone later that morning.

"I do."

"Has anything happened with her memory yet?"

Trin rested his head back against his suede desk chair. "Nah, man, but it's only been one day so I'm still praying."

"Mmm . . ." Arthur commented in a mellow tone before he cleared his throat. "Trin, um . . . do you think things'll get rocky again when she starts to remember?"

The question immediately put Trin on the defensive. "I don't want to talk about it."

"Trin—"

"Arthur, cool it," Trin ordered in his softest tone of voice. He knew his cousin was only concerned, but he also knew that the blame for the problems in his marriage lay mostly on his own shoulders.

The two of them talked for only a short while longer. Arthur sensed Trin's mood and decided to let the subject drop. When Trin hung up the phone, he sat behind his desk with a pensive look on his handsome face.

"Damn, he didn't move a thing out of here," Dom whispered as she sifted through countless garments in her large walk-in closet. Her memory had come back with a vengeance. She began to think about all the work and stories she must have missed out on at the station. All the time with no thoughts of the past and, in one brief instant, they had come rushing back.

Dom found it interesting that many of the pieces she'd aquired during her stay in Chicago complimented the ones she already had. Instinct was an incredible thing, she thought.

Strong hands settled to her shoulders and she felt herself being pulled backwards. She gasped, feeling Trin placing slow, soft kisses against the side of her neck. She pulled away with a jerk, but didn't turn around to face him.

"What?" he asked, clearly confused by her actions, a deep furrow between his long brows.

"Nothing," Dom finally answered. Her uneasiness made any further explanation impossible.

Trin stepped close to her again and trailed one lean finger between her shoulder blades. "Baby, you okay?" he inquired.

Dom turned her head and smiled nervously. "Yeah—yes, I'm fine," she whispered.

Trin wasn't at all convinced. When he caught her arm and forced her to face him, his frown had returned. "I want you to tell me what's wrong with you." His deep voice sounded raspier than usual, but there was no mistaking the concern there.

"Trindy, I told you I'm fine so will you please drop it?"

Trin's frown vanished instantly as he watched her in disbelief. "Domino, you haven't called me that since before . . . the crash," he whispered.

Dom closed her eyes briefly, realizing her mistake. She wasn't ready for Trin to know about her recovery. "I don't know where it came from," she replied lightly.

"I don't care," he whispered, cupping her chin in his large hand. He dipped his head to press the softest kiss to her lips.

When Dom felt his tongue trying to gain entrance to her mouth, she moaned and gave in. The smooth deep strokes of the kiss had her clinging to the lapels of his jacket. Trin untied the satin belt of her robe so he could caress the silky flat surface of her stomach and back. He wouldn't allow himself to become carried away, however, and was soon pulling back.

"I better go take a shower so we can get you to your parents' house," he told her in a quiet voice.

Dom took a deep, shaky breath as she watched him leave. Her thoughts were muddled as she stood there trying to figure out what to do. Should she tell Trin? How would he react when he discovered she remembered everything?

Twelve

"Where is she?" Hamp Carver wanted to know when he opened the door to his son-in-law that evening.

Trin smiled and held his hand out for Dom, who nodded and stepped up to the doorway.

Hamp and Phyllis Carver's attractive features brightened with love and happiness when they saw their only child. Dom pressed her lips together and tried to hold back her tears. The three of them came together in a tight hug and stood there for the longest time, crying and laughing.

"Is this real?" Hamp asked, cupping Dom's face in his large hands.

Dominique smiled at her parents and nodded. "Mmm hmm," she assured them, laughing when they pulled her close and hugged her again.

"Baby, Trin told us about the . . . amnesia," Phyllis said, toying with her daughter's thick curls.

Dom nodded, bursting to tell them that she had recovered. "Yeah," she whispered.

"Well, it doesn't matter," Phyllis said, a light sniffle following her words. "I don't care as long as I have my baby back."

Trin was leaning against one of the porch columns as he watched the Carvers. He didn't think he had ever seen Dom looking so radiant or happy. It was almost as though she remembered her parents . . . really remembered them. A playfully wicked smile crossed his sensuous mouth and he cleared his throat.

"Y'all just forgot all about me. I'm here too, you know?"

Everyone laughed and dried their teary eyes. Hamp placed a hearty clap on Trin's arm. "Thank you for bringing Cookie back to us," he said.

Trin's black gaze narrowed when he looked over at his wife. "I'll never let her out of my sight again," he promised.

Dominique's breath caught in her throat at the intensity of the statement. She clasped her hands together and looked away.

"Let's get off this porch and get some food in our stomachs," Phyllis suggested, waving them all into the house.

"Kyla was my grandmother's name," Hamp was explaining later, while they were having dessert. "She insisted on goin' to that hospital to see Dom, when Phillie had her."

Phyllis laughed and nodded. "Uh-huh. She told me everything I needed to do to get Dom to quiet down, go to sleep, eat regularly . . . she knew everything about babies."

"And so y'all gave me her name?" Dom asked, entranced by all the new information she was receiving. She realized that she'd never asked her parents anything about her father's grandmother.

Hamp nodded. "That's right. She died in the hospital with you in her arms. You were always so fussy, but when she held you, you acted like a little angel."

Dom felt a great sense of contentment wash over her and leaned back in her chair. The napkin slid off her lap and landed on the floor. Both she and Trin reached for it. When his hand touched hers, Dom jerked away.

"Sorry," she whispered, placing the napkin over her lap.

Trin frowned a little, but made himself get over his concerns. The dinner, and the evening as a whole had been progressing beautifully. Unfortunately, Trin knew something was very wrong with Dom for he could sense the distance within her. After the closeness they had shared in Chicago over the last several weeks, he found that he just couldn't bear it.

* * *

"Oh my Lord, you're more lovely than I remembered."

Dom closed her eyes as Martika Salem pulled her into a tight hug. "Thank you," she whispered, relishing the embrace from her mother-in-law.

Martika blinked the tears from her lashes and quickly regained her composure. "I hope you brought an appetite with you, because have I got a spread for you. Grilled pepper steak, broccoli and spinache quiche, cinnamon bread, peach cobbler . . ."

Dom was stunned. "You made all my—it um, it all sounds so good," she said.

"Well, sweetie, it's no wonder. They're all your favorites," Martika replied.

Dominique had been about to reveal as much. Thankfully, no one noticed her slip. When Trin stepped behind her, she flinched when his hands touched the collar of the gray wrap she wore.

Martika noticed the hurt look cross her son's face at Dominique's reaction. "Honey, come with me," she said, pulling Dom close as they strolled toward the living room. "Sweetie, that gorgeous young man across the room is Trin's cousin, Arthur Cule."

Dom's eyes lit up the moment she saw Arthur. She managed to keep her gait steady and unhurried as she approached him. When they hugged, she didn't want to let go.

Martika smiled at the reunion. Hearing Trin sigh as he stood next to her brought the concern back to her face.

"Honey, everything will be fine. You'll see," she tried to console him.

He massaged his jaw and shook his head. "I just don't get it, Ma. All of a sudden, it's like she's cutting me off. That first night back, we—we were so close."

Martika rubbed Trin's back with brisk strokes. "I'm sure you were, baby. But you have to give her time. This is all still new to her—there's got to be a lot of adjusting involved."

"Adjusting . . ." Trin repeated, obviously unconvinced. "I don't know why I'm complaining. After the hell I put her through . . ."

"Trin, stop it," Martika ordered, her almond-brown eyes suddenly flashing with anger. "I'm tired of hearing this self-pity mess from you. That girl loves you, despite the hell you put her through. You just have to give her time."

"Ma, I know what you're saying but I have to face it. I doubt Domino will feel the same about me once her memory comes back. And it may sound self-pitying, but I certainly couldn't blame her."

Martika pulled her son into a tight hug and prayed he was wrong.

"Girl, you don't know how much I missed you," Arthur whispered when he and Dom hugged. "It almost killed me to think I'd never see you again. I know you don't remember, but we were very close. Confidants, you might say."

"I know."

Arthur pulled away, a slight frown marring his handsome caramel-toned face.

Dom smiled at his confusion. "I remember everything," she whispered, pulling him close before he could cry out. "Don't react to what I just said. Trin doesn't know."

"What? Why?"

"I'm not ready to tell him."

"Dom, after all this time? I know y'all were going through some stuff, but can't you get past it?"

Dom rubbed her hands across Arthur's shoulders. "Remind me to tell you *everything* that I couldn't before. This isn't something I can just get over."

"What's up, Arthur?"

Dominique and Arthur pulled apart when Trin walked over. Dom watched the two men shake hands, then squeezed Arthur's arm.

"I'll talk to you later," she whispered as she left her husband's side.

"Damn," Trin whispered, watching his wife speak with his mother. "Let's go get a drink," He suggested to his cousin.

"So, how is it?" Arthur asked, while he and Trin headed off to the privacy of the den.

"It's incredible and it's painful and it's frustrating. And I'm so glad she's back," Trin admitted. "She's going through a lot, though. I know that, but I can't take her shutting me out like this. She's barely said anything to me in three days."

Arthur pushed the den door shut. "You try talking to her about it?"

"No. I don't think I have enough nerve to hear what she'll say to me."

"You without nerve? This can't be Trinidad M. Salem I'm talking to here," Arthur teased.

Trin could barely smile. "It's him, alright. Sometimes she acts like she remembers everything, man."

"Hell, Trin, I thought that would be a good thing."

Trin leaned against the door and groaned into his hands. "Arthur, you knew we were havin' problems."

"And? If she recovers her memory, the two of you can start workin' out this mess."

Trin's eyes narrowed as he watched his cousin strangely. "You say Domino confided in you, but sometimes I wonder how much she actually told you."

Arthur shrugged, folding his arms across the front of the extra-large red football jersey he sported. "I know there were things she kept to herself."

Trin pushed both hands into the deep pockets of his black sweatpants and studied his sneaker-shod feet. "She tell you how I acted when I found out about Spry?" he asked, watching Arthur shrug.

"You mean when you found out in Chicago?"

"I mean, when I found out before she took that damned plane trip."

Arthur was stumped. "Wait a minute. Are you saying, you knew about that . . . before?"

Trin nodded. "I knew everything and I turned on her. For a while she didn't even know what was going on. I said some hurtful things to her. I hid things from her."

Arthur's long, brown brows drew closer. "What are you saying?"

"I'm saying I . . . kept it a secret that I knew about Spry. That night she left I was so angry that I told her I wanted a divorce and to pack her stuff and leave before I said or did something we would both regret."

"What?" Arthur whispered, though he was clearly enraged.

"She was crying . . ." he continued, "I'd never seen her cry that hard. I didn't care though. I threw all her stuff in the suitcase, threw it at the door and told her to get out."

"You cold-hearted jackass." Arthur growled. His handsome features contorted into a sinister expression when he grabbed the neckline of his cousin's gray jersey. "How could you do that to her?" he demanded, slamming Trin against the door.

"I don't know," Trin said, looking as sick as he felt. "All I know is I wanted my wife back and I got her. Unfortunately, everytime I see her, I remember every time I did her wrong. I remember every time, Arthur."

"Trin . . . man . . . ."

Trin could tell his cousin was struggling to find words. "Whatever you're gonna say, please don't let it be 'everything will be fine.'"

Arthur only shook his head. He could offer none of the usual assurances. For the first time, he began to fear that his cousin's marriage was approaching its end.

Dom was relaxing on one of the lounges near Martika Salem's in-ground pool. Dinner wasn't quiet ready, so she had decided to spend time at one of her favorite places.

"I took a chance you'd be out here," Trin called when he found her. "You always liked it out here," he added.

"Yeah, I know . . ." Dom sighed, enjoying the serenity.

Trin frowned. "Domino?"

Dom uttered a hushed curse at her second slip of the evening and pushed herself off the lounge. "Um, yeah, I know I must've loved it out here. It's so peaceful," she said, hoping to ease his curiosity.

She obviously succeeded, judging from his nod. "I better get back inside," she murmured.

"Domino, wait," Trin said, catching her hand as she walked past. When she pulled away from him, he pressed his lips together and cleared his throat.

"Baby, what is this?" he couldn't help but ask.

"You're wondering about my mood?" Dom countered.

Trin didn't like the strange smile she sent him. "I'm concerned," he softly admitted.

Dominique laughed.

"What *is* wrong with you?" he snapped, watching her fold her arms over her snug white jersey dress.

"I can't talk about this now."

"What?" he asked, feeling as though he had heard the words before.

"You don't want to be around me now, Trin," she said, watching him go deathly still. Her lovely light eyes narrowed as she studied the confusion and uneasiness on his face. Her expression softened a bit when he took her hand and pressed a gentle kiss to the back of it.

"There are times I wish you'd remember everything," he murmured against her hand, sounding as though he were talking to himself. "Then you would understand what I mean when I tell you that I can't look at you or myself without thinking about what I did to us. To your trust in me. Then there're other times I pray you'll only remember Chicago . . . like we were just starting out. All those times you asked me to talk to you, I should have. I just couldn't do it without getting . . . Domino,

I'm sorry. When you get your memory back, you'll probably laugh at how pathetic that really sounds."

With that said, Trin kissed her hand again, then placed kisses on her forehead and cheek. He stepped past Dom and went to stare out at the pool. She watched him for the longest time before heading back to the house.

The drapes were drawn in the cozy den a few nights later. The large-screened television blared loudly, but Dom was fast asleep on the sofa. Trin had just finished taking a long, hot shower and was headed downstairs in search of his wife. When he found her in the den, a smile softened his gorgeous features and he stepped into the room.

He pulled her into his arms using infinite care. His intentions were to take her upstairs and put her to bed. Dominique woke at the slight movement, her hands stiffening on his bare biceps.

"Trin, no . . . I'm not ready to go to sleep," she moaned.

"Baby, you were *already* asleep," Trin informed her, not wanting to relinquish his hold.

Dom made a fist and lightly pounded the sleek, muscled wall of his bare chest. "Will you let me stay down here?"

"Domino—"

"Sweetie, there's a movie coming on that I was trying to wait up for," she explained.

Trin sighed. Since he didn't want to sleep without her, he decided to stay downstairs as well. He gently placed her back on the thick sofa and propped her legs up. Then he settled down as well, reclining on the couch with his head on her thighs.

Dom couldn't ignore the queasy feeling in her stomach, and she couldn't deny how good Trin felt lying next to her. Especially with his head so close to the part of her that ached most for him. At that point, they were both wide awake. Trin absently trailed his hand along the length of her calf in a purely possessive manner. He finally stopped to toy with the African beaded anklet she wore.

Dom tried to smother her groan when she felt Trin snuggle

his head deeper against the junction of her thighs. The movie she had been waiting for had just come on. The opening credits were rolling, but she was more concerned with the scene taking place on her couch. Trin began to place moist, open-mouthed kisses to her inner thigh. He teased her for a while before turning over to face her. His strong arms were braced on either side of her body.

As one of Trin's hands ventured beneath Dom's tiny T-shirt, his sexy midnight gaze snapped to her face. "You want me to stop?" he asked.

Dom shook her head, her lovely hazel eyes never leaving his mouth. "We shouldn't be doing this," she cautioned, her voice as soft as the look in her eyes.

Trin nodded once, his eyes never leaving her face. "But do you want me to stop?"

"Uh-uh."

Trin smiled softly at the tiny admission. He caressed the center of her body with teasing fingers. Dom threw her head back and enjoyed the sensation of the caress. Trin smothered her gasps when he pressed his mouth to hers and thrust his tongue deep inside. Dom trailed her hands over the heavily muscled length of his huge thighs, moaning her disappointment when he moved away to push the coffee table farther away from the sofa.

Making love was the only thing on their minds.

Two weeks had passed since Dom had returned home. In that time, she had busied herself becoming reaquainted with her life. She visited family and old friends alike. Everyone was happier than words could express with the knowledge that she was alive and well. Things were progressing more smoothly than she had ever hoped. Everything except her relationship with her husband. Dominique could tell that Trin was confused and hurt by her distance, which intensified even after they'd made love. It was tearing her apart, but the return of her memory brought back the confusion and hurt she had struggled with before the accident.

"Hello? Dominique Salem."

"Honey, do you know how good that sounds in my ear?"

Dom smiled when she heard her friend and news manager Marshall Greene on the other end of the phone. "Marshall? Didn't I just see you two days ago?"

"Yes, you did. But I still need to keep convincing myself that this is real."

"It is, but you can call as much as you need to."

Marshall chuckled. "Thanks, but, um, the reason I'm calling is because after you left, Peaches and I were thinking about having a party."

"Mmm hmm—and I was your inspiration to throw it?" Dom teased.

"That's right, we'd be giving it for you."

Dom was stunned. "Marshall . . . No, Marshall."

"Yes."

"No. That's too much."

"You damn right it is. Girl, you just came back from the dead!"

Dom shook her head at Marshall's bellowing. "You don't have to remind me of that."

"Well, can we throw this party without a hassle from you or not?"

Dominique still thought a party in her honor was a bit much. But the idea was exciting her more and more.

"Oh, alright, Marshall." She finally sighed, knowing he wouldn't give up until she said yes.

"Good. We'll start making the plans right away."

"Whoa, Marshall! Hold it. Now I want this small. I don't need any big throw downs," Dom warned.

"Whatever you say! Whatever you say! We'll give you a call!" Marshall said, quickly dismissing Dom's warnings.

Martika Salem was decked out in an oversized green T-shirt, a pair of bell-bottomed blue jeans, and white Reeboks. A large wide-brimmed straw hat covered her curly silver hair.

Trin had just walked through the tall, wooden gate and found his mother toiling in her impressive garden. She was in the process of retrieving the cherry tomatoes from their vines and inspecting each one for the tiniest imperfections. Smiling, Trin stooped behind her and wrapped his arms around her tiny frame.

"What's goin' on?" he whispered in her ear, pressing a kiss to the side of her neck.

Martika smiled and relished her son's embrace. "Same ol', same ol' with me. But I should be asking about you . . . and Dominique."

The easy smile faded from Trin's handsome face and he sighed. Martika saw that he was about to stand, and she grabbed his hand. "Uh-uh, stay here and make yourself useful," she said, digging in her tool box for a pair of work gloves, which she slapped into her son's hand.

"Ma—"

"Stop whining and tell me what the problem is."

Trin attempted to make use of the gloves that were way too small for him. "Why does there have to be a problem?" he asked.

Martika continued gathering her tomatoes. "Your pretty young wife is finally home and you're here in my garden."

Trin bowed his head and sighed. "I'm scared," he admitted.

The two words caught and held Martika's attention. "Scared of what?"

"Domino's been actin' real funny."

"Is she getting her memory back?"

Trin slapped the gloves against his palm. "I don't think so, but she did call me by my nickname a while back."

"And? . . . Baby, what's the problem?"

"Ma, that was about two weeks ago and ever since then it's like she's been pulling away from me."

Martika, who knew about the heavy problems in her son's marriage, was very concerned by the solemn tone in his voice. More than anything, she wanted the young couple to work past their differences. Unfortunately, their differences had almost been the downfall of the marriage, and the blame lay squarely with her son.

"Are you still seeing Doctor Starks?" Martika asked.

Trin's head snapped up at his mother's mention of the therapist he'd been visiting since before Dom's accident. No one knew about it but Martika.

"I haven't seen him since Domino got back."

"Are you going to?"

Trin tossed the work gloves to the ground and stood. "Ma, I got more important things to worry about, here," he snapped.

Martika, still kneeling on the ground, rubbed her hand along Trin's strong calf. "Sweetie, I know you have other things to worry about, but if Dominique's remembering—"

"She may not remember everything."

"Do you really believe that?"

Trin remained silent. The look in his onyx eyes was very uncertain.

"Honey, this is your marriage and the way you choose to handle it is your business."

Trin looked down at his mother and frowned. "I came here for some advice, so could you please help me a little?"

Martika shrugged. "Alright. Fine. Trin, Dominique may not remember, but I'd talk to her about it anyway if I were you. If you think she's pulling away from you now, imagine how she'll react when she remembers how you treated her."

Dom had been putting it off for a while, but she finally decided to call Belinda. The phone rang four times. Just when Dom was about to hang up, the ringing stopped.

"Belinda Tirelli," said a breathless voice.

"Hi, doctor."

"Dom? Girl, is that you?"

"It is."

Belinda began to laugh. "Well, it's about time, dammit," she scolded.

"You had my number," Dom reminded her.

"Well, Aaron made me promise not to call. We thought y'all could use some time, you know?"

Dom nodded. "Yeah, I appreciate it."

"Mmm hmm . . . So? How is it?"

"It's good." Dom sighed, choosing to get right to the point. "I've, uh, got my memory back," she revealed, frowning when pure silence met her words. "Belinda? You still there?"

"You remember everything? You know it all?"

"I know it all," Dom assured her.

"Oh, thank God! I can't wait to tell Aaron. I bet Trin's jumpin' off the walls!"

Dom gave a weak laugh and sighed. "Not quite."

"Not quite? What do you mean?" Belinda cried.

"He doesn't know."

"Why the hell not?"

"Belinda . . ."

"Yeah? I'm here."

"It's complicated."

"I've got plenty of time."

"I shouldn't tell anybody this," Dom whispered, sounding as though she were speaking to herself.

"Now you have to tell me, because you have me worried. Is this about Trin?"

"Oh, yeah."

"About the problems y'all were having?"

"How—"

"Arthur told me when I called to tell him you were in Chicago."

Dom rested her head against the mahogany headboard and closed her eyes. "Yeah . . . I don't know what I would've done if it hadn't been for him."

"Well, why couldn't you talk to Trin? . . . Dom?"

"Our problems didn't start until he found out about me and Spry."

"What? Are you sayin' he knew before we told him?"

"Yeah, he knew way before. *How* I don't know."

"What happened?" Belinda asked.

"Well, he'd known for a while before he told me. That contributed to our problems. His mood was horrific. Then one night, he just went crazy." Dom said, stopping to clear her throat. "We had a bad fight. I mean a *bad* one, Belinda. We fought right here in this bedroom. He waited until we were home to let me . . . have it."

"What happened?"

"He told me he wanted a divorce and he demanded I pack my bags and leave."

"Dom, stop it! Please now, you have to—have to be confused about this—"

"I'm not confused, Belinda. It happened just like I'm tellin' you. Hell, when I remembered this, I cried my eyes out, so how do you think it's making me feel to actually talk about it?"

Belinda dragged one hand through her braids, unable to keep calm. "I'm sorry, sweetie, sorry. What else happened?" she managed to ask.

"The quick flashes I'd been having were from that night. That was the night I left. Before that, Trin was like someone I didn't know. Someone I didn't want to know. I had no idea why he changed."

"Jesus," Belinda whispered.

Dom sniffed as tears filled her eyes and rolled down her cheeks. "I love him so much, but he was like a different person. I know I should've talked to him about it or told someone, but it was like shock or something. I couldn't do anything."

Belinda cleared her throat softly. "Did he, um . . . did he ever hit you?"

"Uh-uh, no."

"Dom? . . ."

"He told me to leave before he did something he'd regret . . ." she finally confided.

"Shit."

"At first I actually thought it was my fault."

"Honey—"

"I know, I know it wasn't. I was just so confused about everything. When everything about Spry came out, I tried to convince Trin that it was over and that it had happened so long ago. I was, um . . . going to see Spry. I wanted Spry to come back to New York and try and help explain things."

"And?"

"Trin hit the roof. I didn't even have a chance to tell him what I was doing. I got mad and we began to argue. Next thing I knew, I was outside with my suitcase." Dom tried to finish the explanation without crying, but it was impossible.

"Honey, what are you gonna do?"

Dom pulled her bottom lip between her teeth and sighed. "I don't know." She finally replied. "I guess I'll have to tell him something. I can't keep this from him for long."

"Then please don't. This is too serious for that. Maybe it can be worked out." Belinda said.

"I don't know, Belinda. I have to admit that I'm afraid of how he'll react when I come to him with it."

"I'm sorry, Dom."

Dominique's full lips tightened into a thin line. "It's not your fault. It's Trin's for putting me through this shit. Damn that bastard."

Belinda winced at Dom's language, but knew how hard it must have been for her to relive what had happened before the accident. She let Dominique vent her hurt and anger before saying anything more. Dom needed to talk and wouldn't let Belinda off the phone. The conversation lasted almost two hours. The sound of Trin's SUV and the lights on the bedroom curtains caused Dom to hang up. Before she got off the phone, Belinda begged Dom to talk to Trin before any more time passed.

Thirteen

The house was completely dark when Trin walked in through the kitchen. He barely noticed, he was so preoccupied with the fact that his wife was slipping away from him. After a while the silence began to concern him. He practically ran through the house searching every room.

"Domino? Dominique!" he called several times, breathing a relieved sigh when she answered him.

"Upstairs, Trindy!" she called, though her voice sounded faint.

"Domino, you in here?" he asked. He was already reaching for the light switch when he walked through the door of their spacious bedroom.

"Don't turn on the lights."

Trin didn't like the sound of her voice, but he did as she asked. "You alright?" he whispered.

"My memory's back," Dom said after a few silent moments.

Shock rendered Trin motionless and he simply stood near the door. Then he was rushing toward her, pulling her into his arms and sitting with her on the edge of the bed.

Dom relished the embrace only for a moment. Then she braced her hands on Trin's strong arms and pushed herself away. She couldn't see his gorgeous face in the dark, but knew he was frowning. Before he could ask any questions, she explained her reaction.

"Trin, I remember everything. *Everything,*" she emphasized.

A moment or two passed before Trin switched on one of the bedside lamps. Dom blinked rapidly as her eyes adjusted to the light. When she finally looked at Trin, it was obvious that she had been crying.

"Domino . . ."

"Why'd you do that to me? To us?" she asked, her brows rising as she waited for his explanation.

Trin ran his hand over the long, smooth length of her bare leg. "Baby, I'm sorry, I . . ."

"Trin, I've heard that before. I asked you why you did it."

Trin rubbed his hands over his head as he braced his elbows on his knees. "I don't know why. Jealousy, I guess . . ."

"But my marriage to Spry was so long ago and—"

"But you didn't tell me. We were married almost four years and you didn't tell me," he accused.

Dom watched him in disbelief. "Are you saying this is my fault?"

"No, but—"

"But what, Trin? You asked me for a divorce, remember?"

Trin didn't want to remember his monstrous and unforgivable actions. He was too preoccupied with the fact that he was losing his wife again and there was nothing he could do to stop it.

"Domino, are we back to where we were before the accident?" he asked so softly, his words were barely audible.

"I don't know." Dom replied just as softly.

"You were leaving me when you got on the plane, weren't you?"

Dom nodded slowly. "Yes. I needed to go. Then, when you . . . suggested I get out before you . . . I didn't know what else to do."

Trin bowed his head and stood. "Are you gonna leave me now. Now that you remember?" he asked, his back toward her.

"Trin, I don't know what's gonna happen, but we won't get through this unless you talk to me about the way this affected you. I'm always gonna be your cousin's ex-wife. How do I know you won't flip again?"

Trin couldn't answer that question, much as he wanted to. He supposed he shouldn't terminate his sessions with Dr. Starks after all. It was so clear that he had a long way to go before he had a handle on his self-control.

Dom said nothing further on the subject. Trin rejoined her on the bed and they sat there in silence for the longest time. Later, they slept in each others arms.

Trin sighed and turned his face into the crook of Dom's neck. God, she felt and smelled so good, he thought. He hadn't meant to fall asleep after their conversation, but weariness had taken its toll and it couldn't be helped. He squeezed his eyes shut and tried to fight the sunlight streaming through the drapes. After last night, he felt like driving his car off the nearest cliff. How many times? How many times had he said something cruel to her or watched her with looks that practically radiated disgust? He wanted to kill himself for that. He didn't think he would ever be able to look Dom in the eye without thinking of the cruel way he had treated her.

Trin felt Dom moving beneath him and he reluctantly pulled away. When she raised her lovely eyes to his face, he immediately looked away.

"Sorry," he whispered, moving from the bed.

Dom smiled a little as she pushed herself up. " 'Sokay," she whispered.

Trin glanced at his watch and groaned.

"What?" she asked, pulling her bare legs beneath her.

Trin began unbuttoning his shirt. "I gotta . . . get goin' " He mumbled, finding it next to impossible to talk to his wife.

Dom could sense Trin's unease, but she tried to keep things light. "Where're you off to on a Saturday?" she asked, easing off the bed.

"Um . . . me and Arthur planned to go play some ball today," he explained.

"Damn, I'd love to see Arthur again. It seems like a lifetime since that dinner at your mother's."

Trin's sexy, onyx stare narrowed as he watched Dominique pull off her nightshirt. His stare was virtually unwavering as he watched her move around the room gathering things for her shower.

"I'll tell him," he finally said, still watching her.

Dom glanced at Trin and couldn't ignore the heavenly black gaze directed her way. Still, she chose to stick to her decision to take a break from sex and concentrate on their real problems.

"We should all have dinner together," Dom suggested, trying to generate conversation.

Trin remained silent, still watching her.

She cleared her throat. "Is he seeing anybody now?" she asked. "I didn't think to ask when I saw him before."

"I'm not sure."

It was clear that Trin had only one thing on his mind. The last thing Dom wanted was to push him away and have to explain why she needed to abstain.

"Do you need to get in the shower first?" she asked.

After a moment, Trin blinked and looked away. "Nah, I just need to wash my face and brush my teeth. I'll shower when I get back," he said, removing the rest of his clothes.

"Um, Marshall called a few weeks ago. He and Peaches want to throw a party for me."

Trin's handsome face brightened when he heard the news. "Ah, go girl, a party in your honor," he teased.

Dom laughed and waved her hands around her head. "I told him not to go to all that trouble," she said, becoming silent when she watched Trin walk to his closet wearing nothing but his boxers.

"Everybody's glad to have you back. It's no trouble to show you how happy we are," he said, dropping his clothes into a hamper. "So, I guess your memory was back when he called, huh?"

Dom lowered her gaze to hide the guilt in her eyes. "Yeah, I, uh—got it back the day after we got home," she admitted.

Trin leaned against the closet door and nodded. The hurt in his dark eyes was unmistakeable. "So, that's why you started pulling away . . . I guess I was the last to know?"

"Trin—"

"Don't worry about it, Domino. I understand. I can't blame you for not wanting to tell me, considering—"

The phone rang just then. They were both grateful for the interruption, since they didn't know what else to say to each other. Trin headed for the bathroom while Dom moved to answer the phone.

When Trin left for his game, Dom took her shower and changed into a pair of gray shorts and a matching halter top. Though the house seemed as large as some museums she had visited, they had never seen the need to hire any help. Still, it needed a good cleaning, and Dom prepared to dive into the harrowing chore. She had already spent close to an hour upstairs when the doorbell rang.

Dom pulled the heavy door open and found her mother-in-law waiting outside. Martika's lovely face was a welcome sight.

"Hey," Dom sighed, hugging the woman tightly.

"Hey, sweetie," Martika Salem whispered, returning the hug. "How are you?"

"Tired," Dom admitted, massaging her neck. "I've been cleaning this dirty house."

"Oh." Martika scoffed, with a wave of her hand, "you should get Trin to hire you a maid."

"Uh-uh, I'd rather do it myself," Dominique said, motioning behind herself. "Come on in."

"So, where's my baby?" Martika asked as she tossed her burgundy canvas bag on the living room sofa.

"Playin' ball with Arthur," Dom replied, settling to the floor in order to dust the coffee and end tables.

"How are things going?"

"They're goin' . . ."

"Dominique—"

"Martika, I told Trin I got my memory back. I told him I remembered everything, and things are exactly the same as they were the last time we had this conversation."

"He loves you, honey."

Dom threw down the cheesecloth she'd been dusting with. "Martika, I know he loves me. He loves me so much that he just about ruined our marriage with this jealousy of his."

Martika braced her elbows on her jean-clad legs and leaned forward. "Honey, I know it sounds like I'm taking sides—"

"It does," Dom chimed in.

"But finding out the woman you love was once married to a cousin you could care less for can throw you for a loop."

"I understand that, but you don't know how he treated me," Dom whispered.

"You know, we're not gonna have many more hot days like this, so I'm gonna go sit by the pool," Martika finally said, slipping the sandals from her tiny feet.

"See now, you're gonna make me not want to finish up in here," Dom accused in a teasing voice.

"Good. Come on out and join me when you're done," Martika called as she headed out of the living room.

When Dom arrived outside to splash around in the pool, she and Martika continued their discussion.

"So, are you two going to talk or just walk on eggshells around each other?"

Dom sighed and braced her arms on the brick deck that outlined the pool. "I can't get him to really open up about it. This morning he looked like he was in another world."

"He'll come around," Martika assured her.

It wasn't long before Dom saw Trin's Escalade rolling into the driveway. Her light eyes were drawn to his strong calves and thighs when he stepped out of the truck. The heavy muscles rippled as he walked over to the pool.

"Hey, Ma," he called, surprise in his voice. He dropped a kiss to her cheek before his midnight stare settled on his wife. "Hey Domino," he said quietly.

"Hey," she replied just as quietly.

Martika was silent for a while as she observed the scene before her eyes. It was obvious that the couple was still very much in love. Neither wanted to be the one to make the first move toward changing where things stood.

"You know, baby, I was just about to ask Dominique if she thought the two of you would like to have lunch with me. My treat," Martika offered.

With effort, Dom pulled her eyes away from Trin's and smiled at his mother. "Oooo, that sounds good, I'm so hungry," she said, hoisting herself from the pool and shaking the water from her hands. "I'll go take a shower and change. Be right back," she sang, grabbing a towel as she headed toward the house.

Martika smiled and shook her head at the helpless look on Trin's handsome face. His intense dark eyes followed Dom's every move as she switched away wearing a skimpy peach bikini.

"Trin, you look like you could use a shower, too."

"Huh?" Trin grunted, sending his mother a blank stare.

"I'll be fine if you want to take a shower, too."

Absently, Trin fanned his T-shirt away from his chest. "Yeah—yeah, I better. I'll be back!" he called, already sprinting in the direction Dom had taken.

She had apparently raced upstairs for she was nowhere in sight. As Trin got closer to the master bedroom, he heard the shower running. He found Dom's bikini on the counter in the connecting bathroom. He hooked one finger through the flimsy strap of the top and watched it dangle. A smile spread across his handsome face and he stripped out of his shorts and matching T-shirt.

Over the running water, Dom could hear someone tapping on the shower door. When she pulled the sliding glass aside, she couldn't help but smile at the innocent look on Trin's face.

Her eyes slid lower and she smothered her gasp at the sight of his nude, muscular frame.

"Yes?" she whispered.

Trin brought his face close to hers. "My mother sent me to take a shower."

Dom lowered her gaze and smiled. "Oh, well I guess you better do what she tells you."

Trin scratched his earlobe. "Yeah, I like doin' what I'm told."

"Well, come on in," Dom said, her decision to hold off on sex vanishing from her thoughts.

Trin wasn't about to refuse the offer and stepped inside the dark-tiled shower stall. He immediately pulled Dom into his arms and kissed her deeply. The wondrous friction of their naked bodies rubbing together, combined with the water beating on their skin, exhilarated them even more. Trin pushed Dom directly beneath the shower head and pressed her against the wall. He cupped her buttocks in his large hands and pressed open-mouthed kisses to her neck. Dom wrapped her legs around his wide back and begged him to take her.

Trin didn't prolong her need or his. Soon, they were rocking against each other in the throes of sensual bliss.

Martika heard someone call her name. Turning on her chair, she recognized three friends dining at a nearby table. She waved at them and broke into laughter. "Trin, Dominique, I see some ladies I should speak to," she told them, pushing her chair away, "I'll be back before the food gets here."

Dom smiled, and Trin nodded in his mother's direction. When Martika was gone, his black stare returned to his wife. They had been in the restaurant for only ten minutes, but Trin got the distinct impression she had little to say to him. She kept her eyes averted or downcast and he couldn't stand it.

"So, what's wrong now?"

Dom slowly brought her eyes to his face. "'Scuse me?"

"You heard me."

"Trin . . ."

"I'm listening. Domino, you haven't said two words to me since we got out of the shower."

She sighed and folded her arms over her chest.

"Then again, you didn't have much to say to me while we were *in* the shower."

"Will you stop it?" she snapped, pounding her fist against the table.

Trin leaned forward, his long dark brows drawn together. "You stop it. I'm tired of this."

"You're tired? I'm the one who's been getting the silent treatment, orders to leave my own home and threats of divorce, remember?"

Trin winced and looked away. Dom wanted to kick herself.

"I think we should lay off the sex for a while," she said, watching Trin's head snap up.

"And when did you make this decision?" he asked.

"I've been thinking about it since this morning."

Trin toyed with the black curls on his head. "Mmm hmm, and you decided to wait until after our shower to tell me, huh?"

"Trin, sex is not our problem. I think you know that."

Trin lowered his gaze to the table. He gnawed the inside of his jaw and shook his head. "We could've settled all this mess if you hadn't run off and gotten yourself hurt."

"Where the hell did that come from?" Dom asked, rolling her eyes when Trin stubbornly refused to answer her.

Nothing was settled and Martika soon returned to the table. Dominique wouldn't even look at Trin, though he watched her intently.

Later in the week, Trin and Dom were arriving at Marshall Greene's lovely condo in New York City. Though Dom had made Marshall promise not to throw a huge bash, he had completely ignored her request.

"Marshall . . ." she called in a warning tone, when she and Trin stepped out of the elevator and into the plush living room.

Marshall raised his hand in a defensive gesture. "Honey, blame Peaches. She wanted you to have a big blowout."

Dom's pout turned upwards into a smile. "Why don't I believe you?" she drawled.

"I'll find her and you can ask her yourself," Marshall offered, laughing when he held his hand out to Trin. "What's up, man?"

A wide grin crossed Trin's face. "Not much, what's going on with you?"

"Crap" was Marshall's cynical reply. "Y'all come on in and get comfortable. Dom, a lot of people are here to see you, girl."

Dom sighed and looked over at Trin. She held her hand out and he pulled her close. "You up for this?" he asked.

"Yeah, I just wish Peaches and Marshall had listened to me."

Trin smiled and Dom's eyes lingered on the deep dimples creasing his cheeks. Though they had barely been on speaking terms during the past week, it was impossible to notice. Trin kept one arm around his wife's waist in a protective, possessive hold. Dom simply snuggled into the heavenly embrace and let him lead her into the party.

All eyes were drawn to the gorgeous couple when they walked in. Trin was devastating in a black Armani tux, while Dom caught every man's attention in a long, skin-tight tangerine-colored Versace evening gown.

The party was actually quite enjoyable. Everyone was so excited to see Dom, they all wanted the opportunity to hug and talk to her. As a result, she forgot her request for a much smaller get-together.

So much excitement had its effects. Dominique retreated to the secluded balcony and took a moment to get some fresh air.

Trin had decided to have a drink in Marshall's den. He and a few other male guests caught the last few minutes of a basketball game that was showing on the wide-screen TV. Afterward, he began searching for Dom, almost becoming agitated when he couldn't find her. After a while, he spied her on the deserted balcony.

Dom shivered when she felt the teasing fingers beneath the wispy straps of her gown. The smell of Trin's cologne teased her senses when he dipped his head and pressed moist kisses to her neck. She let her head fall back to rest one of his massive shoulders as his large hands rose to cup and fondle her breasts.

Dom enjoyed a moment of the exquisite pleasure before turning to face her husband. As she moved, part of her dress caught and snagged on a ragged edge of the balcony.

"Oh no," she gasped, watching the fine material rip clear up her thigh.

"Hold on," Trin whispered. He patted her hand, signalling for her to let go of the gown. He knelt before her with intentions of freeing the dress from the ledge. One look at Dom's legs weakened him at once.

"Trin . . ." she moaned, feeling his mouth roaming the silky smooth length of her leg. His lips and strong teeth nipped at the lush skin exposed over the lacy tops of her stockings.

Dom braced her small hands on his powerful shoulders and cried out into the warm night air. Trin's grip had moved around to cup her buttocks beneath the torn material of the gown. He set her closer to his sexy, persuasive mouth and his tongue traced the outline of her womanhood through the fabric of her panties. Dominique wanted to surrender to Trin's sensual proposition but the fact that they weren't alone—and other reasons—wouldn't allow her to cast caution to the wind. Reluctantly, she pushed away and left the balcony.

Peaches Greene, Marshall's wife, was headed into her husband's den. Dom saw her and followed.

"Peaches?" she called as she stepped through the doorway.

"Yeah, girl?" Peaches said, turning. Her dark eyes narrowed when she noticed Dom clutching the side of her dress. "Girl, what happened?" she cried.

Dom waved her other hand behind her. "I ripped my dress on the balcony ledge," she explained.

"Dammit, Marshall! I told you we needed to fix that damn thing," Peaches called to her husband, who was approaching them.

"I'll take care of it first thing tomorrow," Marshall promised. "Are you gonna change and come back?" he asked Dom.

Dom glanced toward the hall and saw Trin leaning against the doorjamb. "Nah, I think we're gonna go on home."

"Are you sure?" Peached asked, disappointment evident on her pretty vanilla-toned face.

Dom pulled Peaches close and hugged her. "Yeah, but thanks for the party. I'm glad you and Marshall decided to go all out."

"Well, it was all Marshall's idea and—"

Marshall interrupted his wife by clearing his throat. Dom, however, had already caught on and was shaking her head.

"Listen, I want you to read over that stuff I gave you earlier. We gotta get you back in front of the cameras."

"Mmm hmm." Dom kissed his cheek. "I'll deal with you later," she promised.

Marshall gave an uneasy grin and headed over to shake Trin's hand. When everyone had said their good-nights, the Salems headed down to the parking garage. The ride in the elevator was void of any conversation. Dom kept her eyes downcast. She didn't need to see Trin to know there was a wall of tension surrounding him. When the doors opened, she headed out before him. Just as her hand reached for the car door handle, she heard his raspy, baritone voice behind her.

"What is wrong with you?" he asked.

"Trin, please. I don't want to do this now," Dom whispered.

"Do what? We haven't done anything in almost a week."

Dom took a deep breath and leaned her head back. "I told you that I wanted us to hold off on sex."

Trin rubbed one hand over the back of his neck. "Well, it hasn't been helping and I'm sick of this!" he thundered.

"You're sick?! You're sick of this? Forget you, Trin. At least you have a way to let out your anger!"

Trin raised his hand. "Don't, Dominique."

"What? Don't what?"

"Dom, cool it. I mean it. Just cool it, alright."

"And if I don't?" Dom tested him, losing her temper as well.

"Excuse me? Is . . . is everything alright over here?"

Trin and Dom turned to look at the man who had approached them. He'd obviously been on the way to his car, judging from the keys in his hand. The man was as tall and well-built as Trin. He must have sensed the anger in the air.

Trin's pitch-black gaze was unwavering as he stared the man down. "Get the hell out of here."

"Trin," Dom whispered.

"Be quiet," Trin ordered, without looking her way.

The man saw the annoyance on Dom's lovely face and took a step toward her. "Are you okay?" he asked.

The innocent question irritated Trin to no end. He turned, taking Dom by the arm and putting her in the car.

The ride home was silent, except for Dom's ocassional sniffles as she tried to control her emotions. Trin flew like a madman through the late-night traffic. Dom prayed they wouldn't be stopped by police. She knew Trin would surely be thrown in jail if he turned his temper on an officer.

The moment the car stopped at the front door, Dom jumped out and ran inside the house.

"Dominique!" Trin roared as he rounded the car.

Dom was just about to head up the stairs when she heard Trin call her again. She held down her anger in order to face him.

"How long we gonna keep this up?" he asked, throwing her car keys to a table in the livingroom.

"You tell me!" She threw back at him. "It's like I don't even know you anymore."

"You're the one who started closing me out, Domino."

"Trin—"

"You know I'm right. I know what I said to you. Hell, I think about it every day. I don't need you throwin' it up in my face."

Dom was pacing nervously. "You think about it, but it's not helping. If it were, you wouldn't have acted out tonight."

Frustrated and at a loss for words, Trin wrenched the bow tie from his neck and unbuttoned his shirt. Dom turned away and walked back to the stairway.

Trin didn't want to leave things unsettled between them for yet another night. He went after her. He caught Dom just as she stepped on the third stair. Thinking Trin was still angry, she ran up the stairs and her high heels tangled in the torn fabric of the gown.

The dress ripped even more as she fell on the curving stairway and took Trin with her. Hurt and angry, Dom started to cry. Trin held her close to him and pressed his face against her back.

"Baby, I just want to know what's the matter with you. Just tell me we can get past this. Tell me you want that as much as I do." he whispered.

Dom's crying subsided to soft shuddery sobs. She began to shake all over and Trin tried to turn her around to face him.

"Domino—"

Dom turned and pushed herself away from him. "I'm afraid of you!" she cried, surprising herself and Trin. Her eyes were wide as she watched him move away from her.

Trin braced himself against the bannister and bowed his head. He squeezed his eyes tightly closed. He couldn't believe what he'd just heard. Though he knew he shouldn't have been surprised to hear it, it shocked him just the same.

Dominique didn't know what else to say. It was obvious that Trin was devastated and hurt. She watched him for a while, then gathered her dress and went upstairs.

Fourteen

Dominique frowned and turned onto her back. The sound of the door opening and closing woke her. She could see sunlight fighting to get past the drapes. It was morning and Trin hadn't come to bed the night before.

Her eyes were still opened to narrow slits as she watched Trin walk over to his dresser. He pulled a pair of sweatpants from one of the drawers. He was going to great lengths to be quiet and steer clear of Dom. The look on his very handsome face relayed hurt and sadness. Her heart broke to see him so down, but she was hurting too. She pretended to be asleep and waited for him to finish getting ready.

As he brushed his teeth, Trin found it impossible to look at his reflection in the mirror. His movements were slow. When he left the bathroom, his eyes were focused on Dom. He pulled on the old sweats and a pair of sneakers, then took a seat on the armchair near the doorway. His black eyes were full of sadness and longing as he watched his wife in bed. Ten minutes later, he was gone.

Later, Dom walked out onto the spacious patio and heard music pounding. She realized Trin was hard at work washing his truck out on the lawn. She set her lemonade on the glass table and took a seat on one of the chaise longues.

Marshall had given her a stack of work to go through and Dom figured there was no time like the present. She tried to keep her mind on the paper-stuffed folders while Trin tried to remain focused on his chore. Still, their intense gazes rose ever so often, and they cast secretive looks at each other. Finally, their wanton stares met and held.

"I'll wash your Lexus after I'm done with this," Trin called, his dark eyes narrowed against the sunlight.

"Thanks," she called back. Thankful he'd said something, she tried to keep the mood light. "You should've washed mine first, anyway."

Trin returned her smile. "I'll need to rest up before I get on *your* dirty car."

Dom threw her head back and laughed. "Oh, we got jokes now, huh?" she drawled.

"When it comes to your car, you're damn right."

The teasing lasted only a short while before silence settled once again. Dom didn't mind. She entertained herself by letting her extraordinary hazel gaze slide over Trin's sexy lean body. He wore no shirt and the water and sunlight glistened on the muscles that rippled in his back.

"Do you want anything?" she asked, when Trin glanced toward her and caught her staring.

He pulled his lower lip between his perfect, white teeth and bowed his head. It was on the tip of his tongue to tell her exactly what he wanted, but he managed to restrain himself.

"Can I have some of that lemonade?" he finally asked.

Dom was pleased by the request. It offered her the opportunity to escape his piercing gaze.

Trin watched her hurry back inside and then he leaned back against his SUV. His thoughts went back to the night before. Never, never had he thought he would hear her say she was afraid of him. Then again, what could he expect? Any man who let jealousy come between him and his wife could only expect to hear those words in time. He didn't deserve her, he really didn't. God had given him a second chance with the only woman he ever loved, and he was ruining it all over again.

"Trin?" Dom called, concerned by the set look on his face.

"Thanks," he whispered, taking the glass she offered.

"Mmm hmm."

"Domino?" Trin called, when she started to turn away.

"Yeah?"

Trin set the glass on the roof of the truck and looked down at her. "So, where do we stand?" he quietly asked.

Dom smiled at the humble look on his gorgeous face and shook her head. "I don't know," she whispered.

Trin nodded and rubbed his hands together. "Are you ever gonna feel the same about me?"

"I love you, Trin. I really do." Dom swore. "Please don't doubt that."

An uneasy grin tugged at Trin's mouth when he glanced upwards. "I don't see how that could be if you . . . hate me."

To that, Dom had no response.

Arthur tapped his fingers on his desk and frowned at his cousin. "You're makin' a big mistake, man."

"It's the only thing I can do. It'll be for the best."

"Moving out? That's the best you can do?"

Trin stood from the sofa and pushed his hands into the deep pockets of his slacks. "I can't stay there, man. You don't know how it is seeing her every day *knowing* how bad I did her."

"I still think you're dumb to move out."

Trin shrugged and stubbornly refused to comment.

Arthur propped his chin against his fist. "Did you tell her about the therapy?"

"No."

"Are you going to?"

"Uh-uh."

"Man, why not?" Arthur demanded to know, standing behind his desk.

Trin raised his hands. "I don't want that to be the only reason we stay together. Later, she'll think I used that to get back in her good graces."

"So? If the sessions are helping, what's the problem?"

"I just don't want her to know."

"Trin, man, I think after what just happened, it's obvious that running can cause a world of problems. Ask your wife."

Arthur spent a while longer trying to convince Trin to reconsider his decision. When Trin decided it was time to go, Arthur didn't know if he had succeeded.

Out in the elementary school's main office, two tiny girls with long thick ponytails and dark complexions bumped right into Arthur and Trin.

Arthur smiled and looked down. "Tamara, Tika? Now, I know your teacher didn't send you two to my office."

"No sir," the two little girls replied in unison.

"Well, what's wrong?" Arthur asked.

Tamara Wilson pulled her twin sister close and looked up at Arthur. "Tika's sick and I have to help her."

Arthur smiled and nodded. "I see. Well, you know the nurse will take care of her."

Tamara just shook her head.

Arthur knelt before the beautiful little girls and took Tamara by the hand. "If you go back to class, Tika will be just fine. I promise."

"Uh-uh." Tamara shook her head, her thick ponytails bouncing around her shoulders and cute face.

Trin knelt down before the sisters as well. He tugged on each of their ponytails, causing them to smile. "You know, Arthur, I can understand where Tamara's coming from."

"You can?" Arthur said with a smile.

"Mmm hmm. Then again, Tamara, if Tika's sick and you're not there either, you two could miss out on some pretty big stuff."

"We could?" the girls simultaneously questioned.

"Yep. Your teacher could announce that tomorrow's show-and-tell or maybe an all-day waterpaint day, but you wouldn't know. Maybe you *should* go back to class. Just in case." Trin smiled as he watched the girls consider his advice. He knew there wasn't much they would miss out on in kindergarten, but he also knew how important it was for one to know that the other was safe.

"Okay," Tamara finally agreed.

Arthur smiled and waved to the teacher and nurse who were standing back watching the two handsome men with the girls. After whispering together for a moment, the children parted company.

Arthur clapped Trin's back when they stood. "Don't let Dom get away again, my man. Think about what you could miss out on."

That evening, Dom was being escorted to a table at Corners, an intimate restaurant not far from the neighborhood. Trin had asked her to meet him there for dinner and Dom had arrived right on time.

Trin was lounging back in his chair, stirring his gin. His dark gaze brightened when he saw Dom headed toward him. The tan silk slip dress she wore emphasized every curve, outlining her physical attibutes. Trin closed his eyes and ordered himself not to forget his reason for asking her to dinner. He had decided not to take his cousin's advice afterall and was going ahead with his original plans.

"This was a surprise," Dom said, resting her elbows on the table once the waiter had left with their orders.

Trin cleared his throat. "Yeah, um, I need to talk to you about somethin'. Figured this would be a better place for it."

A small furrow formed between Dominique's brows. "For what?"

"I think I should move out for a little while."

Dom blinked several times in surprise and it felt as though her heart had jumped to her throat. She was shocked and hurt, but felt it was probably for the best. The next minute, she changed her mind. If Trin left, they would never work out their problems.

"I think it's for the best, Domino. I really don't see another way," Trin said, before she could speak.

Dom frowned a bit more, trying to keep her tears at bay. "Yeah, you're . . . probably right."

Trin sipped his gin and uttered a heavy sigh. He offered no other response.

"When are you leaving?"

His gaze snapped to Dom's face and he ground his teeth. It was killing him to have the conversation, but it felt even worse knowing his wife was afraid of him.

"I'll have everything I need out of the house by Saturday afternoon," he told her. His heart broke as he watched a tear escape the corner of her eye when she turned her face away.

Early on the morning Trin had planned to move out, Dom got in her car and hurried to Martika Salem's house. She was torn between wanting to stop Trin from moving and letting nature take its course. She knew she would go crazy just sitting there watching Trin get his things together.

A worried look crossed Martika's face, when she saw Dom on her front porch. "Dominique?"

"He's moving out."

"What?"

"Trin's leaving."

Martika pulled her daughter-in-law inside the house. "What are you saying?"

"Trin's leaving. He's moving out of the house today."

"Honey—"

"I'm sorry I came barging in here so early, but I had to talk to somebody and I couldn't worry Mommy and Poppy with this."

"So you wanted me to be worried?" Martika cried.

Dom rolled her eyes. "Don't even try it. I know Trin confides in you."

"He does," Martika acknowledged after a moment of silence.

"I'm sorry. I know I should be talking to Trin about this, but he's set on moving and he may be right in doing so."

"How do you figure?"

"When he told me about it, all he kept saying was that it was for the best. I don't want him to go, but we can't even talk to each other. How can we even begin to think of getting past this?"

Martika tapped her fingers along the edge of her sofa and contemplated. "Baby, listen to me. Trinidad wants to work this out, you can't know how much."

Dom tugged on one of the strings hanging from her cutoffs. "I'm sorry Martika, but I just don't see how that can be."

"He's been seeing a therapist."

Dom's jaw dropped and she frowned. "What?"

"From the first day he ever clenched his fist in anger , he's—"

"So you did know?"

Martika nodded. "I did. Trin started seeing Doctor Starks, his therapist, right after that."

Dom flopped back in the arm chair. "Trin," she sighed.

"He didn't want you to know and he'd wring my neck if he knew I told you."

Dom smiled at Martika, then stood from the chair and pressed a kiss to the woman's cheek. "Thank you," she whispered before rushing out.

Trin leapt over the bags crowding the foyer and rushed to answer the phone. "Yeah?"

"Trin? Baby, is that you?"

"Hey, Miss P," Trin greeted his mother-in-law.

"Sweetie, is my daughter there?" Phyllis Carver asked.

Trin scratched his head and frowned. "Nah, she skipped out a while back. She'll probably be back soon."

Phyllis sighed. "Alright. Listen, tell her I called about the Labor Day cookout. Tell her to get in touch with me."

Trin frowned. "Labor Day?"

"Mmm hmm, I know it's a ways off, but I always have a pretty big showing."

"Yeah, I know," Trin said, remembering the huge, festive barbecues. "Well, are you at home now?" he asked.

"Yeah, just tell her to call me."

Trin jotted the message on the pad, just in case he was gone before Dom returned. "I'll tell her . . . alright . . . okay, see you soon."

Dom's light eyes narrowed when she saw the back of Trin's Escalade. He had obviously been making headway with his packing, judging from all the boxes inside the SUV. She took a deep breath and made her way inside the house. Another gasp escaped her lips when she saw all the bags filling the foyer.

Trin was closing the strap on one of his bags when he looked up and saw Dom standing there. His hands shook and he stood slowly. "Hey Domino," he whispered.

Dom was speechless for a moment. She couldn't believe how much he had packed. It was clear that he was quite serious about leaving.

"Almost done, I see," she noted.

Trin glanced around as well. "Yeah, I just need to pack this stuff in the truck, then I'll be out."

"Are you sure about leaving?"

Trin's head snapped up, the look in his dark eyes searching. The question threw him for a moment, but he finally managed a nod. "Yeah, I'm sure."

Dominique's courage to fight the separation slowly deserted her. She tapped her keys against her leg and walked over to take a seat on the staircase. Trin continued his packing and little by little, the foyer cleared.

"I'll call you, alright?" He kneeled next to her on the carpeted staircase.

Dom nodded, fiddling with her keyring.

Trin closed his eyes, surprised by the pressure of tears behind them. He pressed a quick kiss to the corner of Dom's mouth. Then he was gone.

* * *

Trin had been gone several weeks. In that time he had again become a workhorse in hopes of forgetting his marital problems. He had, however, resumed regular visits to his therapist and could feel himself becoming more at peace.

Dominique, like her husband, had also become settled in her career. It was surprisingly easy to do, considering she had been away from it for so long. That, plus the fact that she missed Trin, enabled her to dive into her work. The staff at WQTZ were all sympathetic to her situation, though none of them could believe it. The same could be said for Marshall Greene, who thought Dominique was joking when she informed him of the separation. Staying true to form, though, Marshall played the role of news manager to the hilt. He believed living alone had to be driving Dom out of her mind, so he decided to give his best reporter free reign over one of the biggest projects he had.

"I don't believe you," Dom said, her unique gaze unwavering as she stared him down.

Marshall shrugged as he stood behind his desk. "It's all right here," he said, patting a stack of folders.

Dom eyed the stack with growing interest. "Marshall, do you know how old that company is?"

"Old companies go bad," Marshall replied. "In fact, a lot of old companies have made most of their money by being shady from the start. And don't forget they were the ones trying to force that poor old man to shut down his news stand."

"But to accuse Morton and Farber of something like this?" Dom asked, unable to believe the company where her husband was CEO could be involved in anything so underhanded.

"Check it out for yourself. I'm giving you free reign over the story."

Dom smoothed her hands over her silky hose as she recrossed her long legs. "And just where did you get this information? Who would tell you something like this?"

"We got a contact over there."

"Who?"

"Well, it ain't Trin."

Dom rolled her eyes toward the ceiling. "I know it's not. Who is it?"

Marshall opened one of the folders. "Name's Tim Womack. Works in personnel research."

"Research? What is he? A disgruntled employee?"

"That's for you to find out."

"Why me?"

Marshall lowered his gaze. "You're my best reporter. I need my best on this."

"Marshall . . ."

"Hell, Dominique your husband *is* the CEO of the place. I know y'all miss each other and maybe this'll give you the chance to work closely again with the man himself."

"By investigating his company? Yeah, Marshall, this is one way to keep me in his good graces. This isn't a simple human interest story about a small businessman, you know? Besides, don't you see a small conflict of interest here?"

"Hell no. All I see are the facts. The two of you are seperated. You're my best investigative reporter. You've proven time and again that you can be discreet. Practice it now. Choose your own team and work in the background. I want you on this, Dom. Case closed.

"Anyway, Trin probably doesn't have a clue about what's going on over there."

Dom watched Marshall in disbelief. "He's the CEO and he's too smart to let anything criminal slip past him."

"I agree, but you're forgetting one thing."

"What?"

"Honey, Trin is a black man. CEO or not, do you really think they'd tell him all the company secrets?"

Dom had to admit that she was curious. A scandal surrounding the well-respected Morton and Farber would be an occupational windfall for the person who uncovered it.

"Alright, Marshall, you got me interested. I'll take the story."

Marshall rubbed his hands together. "You won't regret this, Dom. You may even get the chance to spend some quality time with Trin."

Dom didn't try to hide her skeptical expression. "I doubt that," she retorted.

"Have you seen him since he left?"

"Uh-uh. Whenever he comes to get more of his stuff, I'm never there."

"Honey, I hope you talk to him soon. Before any more time passes."

Dom nodded her agreement. Unfortunately, too much time had already passed. It seemed that their lives were just zooming right along. She couldn't believe almost a month had gone by. Deep down, she wondered if it was too late for them.

In his stark Manhattan office, Trin was lounging back in his huge suede chair, his feet propped on the polished oak desk. The folder he'd been studying looked like some sort of case history on an employee or possible employee of the firm. After a moment, he frowned and decided he must have received the paperwork by mistake.

"Mary, I have some folders in here you need to pick up. I believe they were left here by mistake."

Mary cleared her throat. "I'll be right in to get them."

Trin gently replaced the receiver on its hook. "And I really don't need any more work," he said, surprising himself with his own words. It was true, though. He would have much rather been with Dom, trying to work things out, than sitting in his office. Unfortunately, it seemed that work would be the only thing keeping him occupied for a long time to come. He could have kicked himself for allowing almost a month to pass since he had spoken with her. Every time he picked up the phone to call, he lost his nerve.

Dr. Starks had said he'd seen progress over the last several visits. He was sure everything would turn out for the best.

Trin couldn't help but wonder if "for the best" meant a more permanent separation.

Mary rushed into the office just then. "Trin, I'm so very sorry about this."

"No problem."

"I should be more careful about where I lay things around."

Trin thought Mary was taking the simple mistake a bit too seriously, but chose not to comment. He had far too many things on his mind to question anything more.

The phone buzzed as soon as Mary left the office. Trin didn't want to answer, but noticed that it was his private line. Thinking, praying it was Dom, he picked up.

"Hello?"

"Trin?"

"Belinda? That you, girl?" He laughed, just as happy to hear his cousin's voice.

"Yeah, what's goin' on?"

"You don't wanna know."

"I already do. Dom told me you moved out."

Trin grimaced. "She tell you what else I did?"

Belinda was silent for a moment. "Yeah," she finally confessed.

"I think it's over for good this time. I messed up even more than I did the first time."

"Ohhh, don't say that. I got faith. I know this is gonna work out."

"Hmph. You know more than I do."

"Well, look, this is why I really called. Me and Aaron are coming home for Labor Day."

Trin laughed. "Get out."

"I'm serious, Dom called and invited us to her parents' Labor Day bash."

"Damn . . ." Trin breathed, impressed and happy with the news. "Where are y'all staying?"

"With Dom. It would be great if you were there too."

"Belinda . . ."

"Alright, alright, I know. But like I said, I've got faith."

At least one of us does, Trin thought. He and Belinda talked for a few more minutes. Belinda tried to steer the conversation clear of Dom, but she knew her cousin's thoughts were planted there. By the time they finished talking, Trin felt worse than ever. He missed his wife desperately.

Fifteen

"Aunt Sharon, I just can't take off all that time right now. I've just been handed a new story and it's proving to be very time consuming."

"Don't listen to her, Sharon. That station bows down to the girl. She just *won't* take the time."

"Mommy . . ."

"Phyllis, don't push the child. She just got back to work. I can understand if she won't take just a couple of weeks to see her old aunt way down here in Cocoa Beach."

Dom leaned back in the armchair. "Y'all are too much," she sighed. For the past hour and a half she had been having a three-way phone conversation with her mother and her Aunt Sharon. Every time they talked, it seemed that Sharon's goal was to get her niece to come visit her in Florida.

"I will make a serious effort to get there as soon as I can," Dominique promised. "I just got a lot goin' on right now."

"I can understand, with Trinidad and all."

"Sharon!"

Dom laughed. "It's alright, Mommy. Stuff is just crazy right now, Auntie."

"I understand, baby. I really do, 'cause if I had a sexy young thing like that for a husband, I wouldn't wanna be too far away from him either."

"Sharon . . ." Phyllis chastised her older sister again, though there was a hint of laughter in her voice.

Dom was still laughing. "Aunt Sharon, Uncle Joe can't be there with you carryin' on like this."

"Ha! I'll talk like this around him if I want to," Sharon assured them. "Plus, he went to a Heat game with some of his friends."

Phyllis joined her daughter in laughter over Sharon's last statement. Dominique was in heaven and couldn't believe how good it felt to be laughing again.

"Anyway," Sharon said, sighing. "Despite your constant refusals to come down here, I took the liberty of purchasing two round-trip tickets for you and Trin."

"Auntie!"

"Hush, child, it's already done. The tickets are on the way to you as we speak. So now it's up to you to either get your butt down here or waste all my hard-earned money."

Dom pushed one hand through her thick curls and groaned. "Oh, Mommy, how did you ever live with this woman?"

Phyllis chuckled. "Honey, all that time is just one big blur."

The three women were in the midst of laughter again when the doorbell sounded. Dominique quieted instantly. It was getting pretty late and she hadn't been expecting any company.

"Honey? You still there?" Sharon asked.

Dom left the cushiony armchair in the den and headed over to the window. "Yeah, somebody just rang the bell," she answered, peeking out from behind the beige drapes. Her breath caught in her throat when she saw the familiar Escalade parked in the driveway. "Uh, Mommy, Aunt Sharon, I gotta go."

"Everything alright, baby?" Phyllis asked.

"Yeah, uh, Trinidad's here," Dom whispered before she clicked off the phone. She rushed to the front door and took several deep breaths before she pulled it open. Yes, Trin was definitely there. He looked devastatingly handsome and undeniably sexy as he leaned against the doorjamb.

"Hey," Dom greeted him in a breathless voice. She stood

there fiddling with the flimsy ties of the strappy T-shirt she wore with white drawstring sleep-pants.

Trin's dark gaze travelled over the length of his wife's svelte form. He cleared his throat and forced his eyes back to her lovely face. "Hey, I, um, hope I didn't wake you. I saw the light on in the den but I didn't want to barge in," he explained.

Dom shook her head, her thick curls bouncing around her dark face. "Oh you wouldn't have . . . Um, come on in," she said, stepping away from the door as he stepped past her.

Trin kept his hands pushed into the deep pockets of his jeans. He went no farther than the foyer.

"I was just in the den," Dom said, whisking past him. The room was in shambles since she had been going through the research on the Morton and Farber story before her mother and aunt called. She didn't want to discuss it with Trin just yet, though. She stumbled around the room, gathering pages of information from the floor and chairs.

"Working?" Trin asked, enjoying the sight of her as she scurried around the room.

"Always," Dom replied with a soft laugh.

Trin nodded, a small smile tugging at the corner of his mouth. "I know the feeling," he informed her as he stood in the den's doorway.

Dom noticed him there and rolled her eyes. "If you're waiting for me to tell you to make yourself comfortable, you can keep on waiting."

"Why?" Trin asked, surprised by the statement.

"This is still your home. You can come in here anytime you please and you wouldn't be barging in."

"You sure?"

"Positive. Get in here."

Surprisingly, they had a wonderful visit. It was almost as though the last month had never happened. They didn't speak of their marriage, though. They both felt the evening had been far too enjoyable to begin such an emotional discussion.

* * *

"That stuff any good?" Trin asked as he peered across Dom's shoulder while she prepared coffee.

Dom was following the directions on the back of the flavor-sealed package. "It's supposed to taste like the stuff they serve in the coffeehouses." She told him.

"Mmm hmm," Trin curtly replied. The smirk he wore added a devilish element to his profile. "I'll ask again—that stuff any good?"

Dom chuckled. "You really should get in touch with your artsy side," she advised.

Trin braced his hands on either side of her along the counter and effectively trapped her there. "You're artsy enough for me," he said, his voice raspier than usual as deep emotion took over.

Dom's lashes began to flutter as the unmistakeable scent of male cologne drifted beneath her nose. She could feel the quiet power radiating from his body through the soft cotton of the hooded sweatshirt he wore. Finally, she turned to meet his gaze. The intensity in Trin's eyes affected Dominique as though he had actually touched her.

"Um, would you mind handing me a coffeepot from the cabinet?" she asked, fearing she would swoon if he continued to stand so close. "Could I get you to do me another favor too?" she asked, once he was on the other side of the kitchen.

"Anything," he replied without hesitation, as he selected a yellow-and-blue ceramic pot.

"Well, Aunt Sharon called just before you got here. She's sending us plane tickets to Florida. I tried to get out of it, but she wouldn't listen. Could you, maybe, call her and make up some excuse about having a meeting or something? I know she won't continue to push if you call."

Trin set the coffeepot to the counter and bowed his head. "You sure you don't want to go?"

Surprise registered on Dom's pretty cocoa-toned face. "After everything that's happened, I didn't think . . . besides, you're a busy man. I know you can't just take off."

Trin shrugged as though he hadn't a care for his position. "There's nothing that I can't get out of for a while," he told her.

"Well, you know how my aunt is," Dom cautioned, fidgeting with the hem of her snug T-shirt. "She's not known for her . . . subtlety."

Trin folded his arms over his chest. "She always means well. And it might help to get away."

"What about all that time we spent in Chicago?" Dom whispered.

"That wasn't a vacation. It was hell."

"Do you think a two-week trip will solve our problems?"

"Baby, I don't think a two-*month* trip would do that," Trin admitted with a humorless chuckle. "I'd just like to get away somewhere—with you. Get away from all the memories here. . . . Besides, I could eat a ton of your aunt's blueberry pancakes," he said, hoping to lighten the mood.

Dominique's laughter filled the kitchen. Eventually, she agreed that the trip might be a good idea.

"Belinda called me at work today. She told me she and Aaron were coming for a visit."

"Yeah, um, you know my parents always have that Labor Day party. I really wanted them here."

Trin was lounging back on the sofa, his long legs crossed at the ankles. "I'm glad you did. I hope I get to see 'em."

Dom frowned. "Well, you're coming to the party, aren't you?"

"You didn't ask me."

"I thought it was understood that you'd be there. But if you want a personal invitation, you just got it."

Trin's long, dark brows drew close as his eyes narrowed. Dom was so close to him and the seductive tone of her invitation was his undoing. He tugged on the edge of her T-shirt and pulled her close until she was straddling his lap. His sensual mouth teased the smooth column of her neck, stopping to nip at her earlobe. In response, Dom gasped and gripped his wide shoulders more tightly.

Trin lowered his black stare to her chest as he brushed the straps from her shoulders. He pressed his handsome face to the deep cleft between her full breasts and inhaled her scent. Dom twirled her fingers through his gorgeous hair and held his head close to her.

"Domino, I miss you so much," Trin whispered against her chest.

Dom closed her eyes and enjoyed the feel of his lips pulling against her firm nipple, which was outlined against the damp material of the T-shirt. Trin disappointed her a while later when he moved away. She watched him take several deep breaths while his head rested on her shoulder.

Trin knew he didn't have to pull away, but he needed Dom to come to him. He felt that if she did, there was hope that she could trust him again.

"I better go," he whispered, patting his hand against her thigh. "Call me when you get the tickets so I can set my schedule." He smiled as she moved off his lap and curled up on the sofa. He stood and gave her an apologetic look. Then he pressed the softest kiss to the corner of her mouth and left.

"Goodness . . ." Dom breathed when she followed her aunt into the guestroom that Saturday afternoon.

Trin was just as amazed, taking in the cool plushness of the third-floor suite. "You sure we're in the right place, Miss Sharon?"

Sharon McDaniels giggled like a school girl as her round, dark eyes sparkled. "I'm positive you're both in the right place."

"When did y'all do this?" Dom asked, walking over to the window and peering down at the stretch of beach visible from the back of the house.

Sharon smiled and looked around the airy room. "I'd been after your uncle to do something with this old attic space for years. After a while, he forbid me to come up here. Until one day, he bought me in here and had done all this."

"Helps to have a contractor in the family, I guess," Trin noted, inspecting the impressive built-in white oak entertainment center.

"Hmph, helps to be married to one," Sharon corrected, a suggestive twinkle in her lovely eyes.

"I'm surprised you and Uncle Joe didn't take this for yourselves," Dom said as she turned away from the window to take a seat on the cushioned sill.

Sharon was heading for the room's white double doors. "This room is reserved especially for lovely young couples trying to find their way back to each other," she announced. "Now you two get settled and dinner will be served in four hours."

Silence followed Sharon's departure. Trin set his suitcase on the bed and cleared his throat. "Sharon still tells it like it is."

"Yeah . . ." Dom sighed, glancing back out the window. "I think I'm gonna take a swim." She pulled her yellow T-shirt over her head and continued to disrobe, unmindful of her husband who stood watching her with his mouth open. Dominique wiggled out of her jeans and underthings, before strolling to the bed. She was searching her suitcase for a bikini when she'd realized what she'd done.

She winced and forced her eyes to Trin's face. "Sorry," she whispered. "Trin?" she called, when he closed his eyes.

Speechless, Trin could only raise his hand before he turned and walked into the private bathroom. A moment later, Dominique heard the shower.

Dom spent a long while at the beach. She took a lengthy stroll and enjoyed the shade from the towering palms that clustered in her aunt and uncle's yard.

"Did I miss dinner?" she asked, finding Trin alone in the kitchen when she returned.

"Sharon says she's prepared a special meal," he announced

as he scanned the sheet of paper he held, "and she says we're suppose to eat down on the beach."

"That woman . . ." Dom sighed.

"I guess we can use all the help we can get," Trin added.

"Well, I guess I don't have to change," Dom decided, slapping her hands to her sides.

Trin's dark, smoldering gaze raked his wife's figure-eight form encased in the devilish cream bikini. A flowing, ankle-length peach floral wrap skirt was slung low over her hips. "Please don't," he requested, then hefted the food basket. "Shall we?"

They left the three-story home, using the short brick stairway that led down to the beach. By the light of the moon and the chic, blue-fluorescent, insect-repelling lamps, they made a pallet and set out the meal.

"Look at this," Trin whispered, joining in when Dom laughed at what he'd found in the bottom of the basket.

Besides a fantastic dinner, Sharon had included a small cassette player with a tape of Luther Vandross's greatest hits.

"I guess we shouldn't disappoint her," Trin suggested, clicking on the radio. He set the volume, then stood and extended his hand.

Dominique accepted and they selected a spot on the beach not far from the blanket. They swayed to one of the many sensual grooves on the tape, when suddenly Dom gasped and stiffened in Trin's arms.

"What's wrong?" he whispered, massaging her waist as he pulled back to study her troubled expression.

"That night," Dom said, pressing her face against the white cotton top that hung outside Trin's khaki shorts, "that night before everything went crazy . . . we danced like this in the kitchen, remember?"

Trin closed his eyes as the memory flooded back. He tried to block out the sweetness of the evening that had been irrevocably ruined.

". . . we were going to make love again when you got back

home, but . . ." Dom's words trailed away and were replaced by a shaking sob.

When her tears began to flow more steadily, Trin gathered her in his arms and hugged her tightly. "Baby, shh . . ." he soothed, dropping kisses to her face. The sweet pecks landed on her mouth and soon they were kissing.

Dom moaned and settled her arms around Trin's neck. She arched against him as she kissed him enthusisatically. Her tongue dueled with his, and her hands ventured beneath his shirt to stroke the muscles rippling in his back.

Trin pulled her high against his chest and carried her back to the pallet. There, he braced himself on muscular forearms and dropped moist kisses to her chest and stomach. His perfect teeth tugged aside a portion of the bikini top and revealed one breast. His nose outlined the sensual roundness and nudged a rigid nipple before his lips closed over it.

"Mmm . . . Trin, Trin please . . ." She brushed his hip in her own silent invitation. When his fingers curled into the crotch of her bikini bottom, she begged him not to stop. Her hands massaged the back of his head as his mouth feasted on her breast. Trin began an assault on her femininity, his fingers invading her body and thrusting with merciless intensity.

Suddenly, surprising them both, he moved away. Dom tugged his hand, silently urging him to continue. After a moment, she realized what she was doing and she reluctantly released him. Several moments of silence passed before they managed to return their attention to dinner.

"Um, Domino I think it might be better if I sleep downstairs or something," Trin said when they returned to the third floor.

"So, I guess you're ready for all Aunt Sharon's questions when she finds you're sleeping outside this room?" Dom challenged, her expression soft and knowing. "And don't even think about using the sofa in here, because it's too small for you and I'm not about to give up the bed," she added, hoping she had covered every excuse.

Trin chuckled. "I guess I don't have a choice. You really okay with it?" he asked, his expression sobering.

"I'm fine with it," she assured him, already opening the door.

They chose their sides of the bed and silently prepared to retire for the evening. Trin was removing his watch when he heard Dom call his name.

"That night after Marshall's party . . . what I said about being afraid of you—"

"Domino—"

"I'm sorry. Sorry I had to say that."

"Never apologize for telling the truth." Trin said, keeping his back toward her. "You have every right to feel that way."

"But I hurt you when I said it, didn't I? Didn't I, Trin?"

"Yeah, Domino, alright? Yes, it hurt, so what?"

"I think that's why I said it. So you'd know what it felt like to be hurt and never see it coming," she said, then slipped beneath the covers.

Trin didn't fall asleep for a long time.

After a huge pancake breakfast the next morning, Trin and Joe went golfing. Dominique and Sharon set out for the slew of shops and markets in town. Everyone returned to the house at around four that afternoon.

"I reserved a table at the best seafood place in town." Sharon announced when they all met in the kitchen.

"What time do we leave?" Dom asked, her attention more focused on the contents of one of her shopping bags.

"It's not far," Sharon was saying as she handed Trin a small card. "Follow these directions and you'll head right to it."

Dom's light eyes clashed with Trin's dark ones. Then they both stared at Sharon.

"You two aren't coming?" Dom asked, looking from her aunt to her uncle.

Joe waved his hand. "Don't ask questions, baby girl," he advised, dropping a kiss to his niece's forehead.

Sharon pushed against her husband's broad back. "Hush, Joe," she whispered, "now you two go on. And you better hurry, 'cause it looks like rain."

Dom pushed her hands into the back pockets of her white Capri pants. "That woman . . ." She sighed, watching her aunt switch out of the kitchen.

Trin smiled and shook his head. "You gotta love her."

"Hmph. She should go into business. I mean, could she be any more obvious?"

Trin's expression turned uneasy. "Um, Domino you're okay with this, right? I mean—"

"Oh, no, Trin, I'm fine with it," she quickly assured him, laughing at the fact that he had taken her seriously. "My aunt can go over the top sometimes, but I love all the help she's giving us."

"Amen," he whispered, his gaze softening.

The seafood restaurant was actually a large ferryboat with an indoor/outdoor dining room. The scene was so lovely and relaxing, Trin and Dom decided to dine outside despite the darkening skies.

"I hope we'll only need this umbrella for shade," Dominique said as they took their seats at the intimate square table.

Trin squinted as he glanced up at the huge green-and-blue umbrella. "We may not even need it for that. I don't see the sun."

"Well, I won't complain about that. This breeze is incredible," Dom noted, as she scanned the menu the hostess had left behind.

Many diners enjoyed the outdoor dining room but the area didn't seem crowded. The boat was also far away from the noise of the crowd milling about the beach and the pier.

"So, I guess you're used to great views, huh?" Dom

remarked when they were enjoying drinks a short while later. "From your condo in the city," she clarified when Trin sent her a questioning look.

He shrugged, his dark gaze following the ice cubes floating in his cognac. "The view's incredible, but I hate the place."

Dom smiled at the creamy texture of her Piña Colada. "Yeah, I guess there's nothing like living in a house," she said.

"No. There's nothing like living with you."

Dominique's fingers stilled on the extra long straw protruding from her glass. "But you felt that you had to leave?" she softly inquired.

"I couldn't stay, Domino. But I can tell you that I left because I'm a coward. I see that now," he admitted, setting the glass aside as though he'd lost his taste for the drink. "Every day I spent around you was more time I spent thinking about how jealous I'd become over something you did before you ever knew I existed."

Dom's eyes were riveted on Trin as he spoke. She almost cursed the waiter when he returned with their orders. Trin's words were effectively silenced.

"What about Chicago?" she asked, when they were halfway through the meal.

Trin's fork stilled in his crab salad. "Chicago?"

"You weren't jealous in Chicago," she explained, unable to meet his probing dark eyes. "You were changed. It was like you were your old self, for the most part."

Trin reclined in his chair and continued to study her. Chicago seemed another lifetime ago, but the night he had learned that his wife had once been married to his cousin was frighteningly vivid.

"Were you changed because of my amnesia, because of your guilt, or were your feelings genuine—completely removed from all that other mess?"

Trin only contemplated the question for a second. "It was my guilt. I asked God for one more chance to make things right. He answered my prayers, and I was determined not to blow it." A smile came to his face then. "You know, I kept expecting you to forget those new memories when you got the old ones back."

Dom smiled too. "The new memories made it hard to believe the old ones ever existed," she said, then leaned across the table with her hands outstretched. "Why couldn't you talk to me then? We were so close. It seemed that we could say anything to each other."

Trin looked out over the blue expanse of water and focused on the setting sun. "Domino, sometimes I think the way I feel about you borders on obsession. Yes, I love you, but it goes so much deeper than that. I don't know how healthy that is but . . . knowing you've been intimate with someone besides me is hard enough to handle. Knowing about Spry made me angry enough to—"

"Hurt me?" Dom interjected, her light gaze unknowingly accusing.

Trin didn't know how to respond.

"How could you do that? Trindy, I've always been a good wife to you. You were everything I wanted—smart, charming, funny, sexy as hell, gorgeous beyond belief . . . and you *knew* that. You knew I felt those things. Then you find out that for a few weeks many, many years ago I was married to a cousin you despise and you turned into a man I didn't want to know. I was afraid to sleep in the same bed next to you." She stopped then, wanting to say more, but unable to form the words.

Trin's dark eyes grew blurred with tears as he watched her cry into her hands.

"I can't do this," Dom whispered. She stumbled out of her chair and ran from the deck.

After the outburst, things were even more strained between Trin and Dominique. Luckily, Sharon and Joe were there to keep spirits high. They treated their guests to the best Cocoa Beach had to offer. Aside from that, Trin kept his distance from Dom. Hearing her voice her feelings so emotionally rendered him more guilt-ridden and remorseful.

Joe grilled out on the last evening of Trin and Dom's stay. Sharon sent her niece to fetch her husband once the meal was ready.

Dom found Trin on the beach. He had his cell phone and was conducting business. She lingered in the background, admiring the authority in his voice as he handled the call. She wanted so much to put everything behind them and move on, but feared that would never be possible.

"Alright, Sam . . . Well, I'll be back tomorrow but let's set up lunch or something later this week. Yeah . . . alright . . . no problem. Talk to you then." Trin ended the call, then clicked off the phone and pushed it into the side pocket of loose-fitting denim shorts.

Dominique watched him bury his face in his hands. Then he folded his arms over his chest and stared out at the ocean.

"Hey," she called, smiling when he turned. "Aunt Sharon sent me to get you for dinner."

"Domino, wait," he called, rushing toward her as she turned to leave. He was about to reach for her, but pushed his hands into his pockets. "I'm, um . . . I'm about to tell you something you probably won't believe. . . ."

"What is it?" Dom asked, fiddling nervously with the uneven hemline of her tan halter T-shirt.

"I'm scared."

The natural arch of Dom's brow seemed to rise a notch. Trin couldn't help but laugh at her reaction. The amusement was brief. He sobered almost instantly.

"Scared?" Dom questioned.

Trin's bare feet trudged the sand as he took a small step closer. "Baby, I don't see how you could ever forgive what I put us through. I don't see it, because *I* can't even forget it, much less forgive it."

Dom waved her hand. "You shouldn't forget it. *Never* forget it because it could easily happen again."

A muscle twitched erratically in Trin's jaw as he fought the urge to swear it would never happen again. "I'm scared," he continued, "because I hurt you that night. I hurt you emotionally with this jealousy of mine. Sometimes emotional hurt can do just as much damage as the physical kind. Many women have ended relationships over it."

"What are you saying?" Dominique whispered, clenching her hands into fists to prevent them from shaking.

Trin squeezed his eyes shut and massaged the bridge of his nose. "I'm saying I'd understand if—"

"Trin! Dom!"

"Sharon's calling," Dominique whispered, thankful for the interruption. She had no desire to continue the unsettling discussion.

Sixteen

Dom's office was crowded with co-workers who hadn't had the opportunity to see her since she had returned to work. Everyone was happy to have her back, though Dom wished they would let her get prepared for the meeting she had in about five minutes.

"Y'all got to go! I mean it. I have too much work to do."

"Girl, what could you possibly have to do?" Edwina Hampton asked in a playfully sympathetic tone.

"Forget you, Eddie. Marshall just dropped a heavy story in my lap a few weeks before I left for Florida."

Eddie rolled her eyes. "Probably that Morton and Farber shit."

Dom's eyes narrowed toward the petite, dark-complexioned lady across her desk. "I don't get it."

Cornell Sims laughed. "Sounds like you did."

"Can someone let me in on the joke please?" Dom asked, scratching her eyebrows.

"Honey, nobody wants that story," Eddie informed her.

"Why not? It sounded hot."

"Mmm hmm," Cornell agreed. "*Too* hot. Nobody wants to mess around with that company. It's too old and too powerful."

Dom pounded her fist to her desk. "I don't believe what I'm hearing here. Y'all are reporters. Experienced reporters. I can't believe you're turning down stories because the company is too big."

"Dom, Marshall didn't tell you the whole story, did he?" Monty Harris asked, stroking the light beard on his face.

Dom raised her hands in a helpless gesture.

"A lot of unfavorable comments have been made about that company. Of course, nothing's ever been proven."

"Well, maybe we got 'em this time," Dom said in a hopeful tone.

Monty shook his head. "I can't believe Marshall's still hanging on to this."

Edwina stood from her chair. "He probably senses a big coup if the station breaks the story. Hell, Dom's husband is CEO of the place. Maybe he figures *she'll* get somewhere."

The phone buzzed, interrupting the conversation. Dom pressed the speaker button. "Yeah, Jessica?"

"Dom, your ten o'clock is here."

"Thank you," Dom said, raising her brows at her co-workers. "You guys heard it. Out."

"Good luck," Cornell said, waving his hand in Dom's direction.

Dom noticed a young man, no older than herself, standing outside the door. He waited until everyone had left before slowly walking into her office.

"Tim Womack?" Dom said, standing and smoothing her hands over her red Lagerfeld pantsuit.

"Pleasure to meet you, Mrs. Salem. Everybody at the firm said Trinidad had a beautiful wife and they were right."

"Thank you, but please call me Dominique."

"Deal."

Dom waved her hand toward an empty chair. "Please," she said.

"I guess you want to know why I'm here."

Dom leaned back in her chair and nodded. "Well, yeah. I mean, droppin' a dime on the place where you make your living. Pretty risky."

Tim stood from the chair and pushed his hands into his pockets. "I was sorry to hear you and Mr. Salem are having problems. I guess finding out your wife was once married to your cousin can throw you for a loop."

Dom gripped the sides of her chair and sat straighter. "What are you—"

"I know all about it." Tim informed her.

"How?"

"Dominique, when your husband got his promotion, a lot of people in that company almost had heart attacks. A black man, no matter how educated or experienced, had no place at the helm of that firm."

Dom couldn't believe what she was hearing. "Trin got that position, though."

"Oh, yeah, he got it because some very influential people wanted him there. They wanted a black man in a leadership position to improve their image. Besides, Mr. Salem had the entire package—prime education, charisma, good looks, beautiful wife, I could go on . . ."

"I still don't get how you know about my marriage to his cousin."

Tim took his seat in front of the desk. "Morton and Farber don't hire anyone without knowing everything about them, their family and their friends. You'd think they were the CIA. They can find out anything. In a way, it's sort of a test all prospective employees must pass."

"What kind of test?"

Tim recrossed his legs. "Some people become very upset when they hear what's been discovered about their private lives."

"Hmph. I bet."

"The way they handle the news is a huge deciding factor with the top brass."

Dom tapped her fingers against the desk. "I guess Trin passed."

"With flying colors," Tim confirmed. "But they don't re-veal everything at once. They wait, revealing choice tidbits when they feel they have to. There was a reason they decided to inform your husband about your previous marriage. Of

REMEMBER LOVE   223

course, they were assuming he didn't know. They were betting on the fact that he didn't and probably hoping he'd end your marriage over it."

"But why?"

"You're a reporter, Mrs. Salem—Dominique. Remember the Hal Lymon story?"

Dom thought for a moment, then her lashes fluttered. "Jesus," she breathed. "You mean they were so threatened by a simple human interest story that they wanted my husband to divorce me?"

Tim shrugged, but it was obvious that he believed it as well. "Luckily that didn't happen. When they dropped their so-called bombshell, your husband was as cool as a cucumber."

You didn't see him when he got home, Dom silently mused. "What's all this got to do with working there?" she asked, hoping to move the conversation from such painful memories.

"Dominique, the prestigious Morton and Farber are not above using blackmail."

"Blackmail? Are you saying they threaten their employees?"

"They threaten anybody who gets in the way of them making money. It's in their best interest to have employees they feel they can completely control. In your husband's case, they didn't need him . . . talking in his sleep, shall we say?"

Dom's bright eyes narrowed. "Why are you doing this, Tim? Are they blackmailing you?"

"Not yet. My reasons are purely selfish. I guess I'm a product of my environment. Can you believe that the company's president wouldn't pay me when I said I'd go to the press if he didn't wire one million dollars to my account by the end of the week?"

Dom propped her elbows onto her desk and shook her head. "So my next question is, can I trust you?"

"You can."

"I don't see how. When this story breaks, you'll be fired. Remember, you didn't get that million dollar bonus you asked for."

Tim nodded. "I can understand your not trusting me, but

maybe after a few more meetings, you'll see I'm dead serious about helping you."

"Okay, but I'm sure you'll understand when I suggest we keep these meetings discreet. I don't want my husband knowing about this yet." Dom watched as Tim nodded again. She hated keeping something so explosive from Trin, but she hadn't decided quite how to handle the situation. She didn't want him knowing how corrupt his company really was.

"I should beat you two for not letting me come meet you at the airport."

"You knew we wouldn't have let you do that," Belinda whispered as she and Aaron hugged Dom when they arrived at her home late that afternoon.

"Plus, we wanted to soak in the reality of bein' back in the dirty apple," Aaron said.

Despite the flippant manner of Aaron's words, Dom could sense the couple's unease. "You guys dreading seeing your people already?" she asked, watching Belinda and Aaron exchange weary expressions.

"Let's just say it's not one of the things we're looking forward to," Belinda told her.

"Well, look at the silver lining," Dom said. "At least you have Trin's support, and he was always your worst critic."

"Amen," Belinda whispered, her lovely dark eyes sparkling with relief.

"Speaking of Trin . . ." Aaron remarked, leaving the sentence unfinished.

"I haven't seen him since we got back from Florida," Dom told them, toying with the gold zipper on her purple-and-mauve chiffon housedress.

"Did y'all get anything settled?" Belinda inquired.

"We got a lot out in the open, but . . . Trin's feeling so guilty and sorrowful. It's like he doesn't even want to talk about working it out. I think he'd feel better if I did ask for a divorce," she said, unable to let the last word pass without breaking into tears.

"Shh . . ." Aaron soothed, pulling her into a slow rocking embrace.

After a few moments, Belinda clapped her hands. "Listen, you two, enough of this. I think we've wallowed in our problems too long. And I don't know about you, but I'm ready to party!" She said, slapping her hands to her jean-clad thighs.

Dom, still in Aaron's comforting embrace, began to laugh. "Then y'all are in the right town for that."

Belinda stopped dancing around the foyer and frowned. "Oh no, baby, I'm not trying to go out on the town tonight. Something small right here at the house will do just fine."

"Well, I'd suggest something by the pool, but it's a bit chilly tonight." Dom was saying, as she tried to think of something.

Suddenly, Aaron snapped his fingers. "Hey, that sounds good," he said, chuckling when his wife and Dom looked at him strangely. "The weather tonight is perfect for a big pot of my chili."

"Oooh, that sounds good," Belinda replied, already rubbing her hands together. "This man makes the best chili." She raved, pulling out her cellphone as she walked off.

Dom threw her hands in the air. "Alright then, chili it is."

"Alright, look here, girl," Aaron called as he hefted the strap of a garment bag across his shoulder. "While I put these bags away, I need you to check your cabinets for the things I need."

"So, you're gonna reveal your chili secrets to me?" Dom teased, as she picked up two of the smallest suitcases.

Aaron appeared to be offended. "Never. It's not just knowing the ingredients. It's knowing the order they're included, when to include them, and how much to include."

"I see, O Great One."

"Hey, I like that."

Much later, everyone was laughing and having a great time. Even Arthur stopped by, and had brought a date along.

Aaron had taken over the kitchen, where the group had gathered to pressure him about his chili's prep time.

Like her guests, Dominique was lightly buzzed and in high
spirits. She was on her knees laughing over something Arthur
had said, when Trin walked into the kitchen.

"What the hell are y'all doin' to my wife?!" he playfully
bellowed as he took in the scene.

"What's goin' on, man?"

"What's up, Trin?"

"Hey, Trin." Dom was last to greet her husband. She tried
to remain soft and poised. Unfortunately, she burst into another fit of giggles.

"I think she got tickled over one of Arthur's crazy jokes,"
Tamara Shaker decided, her own laughter spilling forth.

Belinda was adding more wine to her glass. "Hmph . . . tickled and tipsy," she noted, pointing a finger at Arthur's date.

"Hell, yeah," Aaron agreed, before taking a swig of his beer.

"Well, lemme catch up then," Trin was saying as he accepted a beer from Arthur.

"Alright, Trin, we ain't got no designated drivers here," Belinda cautioned. "You get drunk, you gotta spend the night
like everybody else."

Trin's smile triggered his dimples. "No problem, Bel," he
said, his dark gaze settling on his wife. "Long as Domino
don't mind sharing her bed."

Dominique shook her beer bottle in the air. "No problem,"
she sang, then cast a wicked look in Belinda's direction. "Girl,
I should tell you now that I always wanted to sleep with Aaron."
The room came alive with more laughter. When everyone's attention was drawn back to the chili, Dom pushed herself away
from the kitchen island and sauntered over to Trin.

"You never have to ask to share a bed with me," she stood
on her toes to whisper in his ear.

Trin smiled and turned to face her. "I didn't want to as-
sume," he whispered back.

Dominique's striking hazel gaze settled on the curve of his
mouth. "Consider it a standing invitation."

When she walked away, Trin decided he would be spending the night at home.

Belinda caught up to Trin while he was selecting new CDs for the changer.

"How are you?" she asked, tugging on the tail of his denim shirt.

"Great now," Trin admitted, setting the CDs aside. "I wanted to thank you and Aaron for being here. Domino looks happier than I've seen her in a long time."

Belinda tucked a braid behind her ear. "We want you to be happy too, you know? That's why I called you out here."

"Hmph," Trin replied.

"Sweetie, do you think the mistakes you made took away your right to want your wife back?"

Trin cleared his throat. "It's up to Domino. I'll do whatever she wants."

Belinda pressed her hand against the front of the white T-shirt he sported beneath the denim. "She can't be in this alone, Trin. You have to talk to her. Believe it or not, you have a say in this too."

Trin looked across the enclosed portion of the patio. Dom was waiting to taste Aaron's chili. He chuckled when she took the sample, fanned her mouth and ran into the kitchen.

Belinda smiled at his reaction. "I don't think you'll be able to handle it if you lose her again," she predicted, seeing the love radiate from her cousin's striking black eyes.

After a while, Trin looked down at Belinda and smiled. He tugged one of her braids and walked back inside the house. He found Dom in the kitchen gulping down a tall glass of water.

"Too hot for you?" he teased.

She set the glass down and bowed her head. "I tell you, my mouth was burning before I even *tasted* the stuff," she declared.

"No joke, huh?" Trin said, as he closed the distance between them.

"Honey . . ." was Dom's only reply as she remembered the power of the red hot spices.

"Come over here," Trin whispered as he leaned against the counter and pulled her against him.

Dominique forgot about the chili as the closeness ignited a definite tingle in her erogenous zones. Her eyes traced Trin's fantastic facial features as her hands roamed his muscular forearms, visible below the rolled sleeves of his denim shirt.

Trin stroked Dom's lower lip with the tip of his thumb, then followed the outline with the tip of his tongue. Dom's fingers curled around the neckline of his T-shirt and her lips suckled his tongue. Trin moaned his surprise and lost a bit of the strength in his long legs. Dominique was starved for her husband and it showed. She kissed him with wild abandon, her slender form rubbing against him in an astonishingly wanton manner.

"So, are you going to accept my invitation to bed?" she asked, once the kiss broke and she was pressing wet pecks along his jaw.

Trin cupped her breasts and squeezed them as he suckled her earlobe. "Don't ask silly questions," he ordered in a ragged whisper.

She was already unbuckling his belt and the buttonfly of his white jeans. "Will you accept it now? Please?" she moaned.

Trin rose to his full height and pulled Dom closer. She locked her legs around his back while he headed upstairs. The passionate kiss resumed and they only made it as far as the upstairs hallway. There, Dom found herself pressed against a wall.

"I can't wait," Trin told her, tugging on the gold zipper of her housedress. When he saw that she was completely nude beneath it, his head fell to her shoulder.

Dominique's lashes fluttered madly when she felt his tongue stroking her collarbone. His thumbs manipulated her nipples until they were firm as tiny jewels. His knee thrust between her legs to hold her in place against the wall. Dom's nails raked his crisp, wavy hair and she held him close to her chest. Trin cupped one breast as his mouth worked over the satiny, cocoa-colored mound of flesh. His lips and tongue soothed the nipple as his other hand drifted over her hips and downward.

"Trin!" Dom gasped, when his fingers entered her body two, three at a time. The maddening caress almost rendered her breathless. "Trin, you said you couldn't wait," She reminded him, tugging the belt from his waist.

Trin finished the job, freeing himself from the confines of his jeans and boxers. His hands cupped Dom's full bottom and he thrust upward. The smooth intrusion forced a cry from her mouth. Trin buried his handsome face in the side of her neck and took her with startling intensity. His moans of satisfaction were at times deep and rough and at others soft and tortured. The increasing moisture sheathing his manhood only aroused him more. Dom almost fainted when she felt him grow more rigid inside her.

"Domino . . ." He groaned, his hips thrusting more rapidly as he approached climax.

For several moments afterward, they remained against the wall locked in a sultry embrace. Sounds of heavy breathing filled the hallway for the longest time. Finally, Trin pulled Dom into his arms and headed to their bedroom. They made love for the rest of the night and well into the morning.

"I think I speak for everyone at this table when I say how happy—"

"And relieved."

"And relieved we are that you have accepted our proposal."

"That he *finally* accepted our proposal!"

Trin chuckled and pinned Sam Rutgers with a knowing look. "Was I taking too long, Sam?"

"You? Nah!" Sam replied, joining in when laughter rose at the table.

Trin was having lunch that afternoon with a few colleagues. Two of the men worked for Morton and Farber, the other two were independent businessmen. The men had been tossing around the idea of starting up their own investment firm. They wanted Trin to help bring it all together. After much debate, Trin was finally ready to come on board.

"We should really begin discussing a timetable here, guys," Shawn Hastings suggested.

Again, Sam Rutgers voiced his opinion. "I think we'll be more equipped to produce a firm timetable once Trin tells us when he's going to stun Wall Street and give Morton and Farber his resignation."

Trin shook his head. "Sam, anybody ever tell you you're way too impatient?"

"Don't even try it, Salem," Sam ordered, then turned to his other lunch partners. "We've been after this guy for what? Nine, ten months?"

"Eleven," someone corrected.

Sam shook his head. "Eleven months. Almost a damn year. What more do we have to do to show you how much we want you, man?"

"I'm afraid to ask," Trin replied, grinning devilishly while everyone else burst into laughter. He signaled for the waiter, when he noticed Dominique across the crowded dining room. She wasn't alone. The man with her didn't look familiar, but their conversation appeared intense. Trin couldn't stop the wave of uneasiness that settled in the pit of his stomach, but he ordered himself not to take it seriously.

That order was a distant memory when he saw Dominique reach across the table and squeeze the man's wrist. The strength left his hands and they landed on the table, causing the silverware to clatter.

"Trin? Trin man, you alright?"

"Hey, Trin?"

"Sorry." He finally snapped to. "Sorry, what—what was that?" he said, hoping no one noticed how shaken he was.

Sam was grinning. "We're gonna give you some time to get that resignation together. Then we'll be in touch," he said as he stood from the table. "You coming?"

Trin looked across the room again. "Nah, I'm gonna have

another drink," he decided, shaking hands with each of his lunch partners. Then he settled back and watched his wife.

"You know I wish you all the best. What you've given up . . ."

Tim Womack shrugged. "I knew what I was getting into. Despite the fact that I tried to make money off it, I think this is some dirty laundry that really needs to be aired. Hell, someone would've leaked it eventually, why not me? I deserve to go out with a bang," Tim said, then grimaced. "Maybe I could've phrased that better, huh?"

"I'll say," Dominique agreed, still unable to forget how her life had been affected by the company's meddlings. "Well, you've given me more knowledge on Morton and Farber than I cared to hear. This story is a definite coup for my station, but it's gonna be a shock to the business world."

"Well, I'll definitely be waiting for the story," Tim said, as he stood. "Guess we shouldn't be seen leaving together."

Again, Dom squeezed Tim's wrist. "Let me know when you get settled, alright?"

"You got it," Tim promised before he left the table.

Dom's head was bowed when she walked out of the dining room. She was searching her leather tote for keys, when someone caught her arm.

"Trin," she whispered, seeing her husband standing right next to her. He had been gone when she woke that morning after their sixth round of lovemaking. Vivid memories of their steamy encounter returned and she felt flushed as the images ravaged her mind.

"Are you coming or going?" he asked, hoping his voice sounded light enough.

Dom glanced across her shoulder. "I was just having lunch with Marshall . . . station stuff. What about you?"

"Yeah . . ." Trin sighed, when he heard the smooth fabrication. He felt the slightest pressure behind his eyes then. "Um,

I just came to grab somethin' quick," he lied, ignoring the weakness in his legs.

Dom's smile was brief, and it was obvious that she was eager to leave the restaurant. "I guess I'll see you tonight, then?"

"Tonight?" Trin parroted.

"The dinner party," Dom clarified, smoothing her hands over the sleeves of her burgundy cashmere dress. "Trin, I know you didn't forget that your mother's throwing that big get-together for Aaron and Bel—"

"Oh, yeah. Yeah, I'll be there."

"Alright," she sighed, rubbing her hand along the front of his beige pin-striped suitcoat.

Trin lost his composure when Dominique sauntered from the restaurant. He felt faint and very afraid.

Martika Salem's dinner party was an overwhelming success. Everyone in attendance was elated over Belinda's return to the family. That was especially true for her parents. Samuel and Lillian Cule expressed happiness and remorse over their terrible treatment of their only daughter and her husband. In a move that surprised everyone, Aaron's parents also attended the dinner. Santino and Carmen Tirelli were filled with the same sorrow and eagerly welcomed their son and daughter-in-law into their lives. It was a beautiful, unforgettable evening.

Trin was as happy as anyone for Aaron and Belinda, but he couldn't wait for the evening to end. It was killing him to see Dominique and know she was seeing another man. He had expected her to end their marriage, but being faced with the reality of it actually happening . . . After a while he retreated to the sanctuary of the den.

He let memories of the previous evening fill his mind. Obviously their time together had only meant sex to Dominique while he took it as a sign that she was coming back to him.

"Trin? Trindy? You in here?" Dominique called, uttering a soft curse when her search for Trin hit another dead end. She was about to close the den door, when she saw him reclining on the sofa. "Baby? You sleep?" she whispered.

"No," Trin replied after a few moments.

Dom shut the door softly and walked farther into the room. "Sorry to bother you, but I wanted to talk to you about having lunch together sometime this week. I know how busy you are and I wanted to catch you before you went off to work tomorrow."

"Lunch?" Trin inquired, when a pause occurred in Dom's rambling.

"Yeah," she sighed, smoothing the chic, form-fitting cream gown beneath her as she perched on the arm of the sofa. "There's something important we need to discuss. I thought it might be more pleasant for you if we met over lunch."

"More pleasant for me?" he inquired, folding his arms over the front of his light gray suit.

Dom fiddled with the gold chain belt around her waist. "Mmm-hmm, it's pretty serious."

Trin closed his eyes and leaned his head back against the sofa. "Anytime this week is fine," he told her. He could barely hear his own voice over his heart pounding in his ears.

"Okay. Well the cookout is on Tuesday so I guess we can do it on Wednesday. About one o'clock at Corners?" she suggested, referring to the restaurant close to their neighborhood.

"Fine," Trin said, trying not to flinch when she kissed his forehead. He knew she was about to end their marriage.

Seventeen

Dom went to bed early that evening, hoping to recuperate from such an exhausting week. Belinda and Aaron were dividing their time between all the relatives who wanted a chance to spoil them and welcome them back into the family. Dominique relished the solitude and hoped sleep would visit her quickly. It didn't take long for her light slumber to grow deeper. But in the middle of the night she grew restless, and the slightest noise disturbed her. Then came a soft but distinct sound from outside the bedroom door.

Frowning, Dominique sat up in bed and leaned against the fluffy pillows crowding the headboard. Yes, someone was definitely in the house. She took a few moments to convince herself to go downstairs, then gingerly eased from the bed. It was so quiet when she stepped out of the room that at first she thought she'd been imagining things. But then the sound returned, a little louder this time. She urged herself to continue down the curving staircase. Dom heard another sound followed by what sounded like a low curse.

"Dammit, girl, this is your house," she muttered, holding down her fear as she headed in the direction of the study.

The door was slightly ajar, and to her horror, Dom discovered there was a man there. A tall, well-built man from the looks of him. A twinge of regret flowed through her then and she shook her head. She had left her gun in the desk drawer that he was standing right next to. Then another terrible thought crossed her mind. What if the man had been sent by

Morton and Farber? Perhaps he had come to obtain whatever information she had gathered regarding their shady
dealings. If they had resorted to blackmail, they might very
well resort to actions more fatal. The possibility gave Dom a
surprising flash of courage. She grabbed an iron poker from
its holder in front of the brick fireplace.

Trin had come to the house to get a few things he needed.
It hadn't occurred to him that Dom would hear him milling
around. He heard the soft clatter when Dom grabbed the
poker and turned just in time to see her aim the weapon.

Surprised by the sudden movement, Dominique swung the
instrument wildly. Trin's quick reflexes saved him and he was
able to grab hold to the end of the iron poker. Dom had closed
her eyes. When Trin grabbed the collar of her T-shirt and
forced her arms to her sides, she began to struggle.

"Domino, Domino, it's me. It's Trin," he whispered against
her ear, holding her back next to his chest.

Still terrified, Dominique trembled and took long shuddery
breaths. "Trin?" she gasped, her struggles beginning to subside.

He kissed her neck. "Yeah, baby. Shh . . . it's alright," he
soothed, his raspy voice adding more assurance to the words.

Dom closed her eyes for a moment, enjoying the sound of
the words as a feeling of security washed over her. After a
moment or two, a fierce frown clouded her lovely face.

"You jackass," she whispered, turning in Trin's arms to slap
him. "What the hell are you doing here, dammit? I could've
killed you!"

Trin reached out in a defensive manner. "Baby, I'm sorry,"
he said, rubbing his cheek.

Dom wasn't moved. "You're damned right you're sorry. You
jerk!" she cried, pushing against him and beating his chest with
her clenched fists. "You scared the mess out of me. If you had
never moved out, you wouldn't have to sneak in here!"

Trin blinked, surprised by the comment. "Domino, I'm
really sorry. I only came to get some papers I needed."

She waved her hand to signal that it was forgotten. The look on her face, however, made it clear that she was still quite upset.

"But you're right," he continued, "I should've never moved out."

Dominique smiled then and gave him a guilty look. "Sorry. Sorry I hit you."

"Don't worry about it," he said, knowing she had reason to do that and a whole lot more.

Dom rubbed her hands across the Knicks T-shirt she had worn to bed and felt a shiver course through her from the look in Trin's dark eyes.

"Did you find what you needed?" she finally asked, glancing toward a folder lying on the desk.

He nodded and glanced behind him. "Yeah, just some work from the office."

"The job treating you alright?" she asked, concerned by the tone of his voice when he mentioned work.

Trin shrugged. "Yeah, too good sometimes. They're makin' it hard for me to leave."

Dom leaned against the fireplace mantel. "Why would you want to leave?" she probed.

"Well . . . you never make any *real* money until you're in business for yourself. At least that's what they say."

Surprised by his attitude, Dom decided it was the perfect time to tell him about her latest story assignment. "Um . . . Trin?" she said, growing even more uneasy when he raised his brows and watched her expectantly. "Baby, sit down, there's something I need to tell you."

"What?" he countered, the questioning look on his face slowing turning into a frown.

"Will you sit down? This is important and I better tell you now while I have the nerve."

Trin's long lashes closed over his eyes and he leaned back against the desk. "Does this have something to do with us?"

Dom took a few steps toward him. "Yeah, I'm afraid it does."

"Jesus . . ." Trin whispered, feeling his entire body weaken.

"Are you okay?" Dom asked, closing the distance between them. "Baby?"

"Just say it, Dominique," Trin ordered, bracing himself.

Dom smoothed her hands across his cheeks, before running them across his dark hair. "Honey, if you're not up to talking—"

"Dominique, please, alright? Just say what you have to say. Whatever decisions you've made regarding our marriage, just tell me."

"Our marriage?"

Trin watched her closely. "Yes."

Dom hesitated for a moment. "Well . . . I—I guess you're right. Morton and Farber did do a number on our marriage."

Trin blinked and sent his wife a blank stare. "Morton and Farber?"

"This is about your company."

Suspicious now, Trin folded his arms over the heavy brown crew sweater he wore. "What about it?" he asked.

Dom pressed her lips together, then looked him directly in the eye. "The station's doing another story on Morton and Farber. Marshall asked me to cover it."

Trin shrugged, his onyx gaze still expectant. "Well, that's good, isn't it?"

"Hmph. You might not think so."

Trin leaned forward and cupped the side of her cheek. "Will you please just get to the point?"

"There are allegations of blackmail surrounding Morton and Farber."

"What?"

"Marshall's been gathering information for months now and I've obtained even more. The story seems firm."

"Domino, stop it," Trin warned.

She raised her hand. "Baby, it's true, I swear. They do extensive background checks on their employees, their employees's family and friends. Then they use it to control them if the need arises."

"This is crazy. Besides, they don't have a thing on me, so why should I believe it?"

"Maybe they don't have anything on you, but your wife is a reporter. Smart thing to do is get rid of me before I start nosing around."

Trin moved off the desk and ran his fingers through his hair. "Baby, please . . . Damn, where the hell do y'all come up with his crap?"

"Trin, I know it sounds crazy—"

"You're damn straight it sounds crazy."

Dom dropped her hands to her sides. "I guess I should've waited to tell you."

"It still would've sounded crazy."

"You know, the night we had that terrible fight, before I took that trip . . . I never did ask how you found out about me and Spry."

Trin did a doubletake and shrugged off the question. "Somebody in the family must've told me."

"Must've? You'd remember something like that. Besides, no one knew."

Trin's aggravation mounted when Dominique kept staring at him. "What?" He snapped.

"Did they come to you with this when they found out I was behind the Hal Lymon story?"

Trin leaned against the mantle and faced his wife. "What if they did?"

"Baby, don't you see?" Dom whispered, stepping closer with her hands outstretched. "Honey, it's like I've been saying. Why was my marriage to Spry something they had to dig up and tell you? What the hell did it have to do with you being CEO?"

Trin's expression changed, as though he were remembering the night of the meeting in Gordon Samuels' office. "Yeah . . . what the hell did it have to do with my being CEO?" he whispered, more to himself than Dom. He walked away from the mantel and began to pace the study.

"We were so tight, Trin," Dom recalled in her softest voice.

"I guess that was a threat because I am a reporter. Aside from what happened with Mr. Lymon, you could've slipped and told me something really confidential and I might've been off with it."

Trin leaned against the back of the sofa and covered his face with his hands. "Jesus," he breathed.

Dom knew it would take a lot for Trin to believe everything she had told him, considering how outlandish it seemed. They talked only a short while longer. Trin was very preoccupied by what he'd learned and wasn't much for conversation. Dom prayed she hadn't ruined any possible chance for reconciliation with her news. Before Trin left, he kissed her and promised to see her the next day.

Dominique was on the phone when Trin walked into her office the next day. He closed the door softly then leaned back against it and watched her. His dark gaze was soft as it appraised her svelte frame encased in a chic lavender coat dress. She was an unknowingly seductive vision sitting on top of the desk with her long legs dangling over the edge. Trin crossed his arms over his chest and enjoyed the view. After a while, though, his ear tuned in on her phone conversation. The call could have easily been business related, had it not been for the faint air of extreme familiarity he heard in her voice.

". . . So where are you now, Tim?" Dominique asked.

Tim had relocated to Washington, DC. Dom thought he'd made an interesting choice and warned him to stay out of trouble.

Dom ended the call and began to massage the aching muscles in her neck. Soft rapping against her office door intruded on the relaxing moment.

"Trin!" she gasped, sounding like a schoolgirl when she saw him leaning against the door. She scooted off her desk and hurried across the room with her hands outstretched. "Why didn't you tell me you were coming over?" she asked, pulling him into a sweet hug.

Trin tried to mask his uneasiness, and buried his face in the fragrant dark cloud of her hair. Dom tried to move away, but he held her fast.

"Baby, are you okay?" she whispered, when his arms tightened about her waist.

Trin cleared his throat and released her. "Sorry," he whispered.

"No, no, don't be," she whispered back, her lovely bright eyes filling with concern. "What is it?" She asked, laying her palm against his cheek. "You look like you've been up all night."

Trin managed a smile in spite of his emotions. "Well, you did give me a lot to think about when I left the house last night."

Dom closed her eyes, remembering. "I wished I could've . . . broken it to you a little better than that."

"I don't think there is a *better* way to tell someone they work for a group of crooks," he remarked with a cynical smirk.

Dominique's fingers toyed with his earlobe in an absent manner. Her eyes caressed his handsome face in the most flattering way. When his dark eyes grew just as intense, she looked away.

"So, um, what are you gonna do now?" she asked.

"Well, I already decided to resign."

"Resign?" Dom parroted, looking back up at him. "Have you really thought about this?"

"Extensively." Trin assured her, walking farther into the office.

Dom brought her hands to her forehead. "Trin," she groaned. "I've only been in this business seven years, but in that time, I've done some stories I haven't been too proud of. This is the first time I've actually felt guilty about one."

Trin turned away from the brass shelf that housed his wife's numerous broadcasting and journalism awards. "Guilty? What do you have to feel guilty about?" he asked, not quite believing what he was hearing.

Dom was sitting in one of the chairs that faced her desk. Her elbows were braced on her knees and her chin rested in one palm. "You were already making moves at Morton and Farber when we met, but I know how difficult it must've been to obtain a position like CEO. I mean, a black man your age becoming the chief executive officer of a company whose foundation is based on good ol' boy principles . . . that's quite an achievement."

"So . . . it sounds like I should feel guilty about quitting," Trin teased, kneeling before her.

Dominique shook her head. "You wouldn't be leaving if it weren't for that damn story. I've caused you to give up something you've worked very hard for, Trindy."

"Shh . . ." he urged, brushing his thumb against her cheek. "You didn't cause me to give up anything. Do you really think I'd want to be tied to a place like that?"

"It's just that—"

"Domino, hush," he ordered, tugging one of her curls as he spoke. "Your story had nothing to do with my resigning."

"I appreciate you saying that," Dom whispered, her eyes glimmering with unshed tears.

Trin chuckled. "Baby, I hope you believe that. Because it's true. If that story did anything, it reassured me that I made the right decision to quit in the first place."

A tiny furrow formed between Dom's arched brows. "I don't understand. Have you spoken with someone at the company?"

"Nope."

"Well, Trin, it sounds like you're saying you'd decided to leave a long time ago."

"That's exactly what I'm trying to tell you," Trin replied, his gorgeous dimples flashing when he grinned at her reaction. "Someone made me an offer and I've been mulling it over for almost a year."

"A year?"

"Mmm hmm . . ." He tugged on the stylish wine-colored tie he sported. "They approached me shortly after I thought . . . I'd lost you."

"Oh," Dom replied, her voice little more than a whisper.

"Domino?" said Trin after they'd sat in silence almost a full minute. He ached to ask her about the man he had seen her with, but forced the question aside. "It's really a good job," he said instead.

"Well I hope so." Dom sighed, leaning back in the chair. "After all, you're giving up a job many people only dream about. So, um, can you tell me about it?"

Trin stood and leaned against Dominique's desk. "Well, a few colleagues approached me with an idea they had to begin a new investment firm. They each have a strong client base from their previous positions. Two of the guys are already in business for themselves, but feel a more lucrative opportunity would lie in a merger. To get in on the ground floor of something like that . . ."

"Sounds exciting," Dom admitted. "And what have you got to lose?"

"Hmph. A company that blackmails its employees."

"Yeah . . ." Dom replied, staring unseeingly across the room.

After a moment, Trin frowned and waved his hand before her face. "You with me, girl?"

Instead of answering, Dom moved to the edge of her seat and pulled Trin's hand into hers. "Have you told anyone about your resignation or this new venture?"

Trin's dark eyes narrowed. "Besides you and my soon-to-be partners, no," he answered, with a slow shake of his head.

Dom focused on his hand clasped between both of hers. "Would you be willing to? To talk about it? On camera? You *and* your partners?"

Trin shrugged, finally understanding what she was getting at. "I'd have to discuss it with them first."

Dom took a deep breath and stood. "Trin, you know I've never asked you to reveal things to me for any story, but—"

"You want an exclusive?" he finished, smiling when she pressed her lips together and nodded. He cupped her chin and brushed his thumb across the soft skin there. "You tryin' to get special treatment here?" he teased.

"Special treatment? *Me?* No . . . just trying to look out for my co-workers. I'm strictly background help on this."

"Mmm hmm."

Dom's expression grew solemn. "To get these guys for everything they've done? Everything they've done to us? Yes," she admitted, her gaze unwavering. "I know it's unprofessional, but this is personal for me."

Trin nodded and leaned down to place a kiss at the corner of her mouth.

"Do you have a few more minutes?" she asked, her fingers curling around the lapels of his dark, pin-striped suit coat.

Trin pressed another kiss to her mouth. "I have as long as you need."

Dom smoothed her hands across his chest. "Good. I have something I want to run past you and Marshall."

"Marshall?" Trin repeated. He had hoped his wife had something more private in mind.

Dominique was already pulling him out of the office. "We'll have to have your partners' cooperation, too, for this to work. But, I think we can do it." She rambled on until they arrived at Marshall's office door.

"You got a minute?" she called, watching Marshall stand behind his desk.

"Yeah, what's goin' on? Hey, Trin," Marshall said, rounding the desk to shake hands.

Dom sighed, rubbing her hands together as she watched Marshall and Trin. "Trin's resigning from Morton and Farber," she announced, smiling when Marshall gasped.

"Well, does it have—"

"It has nothing to do with the story. He made the decision well before," Dom informed her news manager. "He has a new business opportunity he wants to take advantage of. The offer was made almost a year ago. What I want to do is get Trin and his partners on camera to talk about this new venture. Trin can announce his resignation. That way, when everything is revealed about Morton and Farber, he'll be gone and—"

"None of the fallout would touch him," Marshall finished. "You think we could pull it off?"

"It's worth a try. Besides, we've got quite a bit of time before the story airs. Sure, there are gonna be questions—whether he knew what was going on and such—but that's to be expected and I think he'll still come out on top."

Marshall was nodding and his small dark eyes were sparkling with excitement. "I like it," he said, just as his phone buzzed. "Don't move!" he ordered, rushing over to take the call.

Trin reached for Dominique's hand and toyed with her fingers. "I can't believe you're doing this for me."

"Why?" she whispered, with a quick shake of her head. "I don't want this mess overshadowing you. I think we've been hurt enough by those people, don't you?"

"Amen," Trin sighed, feeling as though he could drown in her scintillating stare. He cleared his throat and dragged his dark eyes away from her face. "You know, um, I'm not too hot about being on TV."

Dominique chuckled and brought her hand to his cheek. "Only someone so gorgeous would be squeemish about being on television," she teased, loving the boyish embarrassment she saw on his face. "Listen, don't worry about it. I'll be right there to coach you. I'll review all my questions with you and your partners so there won't be any surprises."

Trin pulled her hand away from his face and pressed a kiss to the back of it.

Marshall ended his call and clapped his hands. "Alright now, you two, where were we?"

Trin was behind the bar pouring himself a cognac, when he heard the knock against the door. "Come in!" he called, watching the company President, C.O.O. and C.F.O. enter his office with guarded expressions. "Thanks, Mary. Goodnight," he told his assistant. He headed to his desk while she closed the door.

Drink in hand, Trin snatched a sheet of paper from the desk and handed it to Jarvis Hamrick. He enjoyed the strong drink and waited. When he heard Jarvis utter a low curse, a smile came to his face.

"What the hell is this?" Jarvis whispered, shoving the sheet at Gordon and Henry. "What's the meaning of this, Trinidad?"

"I have a better question," Trin replied, pinning the man with a bitter glare. "What was the meaning of that scene in your office more than a year ago?"

Jarvis was stumped. "What scene? I don't have time for riddles, young man."

"Then I'll spell it out for you. What were you trying to accomplish by informing me of my wife's previous marriage to my cousin?"

The confusion cleared from Jarvis's face and he appeared to be rooted to his spot. Gordon and Henry stood with shocked expressions. The only sound in the room was the faint hum of the central heating.

Trin appeared calm, though he was growing more enraged as he remembered. "Why'd you do it? Was she too much of a threat, being a reporter? Was I suppose to divorce her? Get her out of my life?"

"Trin—"

"What?" he thundered, reaching across the bar to slosh more cognac into the beaded glass. "That's it, isn't it? You came to me with this shit right after you discovered that story on Hal Lymon. Obviously, my wife's career was unsettling someone high up in this son of a bitch."

Henry Thornton swallowed past the lump lodged in his throat. "Trinidad, if you just calm down and listen—"

"Sorry Henry, but there isn't much of an explanation for this. It's pretty cut and dried," Trin said, tossing back the drink.

"Trinidad, are you telling us that marriage is something

you would've preferred never knowing about?" Gordon Samuels probed.

"Oh, yeah," Trin answered without hesitation.

"Well, we felt differently," Jarvis retorted.

"And who the hell are you to make a decision like that?" Trin snapped, grimacing when the man flinched. "If anyone had to tell me this, it should've been my wife."

"But she didn't."

"And you took a huge gamble that I didn't know. Tell me, what else did you have in that bag of tricks? Surely there must've been another big secret to be revealed if your first one didn't do the job."

Henry raised his hands. "That was it. We swear."

"Bastards," Trin muttered. "I suppose when I didn't quit and storm out of here, you figured that was it, huh?" he inquired, watching the three men with loathing in his eyes. "Did you really think I'd keep working for you after that?"

"We hoped you would. We still do."

"Give it up, Henry," Trin ordered, running one hand over the back of his silky hair. "Thanks to this shit, I made a pure mess of my marriage. I want my wife back and it's obvious she can't be in my life if Morton and Farber is, so this is most definitely goodbye."

The room fell silent for several minutes. Then Henry whispered a fierce curse.

"You two bastards have caused us to lose a great asset to this company and you know it," he told Jarvis and Gordon. "I've stood by and watched you and the boys upstairs pull this crap for years. Now you've really done it. Do you know what a negative spotlight this is gonna put on us?"

"Hmph. Henry, believe me, my resignation is the least of your problems," Trin muttered, waving his hand toward the stone-faced threesome. "I've got nothing else to say to you all. Goodnight."

Gordon and Henry seemed to accept the defeat, but Jarvis wasn't about to leave so quietly. He shook off their warnings to let it go and went to stand before Trin.

"You conceited, arrogant bastard," he drawled. "Do you know how many men would kill to be where you are? Good men who've paid their dues just like you? Men who would understand how volatile it could be having a reporter for a wife in a delicate business like this?"

Trin gnawed the inside of his jaw. "Leave my wife out of of this." His voice grated as he sent Jarvis a scathing glare.

"Your wife is dangerous. You are so young and naive, you don't realize that rules are often broken in a business like this! The last thing we need is a nosy little bitch snooping around our company. Hell, forget snooping. All she has to do is screw the CEO and she has her exclusive!"

Trin hurled the beaded glass toward the fireplace and it shattered just as he wrenched Jarvis into an iron hold. Trin grasped the collar of Jarvis's shirt so tightly, the man gasped for air.

"You have no idea what I put her through. I took someone so remarkable, so incredible, and I treated her like garbage," he growled, bringing his face close to Jarvis's. "I treated her like she was nothing. All because of some old news you jack-asses saw fit to dig up and throw in my face. And I let you. I let it happen. I could've killed her over this bullshit, when it was you who deserved it all along."

Henry and Gordon finally swallowed their fear and rushed over to help Jarvis. The man was on his knees, grasping and beating against Trin's hands. The expression on Trin's face had twisted into something sinister and vengeful. Through Gordon and Henry's combined efforts, they managed to talk Trin down. They were afraid to breathe sighs of relief when he let Jarvis slide to the floor.

The haughty, stern, well-known businessman was a shaking mass as his colleagues helped him out the door. Trin closed his eyes and regained his composure. Afterward, he helped himself to one last drink, before grabbing his briefcase and strolling out of the office.

* * *

Dominique waved and removed her coat as she hurried across the diningroom. When she reached the table where Trin waited, she cupped his handsome face and kissed his mouth. Trin uttered a tiny moan the instant her lips touched his. His hands spanned her waist and he savored the lingering kiss.

"I was surprised to get this invitation," Dom noted when she stepped back.

"Surprised?" Trin parroted. "I thought you told me you wanted to get together for lunch."

Dom only shrugged and rubbed her hands across the front of the short-sleeved black crew top that outlined the muscular expanse of his chest. "I don't care whose idea it was as long as I can eat," she decided, turning to the table.

"Here," Trin whispered, taking Dom's red cashmere coat and tossing it on a nearby chair where his leather jacket lay.

"So, what's going on?" Dom asked, selecting a menu.

"Excuse me?" Trin countered, watching her strangely.

Dom smiled at the waitress and placed her order. "Have you spoken with your partners yet?" she asked once they were alone.

Trin shrugged. "They were already talking about going public when I asked them about talking to the press. Seems they were waiting for me to come on board before making the announcement."

"Hmph. Well, this is going smoother than I thought it would."

"I turned in my resignation."

Dom looked up and leaned across the table. "How'd it go?"

Trin tapped his half-empty glass against the table. "Started civil, ended savagely."

Dom winced. "What happened?"

"Let's just say they pushed my buttons and my temper got the better of me."

"Ouch. Did the paramedics have to be called?" she asked, her lovely eyes roaming the powerful line of his biceps and muscular forearms.

Trin smiled. "It didn't get quite that bad."

"Thank goodness."

Silence settled between them again. Trin waited, hoping Dom would get to the main reason for the lunch. He judged from her relaxed demeanor that she was in no rush to get to the point. He couldn't help but feel a bit anxious as his worries got the better of him. Finally, he resigned himself to the fact that she probably wanted him in a calm mood when she told them their marriage was over.

"Trin, I'm so sorry things turned out so badly."

He waved his hand. "I'm glad it worked out the way it did. I finally took my anger out on the people who really deserved it."

Dom rubbed her hands across the soft, extra-long sleeves of her red cotton top. "Um, did they admit to anything?" she softly inquired.

Trin crunched an ice cube between his teeth. "Oh, yeah."

The meal arrived before anything more could be said. Dom's focus was quickly diverted to the delicious food. Trin smoothed one hand across the silky material of his top and studied her closely. He listened as she raved over the tenderness and perfect seasoning of her grilled chicken breasts.

Several minutes passed before Dominique looked up from her plate and noticed that Trin wasn't eating. "What's the matter?" she asked, taking in his stony expression.

Trin ran his hand across his dark hair and took a deep breath, hoping to keep his voice from shaking. "I'm waiting for you to tell me what you wanted to discuss."

"What I wanted to discuss?" Dom parroted, watching him send her a cool smile. She set down her fork and regarded him with a confused look. "I thought we already covered what I wanted to discuss."

Trin closed his eyes. "Already covered it, Domino?"

Dom stretched her hands out across the table. "The story?" She reminded him. "You know everything, so . . ."

"So, what?"

"Trin, what in the world are you so uptight about?" she snapped, tiring of his mood.

Trin massaged the sudden tension in his neck. "We were supposed to be discussing the marriage," he explained, his tone and expression weary.

"Our marriage?"

"Maybe I should say, our divorce."

"Dammit, Trin," Dom whispered, smoothing her hands across her black pants, "what is it with you and that word? Is that what you want?"

"Are you crazy?" he whispered, leaning across the table to pin her with an angry glare. "Hell no, Domino. Hell no I don't want that!"

Dominique's hazel eyes were sparkling with tears of frustration. "You don't want it? Then why do you keep bringing it up? If I wanted a divorce, don't you think I would have asked for one by now?"

"I don't know, baby. I guess that would depend on how long you've been seeing your friend."

Dom shook her head, sending a slew of heavy curls into her face. "Could you explain that?" she requested.

"I saw you with him, Domino," he said, rubbing his temple where a dull ache had formed. "That day I just happened to bump into you at Jabrill's Restaurant? I know you weren't meeting with Marshall."

"Jabrill's?" Dom repeated, thinking back to the day in question. When she realized what Trin was referring to, an uproarious fit of laughter ensued. Several people glanced around.

"Are you ready to be serious now?" Trin asked, his palm propped against the side of his face as he glared across the table.

Dominique finally pulled her forehead from the table and pinned her husband with an amused gaze. "I'm sorry, Trindy. Baby, um, hmph . . ."

Trin's expression was somber. "I'm listening."

Dom moved closer to him. She perched on the edge of the chair that held their coats. "Honey, the man you saw me with that day, his name is Tim Womack. He worked in the human resources department of Morton and Farber. Employee research was his speciality. Tim was Marshall's contact at the firm. He's how we discovered what they were up to."

Trin's midnight gaze searched Dom's face for a full minute. Then he bowed his head. "Dammit . . . Domino—"

"It's okay," she assured him, rubbing her fingers through his dark curls. "I should've told you this when I was going into all that stuff about the story. I have to admit, though, that your reaction to the possibility of my seeing another man has me a bit suprised."

"What do you mean?" Trin asked, his gaze holding a trace of unease.

"You didn't explode. You kept quiet about it all this time. You seemed so reserved, calm . . . not what I'm used to."

Trin shrugged. "I'm making a serious effort to learn how to deal with my temper."

"I know," Dom said, then quickly shook her head, not wanting him to suspect she knew about his therapy. "I'm sorry you were worried." She stroked the side of his face.

"Salem!"

Trin and Dom turned to see Sam Rutger bounding toward them. Trin pressed a quick kiss to Dominique's hand, then stood to greet his partner.

"Sam Rutger, this is my wife, Dominique Salem," he announced, grinning at the awestruck expression on the man's dark, angular face.

Sam pulled Dom's hand into a warm grasp. "I've heard people comment on how lovely you are. But words don't hold a candle to seeing how beautiful you really are."

Dom smiled, feeling the blood rushing to her cheeks. "Thank you," she managed.

"My partners and I can't wait to work with you."

"Oh yes," Dom replied, her thoughts instantly back on the story. "Yes, I'll be in touch with each of you to set up the best time for a meeting and the actual taping."

"I think I speak for everyone when I say we can't wait."

"Neither can I," Dom said, trying not to laugh at the silly

expression her husband made behind Sam's back. "I'll see *you* later," she told Trin, smiling as he passed her coat and purse across the table.

Eighteen

"Poppy?! They didn't have the brand of charcoal you wanted, so I had to make a substitution!" Dom called, walking into the huge kitchen through the back door of Hamp and Phyllis Carver's lovely Jamaica, Queens home.

Food was bubbling and simmering on the stove, but her parents were nowhere in sight. "Poppy? Mommy?" Dom called.

"They're in the den."

She jumped, hearing Trin's raspy voice behind her. "Oh," she managed, slapping her hands along her denim-clad thighs.

A sexy, devilish smile crossed Trin's mouth and he leaned against the doorjamb. His onyx stare took a leisurely trip across the buckles of her black sandals. He enjoyed the way her bellbottomed jeans formed to her fantastic body and how her full breasts pressed enticingly against the snug black T-shirt she wore. "One of Mr. C's brothers is trying to get here and he needed some directions."

"Mmm . . . must be Uncle Henry. He's always forgetting the way."

Trin didn't respond and silence descended over the kitchen. Dom couldn't tear her eyes away from him, thinking how sexy he looked in the black jeans and gray T-shirt he sported. Finally, she managed to turn her concentration to taking the groceries from the plastic bags that crowded the oval mahogany table.

"I guess you're the first one here, huh?" Dom asked, a hint of nervousness tingeing her low voice.

Trin took a step closer. "Yeah, I wanted to talk to you before everyone else got here."

Dom's hand faltered over one of the bags. "'Bout what?"

Trin cleared his throat and walked up behind her. "I talked to Henry Thornton last night."

"The company president, right?"

Trin nodded. "Mmm hmm. I'm worried about him."

"You're . . . worried about him?"

"I know it sounds crazy—"

"No, I know you two were friendly."

"It's not that. I just don't know how he's gonna handle it when this stuff comes out."

Dom leaned against the kitchen table. "You having second thoughts?"

"Hell no." Trin retorted, with a wave of his hand. "I don't know. It was just something in his voice."

"Honey, I'm sure Henry Thorton's been through work-related upsets before. Don't you think you might be reading too much into this?"

Trin rested his hand on the table beside Dom's hip. "We didn't get a chance to talk that night I resigned. Last night I had a chance to find out where he stood in all this."

"And?"

A rueful smirk tugged at Trin's mouth. "There wasn't much he stood for anymore. He said that although he didn't approve of what was going on, he didn't have the nerve to do anything to stop it."

Dom's smile was sympathetic and she reached up to pat his cheek. "I'm sorry," she whispered.

Trin shrugged. "It's not your fault."

"Did you tell him about the story?"

"Yeah, but I didn't tell him it's you who's breaking the story."

"How'd he take it?"

Again, Trin shrugged. "Shocked at first, then he started crying about how he was ruined."

"Baby, I'm so sorry. I know how much you liked him."

"Well, in business you make and lose friends. I hope this thing with Sam Rutgers is successful. But I still hope to start something of my own one day."

Dom frowned. "Your own? Business?"

Trin smiled serenely and nodded. Dom rolled her eyes.

"Oh goodness, you in total control? Heaven help us!"

"Only in business, Domino. Only in business," he assured her, his expression serious.

Dominique thought she'd melt as his words touched her ears. "Trin . . ."

He stepped closer and pulled her toward him. "I just want to know where things stand with us."

Before she could answer, Hamp and Phyllis Carver walked into the kitchen. A crowd of people followed them. The party had begun.

"Why was Aaron frowning when he got here?"

Belinda Tirelli rolled her eyes away from Dom and looked toward her husband. "Girl, he wants to drive from New York all the way back to Chicago," she explained.

Dom glanced across the yard toward Aaron, who was lounging back having a drink with Trin. "Is he suddenly afraid to fly or something?"

"Nooo, he started talkin' about how we rarely have any time off, so we should make the most of it."

"And what'd you say?"

Belinda propped one hand on her hip. "Honey, I said I'd much rather spend that extra time kicked back at home before returning to the office, than cooped up in a car with him trying to figure out a road map."

Dom burst into laughter. "You two are crazy!" she cried.

Belinda appeared skeptical. "Hmph, Aaron's the one," she said, before laughter affected her as well.

"Damn, look at these two fine sistahs over here talkin' about me."

Belinda and Dom turned and saw Spry Cule approaching them.

"Spry!" Dom called, happy he had accepted her invitation to attend her parents' barbeque.

"What's up, girl?" Spry greeted, pulling Dom close and kissing her cheek. He let her go and pulled his cousin in for the same treatment.

"Mmm hmm," said Belinda, enjoying the soft kiss. "And why would you think we were talkin' about you, boy?"

Spry pretended to be confused. "Well, y'all were smilin', right? Women only smile like that when they talk about *me.*"

Dom tapped Spry's shoulder. "Uh, we were laughing Spry."

"Mmm hmm," Belinda confirmed, "and there's a *big* difference. Hey, maybe we were talking about you after all."

Spry rolled his eyes. "Funny," he said, watching Belinda and Dom break into another fit of laughter.

Aaron Tirelli's brown gaze slid from the laughing trio, across the yard to Trin. Aaron watched his friend tap a beer bottle on the wooden arm of the chair he occupied. "Easy, man." Aaron cautioned.

"What?" Trin replied, his dark eyes never straying from Dom and Spry.

"I can see you're about ready to go off," Aaron noted, taking a swig of his beer.

Trin kept his slanting stare focused ahead for a moment longer. Then he chuckled. "Nah . . . I'm just debating."

"Debating what?" Aaron asked, watching Trin shrug.

"Whether or not to start trying to make peace with Spry. I mean, I know Domino is mine. I know she loves me and we're gonna work this out."

"But?"

"But . . . nothin'. Nothing, that's it," Trin answered, sounding as though he'd just made a profound realization. "I've got Domino and that's what I wanted. All that shit from the past is irrelevant."

A wide grin brightened Aaron's darkly handsome face. "Man, I think it's time for you to follow your own advice."

"Me too," Trin agreed, standing from his chair.

Dominique was laughing over something Spry said, but suddenly grew silent when she saw Trin headed toward them. "Oh no," she whispered.

Belinda heard her and followed the line of her gaze. She repeated Dom's words of woe.

Trin walked up and lightly placed his hand against Dom's tiny waist. He smiled slightly when he nodded toward Spry. "Can I talk to you, man?"

"Trin . . ." Dom said, resting her hand against his chest.

He smiled and pressed a lingering kiss against her ear. "Nothin' to worry about," he softly assured her. "Spry?" He called again.

"Lead the way," Spry urged, a solemn expression on his dark handsome face.

Dom watched the two men walk toward her parents' home. Then she turned to Aaron. "Go with them," she pleaded.

"No need," Aaron said, his smile quite reassuring.

"I guess you don't want any witnesses, huh?" Spry commented when Trin took them into Hamp Carver's study. The room was located on the other side of the house.

Trin smiled and closed the heavy mahogany door. "Same ol' Spry. Always got jokes."

Spry shrugged. "Not always."

"I heard about what you're doin' with the kids. I was impressed."

Spry bowed his head, acknowledging the compliment. "Thanks, but I know that's not why you brought me in here."

Trin ran his fingers along the sleek line of his eyebrow. "No, I wanna talk about Dominique."

"Trin, nothin's gone on there for a long time. That was way before she ever knew you."

"I know. That's why I want to apologize."

"Thanks man, but you should be sayin' this to Dominique," Spry suggested.

"I have and I will be for a long time," Trin assured his cousin. "But I've been pissed at you for a long time for things you had nothin' to do with."

Spry took a seat on one of the arm chairs, which flanked the fireplace. "I don't get it."

"Man, ever since I've known you, you've had jokes. No matter what type of horrible, messed up crap was goin' on, you had jokes. I guess I was jealous."

Spry let out a short, loud burst of laughter. "Hell, man, that was all I had. You were the one with the best toys, phat clothes, a car when we were in high school. Hell, kid, you had it all. I should've been the jealous one."

Trin shook his head, bracing himself against the huge desk. "Yeah, I had everything, but my father."

Spry grew serious. "Uncle Max died when we were little. You know you couldn't do anything about that."

"I could get mad as hell," Trin reminded him.

Spry smiled. "Amen. But man, Arthur is my brother and you never acted jealous of him."

Trin nodded. "I know, but Arthur was like the mediator. He could relate to you and me at the same time. You always wanted to clown and after a while, I didn't want to be bothered."

"So, how long are you gonna hate me for marrying Dom?"

"Forever," Trin admitted with a chuckle. "I tell ya, man, I could've killed you when I heard you and she were once married. I could've killed *her*."

"And now?"

Trin's deep sigh filled the room. "When I thought I lost her. When I thought she was dead. I prayed to God every night to just give me one more chance with her," he said, moving away from the desk and beginning to pace the room. "God answered my prayers and I messed up again. I guess it wasn't bad enough for her to brush me off for good, though. I'll do everything I have to to keep her with me, man."

"So, this talk was for her benefit?" Spry asked, leaning forward in his seat.

"A little, but I really thought it was time for us to get this mess cleared up. It's gone on for too long."

Spry stood and held his hand out toward Trin. "You're right," he said.

Trin took his cousin's hand and they shook vigorously. They talked for a long while, and though they didn't become best friends, a lot was solved.

Later, Trin found his wife back in the den with the phone in her hand. A light smile touched his face as he watched her as she lay curled up in an armchair.

"So, what did you think?" She was speaking into the receiver, unaware that she was being watched.

Marshall had just reviewed Dom's copy for the Morton and Farber story. He was very pleased with her work and ordered her to relax and take care of things with her husband.

When she finally set her cell phone aside and leaned her head back against the chair, she closed her eyes briefly, then opened them and looked directly at Trin. He glanced across his shoulder and pushed the door shut.

"Can we talk?" he asked.

"Mmm hmm," Dom replied with a nod.

"I talked to Spry."

"Yeah, um, what hospital is he in?"

Trin chuckled in spite of himself. "It wasn't even like that. It was good. We had a good conversation."

Dom toyed with one of her bouncy curls. "And now it's my turn, huh?"

"Our turn."

"Are you ready to really talk this time?" she asked.

"Hmph. I better be, because I want my wife back."

Dom shook her head. "You never lost me. I only wanted you to tell me what you were thinking. That's all I wanted from the very beginning."

Trin dropped to the sofa on the opposite side of the room. "You wanted me to talk about my jealousy . . . I wasn't ready. I couldn't look you in those pretty eyes and explain why I asked for a divorce. Like there would be any explantion good enough."

"Can you tell me why now?" Dom asked, a lone tear escaping the corner of her eye. "Did you hate me that much for marrying Spry? Or did you just hate me?"

"I never hated you, but when I found out you were married—*married*, Domino—to another man, that he could . . . have you anytime, the way I could—I just snapped."

Dominique wiped her eyes. "But it was so long ago. We were a couple of intoxicated college kids. You didn't have to feel threatened by that."

"Just knowing that he had you, that he'd been where I had been *before* me. Baby, that tore me apart."

"Trin, you knew I was no virgin when we met."

"Just knowing it was Spry," he whispered.

"Baby, Spry was never in my heart. Not really, not like you. You're the only one who's ever been there. That's what should've counted."

"Obviously, I wasn't thinking that way."

"And now?"

Trin left the sofa. "And now, I can admit what a jealous bastard and jackass I've been." He closed the distance between them and dropped to his knees before her. "I don't expect you to believe much of what I say, Domino. But just so you know, I am doing everything I can think of to help myself and understand why I hurt you like I did."

Dom cupped the side of his handsome face. "I know," she told him.

He shook his head. "No, you don't."

"I know about the therapy," she informed him, smiling when his intense dark eyes snapped to her face.

"Ma," he groaned, bowing his head.

Dom kept her hands against his face and made him look at

her. "She didn't mean to tell me, but she couldn't bear to see this tear us apart. Don't be upset with her."

Trin pressed a kiss to her palm. "I'm not, I just didn't want you to think I was using it to get on your good side."

"That's why I didn't say anything. And for your information, you were never on my bad side."

Trin stared at her for a moment before lowering his head to her lap. Dominique pulled her fingers through his soft, black curls and pressed a kiss to his head.

"I, um, I should apologize too," she whispered, taking a deep breath when he looked up at her. "I should've told you about Spry."

"Domino, you—"

"I should have. I'm not saying that I asked to be treated the way I was, but you're my husband. This is something you needed to know. A secret like that . . . we almost didn't survive it, Trin. You had a right to know, and I should have told you. Especially when I discovered Spry was your cousin."

Trin looked down and smoothed his hands across her thighs. "Domino, I want to work this out. But do you think we can just end all the apologies here and move on?"

Dom leaned forward and pressed a kiss to his forehead. "That sounds very good to me, but I don't think I can handle being away from you much longer."

Trin's pitch-black gaze narrowed, and he watched her closely. "You want me to move back in?" he whispered, thinking he had misunderstood her.

"I never wanted you to move out."

Trin's mouth fell open. "Why didn't you stop me, then?"

Dom shrugged. "You seemed so set on doing it. I didn't know how to tell you that I didn't want it."

"I'll be back tonight," he promised, pressing soft, moist kisses to her neck.

Dom started to wrap her arms around his neck, when he surprised her and pulled away. "What?" she asked.

Trin reached into his pocket and pulled out a small black velvet box. Dom gasped when he opened it and she saw her familiar, six-carat Baguette diamond wedding band. "Trinidad," she breathed. "I didn't know what had happened to it . . ."

"When you left that night . . . you left it behind," he said, pushing the dazzling ring onto her finger. "I hope you agree when I say it's time you start looking like my wife again, even if we are still trying to work this out."

Dom pressed a kiss to his cheek and hugged him tightly.

"I love you so much, Dominique," he whispered, hugging her back.

"I love you too, more than anything," she whispered back.

They remained locked in the embrace for countless moments. Finally, Dom pulled away, a wicked gleam brightening her extraordinary gaze.

"Baby, did you lock the door?" she asked.

Trin frowned a bit. "Yeah . . . why?"

Dominique pushed him back on the floor and rested on top of him. "Let's start working this out."

"So, are they all married?"

"All but one."

"Mmm mmm mmm. That's a gorgeous group. I don't think they'll have any problems drawing business."

"They're opening an investment firm, Janice, not a strip club."

Janice Redd waved off Dominique's remark, her dark almond-shaped eyes trained on the conference room door. "Well, I can't wait to start playin' the market."

Dominique rolled her eyes at the suggestive comment. "I gotta get back in there."

"Need some help?" Janice offered, ready to fall in step beside Dom.

"Nah, I gave them some time to go over my questions for the interview. They should be done by now," she said, already heading toward the double doors at the end of the corridor. After smoothing her hands across the long sleeves of the figure-flattering tan dress, she stepped inside the room.

"How do things look, gentlemen?" she called, whisking toward the huge oval table in the center of the room.

Each one of the devastating men at the table took the question literally.

"From where I sit things look quite lovely," Simon Frakes, one of the partners, remarked.

"Beautiful," Sam Rutgers added.

"Absolutely incredible," Jeremy Wallace, another colleague, agreed.

Trin interrupted. "Guys," he reminded them, "the woman's husband is in this room, you know?"

Dominique resisted laughing at the boisterous comments. She nodded once to acknowledge them before waving her hands toward the table. "I can only hope the questions for the interview look just as good."

"We're very pleased," Russell Avery, another of Trin's colleagues, told her.

Dom clasped her hands and pinned the group with a skeptical gaze. "You're sure? No questions you feel uncomfortable answering?"

"Not one," Jeremy Wallace further confirmed.

Dominique couldn't help glancing at Trin, who occupied the seat farthest from her. He had been virtually silent since the meeting began almost an hour earlier.

"Well, are there any questions you'd like me to address? Something I didn't put on the list?" she asked, watching the men shake their heads. "I am a professional, guys, you can tell me if you're displeased."

Sam Rutgers shrugged. "We have no problems with your work, Dominique."

Dom wasn't quite convinced that the group of top-notch, hard-nosed businessmen had no concerns. She sent her husband a helpless look. Trin chuckled, drawing his partners' attention.

"I think my wife is trying to tell you guys that you can feel free to criticize or question her without making me uncomfortable. Am I right?" he added, smiling more broadly when she nodded.

Simon Frakes gestured toward Trin. "You think we're afraid of this guy?" he teased.

"I'm sure this is rather awkward." Dom pointed out.

"Dominique, we assure you that we have no problems with anything so far," Jeremy reiterated.

"We'll definitely speak up if we do," Russell added.

"Alright, I'll drop it." Dom sighed, flipping to the next page on her legal pad. "The only thing we need to discuss now is the time for the interview."

"Our schedules are practically clear right now. Any time is good for us," Sam said.

"You all are by far the easiest group I've ever had to work with," Dom told Sam.

"We aim to please," he said.

"How about the day after tomorrow?" Dominique proposed, focusing on the appointment book next to her pad. "Noon?" she added, watching the group nod and notate the date on their electronic calendars and date books. "Trin?" she called, waiting for him to make the decision unanimous.

He lifted his hand from the table and shrugged. "No problem," he replied.

Dom made an effort to ignore Trin's smile. She prayed she could get through the rest of the meeting without him affecting her hormones any further.

"So, we're set for Thursday at noon," she reconfirmed, circling the date. "If there's nothing else we need to discuss, gentlemen, I have everything I need. But please feel free to call me with any questions you have."

"Does that go for me too?" Trin asked as his partners were walking out the door.

Dominique pushed a stray curl from her forehead and smiled up at him. "I'd prefer to see *you* in person," she whispered.

Trin's smoldering onyx stare narrowed with wicked intent. "I'll keep that in mind," he said, sending her a devilish wink and smile before he turned to leave.

Dominique moved to gather the loose papers from the table. When she turned, Trin was still there. He was leaning against the closed door, both hands inside the deep pockets of his navy blue pin-striped trousers.

"Was there something else, Mr. Salem?" she asked, taking note of the humorous smirk on his gorgeous face.

"There *was* one more thing," he admitted as he strolled toward her.

"Oh?" Dominique inquired, setting her papers aside and smoothing both hands across her hips. "Something I forgot to cover?"

Trin's big hands encircled her tiny waist. "Mmm hmm. Me," he said, pulling her against his chest.

Dominique could only respond with a tiny whimper as his mouth slanted over hers. His tongue traced the outline of her full, parted lips before thrusting inside. The deep kiss forced several soft moans from her throat. Trin massaged her back with soothing, langourous strokes before moving his hands to cup the sides of her breasts.

"Trin . . ." she gasped, feeling his breathtaking arousal grow more pronounced.

"Should we be expecting company?" he asked, his hand already moving beneath the hem of her dress.

Dom's lashes fluttered madly when she felt his fingers slip inside her panties. "I—we have the room for another hour. I thought the meeting would take longer," she explained, gasping when she felt him stroking her intimately.

"I guess that'll have to do," Trin decided, taking a seat in one of the chairs and pulling her down with him.

She straddled his lap and favored his strong jaw with the softest kisses. Trin buried his face into the fragrant valley between her breasts, but wanted more.

"Baby, wait," Dom cautioned, knowing he was seconds away from ripping the delicate buttons along the front of her dress. "I have to walk out of here, you know?"

Trin's hands massaged her thighs and he watched as she unbuttoned the bodice with maddening slowness. He uttered a ragged groan when the lacy white bra was revealed. His lips sought one breast, while his hand cupped the other.

Dom threw her head back and rubbed herself against his arousal. Trin treated her to an expert's kiss, suckling one firm nipple with shocking thoroughness. His thumb brushed across the other before slowly circling it in the same manner as his tongue favored its twin.

"Dammit, Trin," Dom whispered, as she unbuckled his belt and handled the zipper and trouser fastening. A moment later, she'd freed him from his boxers and stood to pull the dress over her head.

"Mmm . . ." Trin grunted, when she settled over him and began to move. He returned to her breasts and treated them to more kisses. He savored the seductive movements of her hips as she satisfied him . . .

"I think we should give a little party or something for you and your partners once the stories air," Dom mentioned later as she fixed her garters.

Trin zipped his pants and shrugged. "Sounds good to me. I'll tell Simon."

Dom frowned when she heard the name of one of his partners. "Tell Simon? Why?"

"Well, his wife loves doin' that kind of stuff."

"Is that her job or something?"

"Nah, she doesn't work, but she handles the parties whenever Simon throws something for business or whatever."

"But this is *my* idea," Dominique told him, clearly pouting. "I want to see it through."

Trin didn't realize how seriously she was taking the matter. "Baby, it's not a problem for her," he said as he jerked into his suitcoat. "Like I said, she's not working so it only makes sense for her or Jerry or Russell's wife to handle it. They're all housewives."

"What are you trying to say?" Dom snapped, folding her arms across her chest as she glared at him. "You think just because I have a job it means I can't arrange a party for my husband's business associates?"

"Whoa, baby. Hold on a minute," Trin whispered, his hands raised defensively. "I didn't mean to imply that. If you want to handle this, I'm fine with that. I love you."

Dom leaned against the oval table and watched the door close behind her husband. Her lovely dark face clouded with a pensive look.

Nineteen

"And will you be having dessert as well, ma'am? . . . Ma'am?"

Phyllis Carver exchanged a quick glance with the waitress before leaning forward. "Baby?" she called to her daughter, brushing her hand. "Dominique?"

"Huh?" Dom grunted. She looked up and noticed the questioning expression on her mother's face. "Sorry, what was that?"

"Um, may I get you any dessert, ma'am?" the young waitress asked, with an encouraging smile.

Dom dragged one hand through her curls. "Did you get something, Mommy?"

"Cheesecake."

"Mmm. I'll just have coffee. Thanks," Dom said, reaching for a packet of sugar.

"Honey, what's wrong? You're a million miles away."

Dom fiddled with the sugar packet a moment longer. "Mommy, how long did you work after you had me?"

"After I had you?" Phyllis parroted, taken aback by the question. A second later, her expressive walnut-brown gaze brightened. "Baby, what are you trying to tell me?"

Dom frowned at the excitement in her mother's soft voice, then realized the misunderstanding. "Mommy, no. It's not that," she said, watching her mother deflate a little.

"You mean, you're not pregnant?"

"I'm not," Dom confirmed, with a breathless laugh. "If you can hold out a little while longer . . . I'll see what I can do."

Phyllis raised her hand. "So what's all this talk about how long I worked?"

"I guess I should've asked how long you worked after marrying Daddy. How did your role as a wife affect your role as a working woman?"

"Honey, is something wrong? Are there more problems between you and Trin?"

"No, no, things are great. Trin is incredible and I'm on cloud nine."

"Then why are you talking this way?" Phyllis asked, toying with a glossy lock of her bobbed hair.

Dom grimaced and tossed the tiny sugar packet into her water glass. "I've been feeling guilty lately."

"Guilty? Why?"

"Mommy, Trin's done so much to set things right with our marriage and I feel I should be doing something too."

"Doing something like what? Quitting your job?"

"My career was the . . . catalyst for most of the things that went wrong," Dom clarified.

Phyllis leaned back in her chair. "Now I *know* Trin doesn't believe that."

Dominique tugged at the zipper tab on the snug orange top she sported. "He would say he doesn't, but deep down, we both know it's true," she said, her voice trembling a bit. "I love him for not saying it. Even when he was treating me so coldly, he never attacked my career."

Phyllis appeared confused. "Then, honey, why are *you* stressed over it?"

"Because I don't want to go through that again. I'm scared to death of going through that again."

"Dominique, I don't believe I'm hearing this. How long? How hard have you worked to get where you are? Aren't you the one always talking about how far you still have to go? How much more hard work you need to put in to get where you really want to be?"

"Yeah, Mommy, but I've worked hard to get my marriage back too."

Phyllis rolled her eyes. "Honey, if Trin isn't complaining, what sense does it make to create a problem?"

"But I don't think I'd be creating a problem," Dom said as the waitress set coffee before her. "I think he might even be happy about me quitting. All his partners' wives are at home for their men at all times. Completely accepted, respected, gracious—"

"Boring," Phyllis interjected. "Dominique, you're forgetting something. You're a very beautiful girl, but do you think that's what's kept Trin with you all this time? You have a high-profile and exciting career. People know you and respect your ethics and drive. A man sees that and is both intrigued *and* aroused."

Dom rubbed her hands over her long sleeves. "I hear what you're saying," she finally replied.

"But are you listening?" Phyllis challenged, shaking her head when Dom looked her way. "Just don't make any quick decisions before you talk to your husband."

The Morton and Farber exclusive had been promoted with surprising subtlety. WQTZ's top executives wanted to keep a lid on the inevitable shock the story would generate throughout the media and business worlds. Still, the brief previews for the event had already caused quite a stir.

Trin and Dom were relaxing in his study where they'd decided to view the broadcast. Trin was lounging in the cushiony swivel chair behind his desk while Dominique occupied the sofa across the room. Several times during the newscast, she glanced at him. The set expression on his face revealed nothing. Dom clutched a throw pillow to her chest and twisted one corner in an effort to soothe her raging nerves. Once the piece ended, Trin clicked off the television.

Dom loosened her grip on the pillow and set it aside. She

drew her knees to her chest and looked over at her husband. "Well?" she whispered.

Trin set the remote on the desk and tapped his fingers against the shellac surface. "Come over here," he softly ordered, after a few silent seconds.

Expelling a deep sigh, Dom inched off the sofa and made her way to the other side of the room. When she stood next to Trin's chair, he reached for her hand to pull her onto his lap.

"Incredible," he whispered against her ear as his teeth tugged on the lobe. "Very impressive," he added, his tongue soothing the sensitive area below her ear.

"Well, I did have help." Dom slowly reminded him, arching her neck closer to the enjoyable caress.

"Mmm . . . but your hard work breathed life into the thing," Trin pointed out.

"Trin?"

"Hmm?"

Dom eased her arms around his neck and faced him more fully. "Would you prefer it if my life—my work weren't so hectic?"

"What are you talkin' about?" Trin murmured. "You're sexy as hell when you're workin'. I never knew that until I had the chance to see you in action."

Vaguely, Dom recalled what her mother had said. Trin's words filled her with twin feelings of confidence and power. She didn't have long to dwell on that, though. Trin gripped her hips tightly and sat her on top of his desk. He tugged on her skimpy shorts and she wriggled out of them. Her top and bra followed. Afterward, Trin was covering her satiny, dark chocolate skin with hundreds of sultry kisses . . .

"Dominique, this is so lovely. Elegant but unpretentious, informal but chic."

"Thank you, Peaches. That means a lot coming from a master party-planner such as yourself," Dom replied, tilting her wineglass toward the vanilla-complexioned beauty.

"Well, thanks for inviting us," Marshall said as he popped a shrimp puff into his mouth.

Dom smoothed her free hand across the scooping bodice of her casual turquoise gown. "Well, I need at least a couple of people here that I know."

"Please, honey, you've charmed the pants off everybody in this room," Peaches remarked, glancing around at the smiling guests filling the living room.

"Well, I guess," Dom slowly agreed, tiny goosebumps lining her bare arms. "They do seem pleased, but I'll admit, planning this thing was incredibly tedious."

Peaches took a canapé from Marshall's plate. "Parties always are. Trust me, though, you did a great job. Pulling this off with everything else you had on your plate, very impressive."

"You're so good for my ego," Dom drawled, her striking gaze sparkling with excitement. "I'll probably be doing this a lot more now. I think I'll be able to do a much better job when I don't have such a hectic career," she added.

"What's goin' on, y'all?" Trin said in greeting as he joined the group.

"Trin, your wife sure can throw a party," Peaches said.

Trin's dimples flashed a bit deeper and his smile brightened. "Yes, she can," he agreed, pulling Dom against his chest. "Just this morning I was telling her how incredible she is."

Dom cleared her throat softly when Trin's fingers disappeared beneath the straps of her gown. Of course, she knew the illicit circumstances surrounding the seemingly innocent compliment.

"Oh, looks like we have some more people arriving," She announced, hoping to dispense the flustered feeling surging through her. She and Trin excused themselves and went to greet their new guests.

"I had no idea that company was so scandalous."

"Hmph, I don't think anyone did."

"Imagine all the lives they must've affected with those kind of tactics."

"Dominique, I know you've probably heard this several times already, but you did an incredible job on that story."

"Thanks, Katy," Dom replied, patting the woman's hand.

Katy Wallace, Jeremy Wallace's wife, shook her head. "It must be so remarkable, a job like yours."

"Remarkable and hectic," Sandra Avery, Russell Avery's wife, noted.

Dom nodded. "You are so right about that."

"Still, the adrenaline rush you must get," Julia Frakes, Simon Frake's wife, said. "Especially when all the pieces start to fall into place."

"It is exciting, I'll give you that," Dom admitted with a shrug. "But managing a household and a family, there must be an even greater reward in doing that." She watched as the wives of Trin's business partners all grimaced.

"Honey, there are many days I wish I could escape to an office," Katy said.

Julia nudged Dom's shoulder. "That's for sure. We don't mean to say that working outside the home is like a vacation, but ours is not the glamour life most women think."

"But I believe we can all agree that we love it." Sandra interjected.

Katy closed her eyes and nodded. "I do. I really do. I love being there for Jerry when he gets home."

"I'll second that. As busy as Russell gets, I'd probably never see him if I worked." Sandra added.

Dom enjoyed the conversation more than she realized. Though the three housewives acknowledged that their lives were far from perfect, it was obvious that no other life could compare.

Trin locked up after the caterers left and went through the house shutting off the lights. He removed the casual cream suit jacket and tugged the hem of the olive green crew shirt from the waistband of his trousers. He'd seen Dom headed toward the kitchen and set out to find her.

Dominique had retreated to the solace of the deserted patio once all the guests had gone. She heard Trin's footsteps behind her and shivered when his hands smoothed down her bare arms.

"The caterers gone?" she asked.

"Mmm . . ." Trin confirmed, his mouth brushing the nape of her neck. "Thank you, Domino. I'm glad you did this."

"Hmph. Thanks."

The unenthused response brought a frown to Trin's gorgeous face. "What is this?" he whispered, turning her toward him.

Dominique's gaze faltered. "I just think I could've done a much better job if I weren't so busy."

"Domino, what are you talkin' about? The party was great, everyone had a good time. You threw a fantastic party despite all that stuff with the Morton and Farber story."

Dom shook her head. "Trin, I'm always busy. Don't you ever get tired of that?"

"What? Your high-pressure career?" Trin teased, underestimating how serious she was.

"I'm always on the go, chasing after the next big story," she rambled, grimacing at the words. "Wouldn't you like it if I were more available to you?"

Trin favored her with a playful smirk. "Domino, if it makes you feel better knowing this, I'll admit that I'd love to have you at my beck and call twenty-four seven."

Dom wanted to say more, but she wasn't given the chance. Trin dropped a few quick wet kisses to her mouth before he stepped behind her and pushed the dress straps from her shoulders.

"Now shut up and let me thank you for my party," he ordered, when she stood before him wearing nothing but a pair of black panties.

Dom practically melted beneath his sexy, onyx stare. She was happy to let him have his way.

* * *

By morning, the tables had turned and Dominique was thanking her husband for an exquisite night of lovemaking. She had disappeared beneath the covers and was ravishing him with an erotic treat. Trin held one hand over his eyes while the other ventured beneath the covers to play in Dom's curly hair. His hips simulated slow thrusting movements in response to her lips and tongue. His tortured groans and sighs of enjoyment spurred Dom onward, and she grew more bold in her task.

"Domino, wait," he groaned.

"What?" she replied, her voice effectively muffled.

"I want this to last," he said, hoping she would still her movements.

Dominique enjoyed teasing him. "It'll last as long as you do."

Trin chuckled. "You're too good at this. You know that, right?" he teased, then moaned as the almost unbearable pleasure reasserted itself.

The phone began to ring and was ignored until the machine clicked on. When Mary Hill's voice filled the room, Dom emerged from beneath the covers.

Trin uttered a fierce curse as he lifted the receiver. "Mary?"

Dom braced on her elbow and traced Trin's abdomen. The impressive array of chiseled muscles flexed as he spoke into the phone.

"What?" Trin whispered, his entire body tensing. "When?" he asked.

Dom ceased her play and listened as the call went on. Shortly, Trin was replacing the receiver.

"What?" she inquired.

Trin brought one hand to his mouth and shook his head. "Henry Thornton . . ."

"The President of Morton and Farber?" Dom supplied in an encouraging tone.

Trin nodded. "He, um, he's dead. Killed himself."

"What?!" Dom shrieked, sitting up in the middle of the bed.

"Mary said it happened last night. His wife found him with a gun . . ."

"Oh, my God."

"I should go," Trin whispered, appearing dazed as he pushed himself up. "I should go see his family. Find out if I can do anything."

"Right. I understand," Dom said, rubbing his shoulder. "Do you need me to do anything?"

Trin reached for her hand and pressed it to his chest. "Will you come with me?"

"Baby," Dom groaned, her heart aching, "Sweetie, I don't think that'd go over too well."

"I don't care about that," Trin said, his brooding expression a perfect match to the sound of his voice.

Dom raked her fingers through his silky hair. "You don't care, but they might."

"I should be back by lunch, then. Will you be here?" he asked, his bold raspy voice sounding almost faint.

"Course I'll be here," she promised, squeezing his hand.

Trin kissed her mouth, then left the bed. When Dom heard the shower, she closed her eyes and whispered a curse.

"I knew it. I knew you were thinking of doing this," Marshall groaned, running both hands over his bald head as he paced the office.

Dom clasped her hands next to her chest. "Then you do understand?"

"Hell no!"

"Marshall, please. I really need you to understand this."

"Understand why you're resigning?" Marshall replied in utter disbelief. "Sorry, Dominique. I can't understand that. Other stations, hell, national networks were trying to snatch you before any of this Morton and Farber crap. Now, they're practically droolin' they want you so bad. And you're telling me you're ready to give it up?"

"I'm trying to put my priorities in order," she explained, following Marshall across the room. "Right now, my career needs to take a backseat."

"Trin makin' you quit?" Marshall asked in a knowing tone.

"He has no idea I'm even doing this."

"Then what the hell brought this on?"

Dominique pushed back her thick curls and went to stand before the office windows. "I just want to concentrate on my marriage for a while. We almost didn't make it through all that drama, Marshall. I can't let that happen again."

"Honey, quitting ain't gonna help."

"Yes, it will," Dom snapped. "Before the accident, we hardly saw each other. With my being home, we'll have more time together. I can concentrate on my husband and my home and—"

"Alright, Dom. Dammit, alright." Marshall interrupted, waving his hands around his head. "I can't listen to anymore of this, alright?"

Dom turned to face him. "Thank you."

"Don't thank me yet," he advised, snatching her typed letter of resignation from his desk. "Take this mess and take off as long as you need to play housewife or whatever. You've certainly earned a vacation," he said, shoving the paper into her hands. "I'm not letting you quit," he added, turning his back towards her.

Dom decided to give Marshall time to adjust to her news. She placed her resignation back on his desk and left the office.

It had been a long and exhausting day. Henry Thornton's suicide and the Morton and Farber exposé had hurtled the business world into a scandalous whirlwind. Ironically, the entire situation had given Trin and his partners a tremendous jumpstart to their new organization. Everyone, it seemed, was eager to work with Morton and Farber's former CEO and his new associates. Though the entire ordeal had been draining, Trin knew he had no desire to be where he had been one year earlier.

The house was practically dark when he walked in through the front door. Trin tossed his keys on the message stand in the foyer and set his briefcase down on the floor. He strolled to the entryway and leaned there, massaging his tired eyes. He looked around and noticed candlelight dancing against the walls and ceiling. His dark gaze narrowed when he glimpsed Dominique on the stairway. He squeezed his eyes closed for a moment, thinking he was imaging things. He realized it was no hallucination. She was there, lying back on the stairway. He took in the coral-colored, slip-style nightie she wore. The devilish see-through ensemble had a tight bodice which seemed to force an ample portion of her buxom over the lacy cups.

Trin smothered a moan when she stood. The daring piece of lingerie barely covered her derriere. A smirk tugged at the sensuous curve of his mouth as he pushed himself from the doorway.

"For me?" he inquired, closing the distance between them as he removed his suitcoat and loosened his tie.

"Of course," Dom whispered, smoothing her hands over her hips.

Trin stopped before her and reached out to trace the lacy fabric. He followed the outline of one breast, his thumb massaging the nipple as he pulled her close. "Just what I needed," he muttered, and kissed her deeply.

Dom arched against his tall, athletic frame. Her arms circling his neck, she kissed him back with equal enthusiasm. She suckled his lips and mimicked the sultry thrusting motions of his tongue. A sound resembling a low growl rose from deep within his chest then. A moment later, he'd scooped her into his arms and was heading upstairs.

"Trin, no," Dom gasped. "I don't want to go up yet."

"No problem," he told her, and pressed her against the banister. His hands cupped her bottom as he rained kisses upon her chest.

"Trin, wait," she whispered when his fingers ventured beneath the hem of the lingerie. "Wait," she moaned, even as her thighs parted for his seeking fingers. Fearing she was seconds away from completely discarding her plan for the evening, she suddenly shoved his hands away.

A sinister frown clouded Trin's gorgeous face when Dominique pushed him back.

"How about a drink?" she suggested, already bouncing down the staircase.

Trin caught her waist before he made it halfway down. "No," he grumbled against her shoulder.

Dom turned in the embrace and graced him with a dazzling smile. "Well, that's fine, since dinner's ready."

"Save it," he ordered, swinging her back into his arms and heading up the stairway.

Dom pounded her fist against his shoulder. "Trin, come on, now. Stop."

A fierce, low curse passed Trin's lips and he let Dom slide down his body. Surprising her, he trapped her against the curving oak banister and fixed her with a stern glare.

"I'm in no mood to be teased tonight, Domino," he said.

Dom took heed of the warning and nodded. "I don't mean to tease you, but we need to talk. There's something serious I have to discuss with you. Tonight."

Trin's expression went from stern to disbelieving. "Talk? You expect to have a serious conversation dressed that way?" He asked, watching her glance down at her X-rated attire.

"I wanted you to be relaxed while we talked."

Trin laughed shortly. "Domino, what you're wearing is doing everything *except* relaxing me."

Dom brushed the back of her hand across the slight shadow darkening his face. "Ah, baby, just try to restrain yourself for a little while. I promise to make it worth your wait after we talk."

Trin knew he'd make no headway convincing her to change her mind. He rolled his eyes, silently giving his consent. Aggravated and aroused, he followed Dom to the dining room and took his place at the table. For the next five minutes, he watched her bring the dinner out. The wispy teaser she wore did nothing to assist him in resisting his basest instincts. After a moment, he went to the buffet and prepared a stiff drink.

"Okay," Dom called, when everything was set.

"How long do I have to wait before you get to the point?" Trin asked, once he'd resumed his place at the table.

Dominique replaced the cover on the untouched spinach quiche and accepted that they wouldn't get around to eating. "I gave Marshall my resignation today," she announced.

Several seconds passed before Trin acknowledged the statement. "You resigned?" he replied, bracing his elbow on the arm of his chair. "May I ask why?"

"I did it for us. For our marriage."

"What does your job have to do with our marriage?"

Dom couldn't believe he'd asked such a thing. "Trindy, it has everything to do with our marriage. Aside from it being a threat to the powers-that-be at Morton and Farber, it's proven to be so hectic we hardly have any time together. Besides, I—what are you doing?"

Trin was checking his watch as he dialed his cellphone. "Uh, yes, Marshall Green please . . . Trinidad Salem."

"Trin!" Dom whispered, rushing over to grab the phone. "What are you doing?"

Trin clasped one hand over both her wrists and forced her to remain still while he conducted the call. Dom stomped her foot, when she heard him greet Marshall.

"What's goin' on, Trin?"

"Dominique just told me she resigned."

"Hmph. Yeah, I'm lookin' at this piece-of-crap letter of hers right now," Marshall said.

"Well go on and toss it," Trin ordered, his dark eyes roaming Dominique's bare thighs. "It won't be happening."

"She changed her mind?"

"She realized she made a mistake. She'll be back in a few days."

"Thank God," Marshall said.

"Talk to you soon, man," Trin called before he clicked off the phone.

"You had no right to do that," Dom snapped, wrenching herself out of his loose grip. "So it's okay for you to quit your job, but not me?"

"What do you plan on doing, Domino?" he calmly inquired, though his expression was probing.

Dom stood a bit straighter. "I'm gonna stay at home. Be a housewife—a *real* wife to you," she proudly replied.

Trin appeared stunned for a moment. Then he was laughing uncontrollably. Dom's temper heated and when she saw him wipe tears from his eyes, she stormed out of the dining room. Trin tried to call out to her, but his laughter got the better of him. When he caught up to her, she was halfway to the den.

"What the hell is so funny about me putting you and our marriage first?" she demanded, her voice carrying in the long corridor.

"Baby, I'm sorry," Trin was saying, his hands raised, "but you being a . . . housewife is crazy."

"There's nothing wrong with choosing to focus on your family, Trin! A lot of great women have chosen that lifestyle. My mother, yours!"

"That's very true," he conceded, slipping his hands into his trouser pockets as he walked toward her. "I didn't mean to imply that there was anything belittling about it."

"Then why the sudden laugh attack?"

Trin couldn't believe she was actually considering something so drastic. "Domino, why don't you take a step back and look at your career? Damn, baby, you are a phenomenal broadcast journalist in a field not too well-known for its avid recruitment of the African-American population. Hell, I'm willing to bet your value has shot up like a rocket since that Morton and Farber story came out. Am I right?" he asked, waiting for her nod. "And you're just going to give all that up?"

Dom nodded. "I just can't take it any more," she sighed, leaning against the wall. "What happened to Henry Thornton and our marriage. Trin, you know as well as I do that if it hadn't been for my high-profile job, they wouldn't have seen me as a threat and—"

"Hold it," he ordered, taking her arm and pulling her with him to the den. There, he placed her on the sofa and threw an afghan over her. "I can't concentrate on a damn thing with you bouncing around in this," he mumbled, tucking the cover beneath her hips.

"Trin—"

"Uh-uh. It's my turn to talk," he said, raising his hand for silence. "Now, have I ever given you the impression that I wanted you to quit or that I thought your job was a problem? Even when I was actin' like a damn fool? Did I ever demand you quit?"

"No."

Trin couldn't hide how furious he was. "Then why the hell are you doin' this?" he demanded.

"I told you!"

"What? Henry Thornton's suicide? Domino, the man was very disturbed before that story ever came out. I told you that, and I thought we decided to stop apologizing for what happened and move on?"

Dom fiddled with the pattern on the afghan. "I have moved on."

Trin folded his arms across his broad chest. "Is that right? You quitting your job for me because it might ruin our marriage doesn't sound like you're movin' on, Domino."

"Alright!" she cried, leaving the sofa with the afghan trailing behind her. "I feel uneasy about this whole thing."

"Uneasy?" Trin queried, walking toward her. "About us?"

"Trin, before everything that happened, our marriage was great but we were still like two ships passing in the night sometimes. My job was very hectic and it'll probably be even worse now. It's time consuming and I don't want anything else coming between us because of it." She turned then and pointed her index finger toward him. "Whether you want to admit it or not, my job was a very big factor in what happened. I admit that I should've been more honest about my past. But those bastards never would've gone after us had I not been a reporter and potential threat."

The only sound in the room was Dom's heavy breathing as she struggled to calm herself. Trin gave her a few moments before he took her hand and pushed her to an armchair.

"Look at me," he ordered when he kneeled before her. "Can you honestly admit that you'd be happy cooking and cleaning while I'm gone for most of the day?"

"I thought your partners' wives made it sound pretty wonderful."

Trin smoothed his hands over her dark thighs and shook his head. "It's easy to think that way if you have nothin' else to compare it with. Baby, as refined and lovely as they are, every one of them went to college looking for a husband. That was important to them, just as digging for news was important to you. Now can you tell me that you'd truly be happy livin' that life?"

"No. But I could learn to love it."

Trin squeezed her thigh. "Dammit, girl, I don't want you to have to learn to love it. Not when you already have something you love."

"But wouldn't you like having me at your beck and call?" Dom asked, scooting to the edge of the chair.

Trin brushed his thumb across the lush curve of her mouth. "Baby, you already are. Believe me, I have no complaints where our sex life is concerned. I have no complaints about anything."

"But—"

"You do realize we could go back and forth on this for hours?"

Dom closed her eyes and nodded. "Trin, I just don't want us to go through what we just got out of. It was scary and it was . . . complex, I—"

"Shh . . ." he soothed, pulling her into a tight hug. "Shh . . ." he repeated, when she sobbed against his shoulder. "Baby, I can't promise we won't ever hit another snag, but I love you," he vowed, rocking her for a few more minutes before he moved back to look at her. "Corny as it may sound, I think that counts for a whole helluva lot."

Dom laughed softly when he brushed the tears from her cheeks. "I love you too," she whispered, hugging him tightly and pressing a kiss to his ear.

"So can we consider this conversation over and done with?"

"I won't mention it again. Your workaholic wife is back to her senses."

Trin rolled his eyes. "Thank you."

"Trin?"

"Yes?"

"Um, what'd you mean when you told Marshall I'd be back to work in a *few* days?"

Trin cleared his throat and pulled her off the chair to straddle his lap. "I meant that for the next few days we're going to be prisoners in our own home. No phones, cellphones, faxes or e-mails."

Dom snuggled into his lap. "What about work?" she whispered, her light eyes caressing his devastating features.

Trin shrugged. "The only thing we'll be working on is making love in every room of this house."

"We've done that already."

"It's been a while," Trin countered.

Dominique giggled. "We have a lot of rooms."

"Damn right and I wasn't even counting all the closets and hallways."

"Oh? There's work to be done there too?"

Trin began to favor her collarbone with whisper-soft kisses. "Extensive meetings," he informed her.

Dom fixed her husband with a wicked stare. "You think a few days will be long enough?"

Trin lowered her to the floor. "I don't know, but I can't wait to find out."

Dear Readers,

Remember Love was exciting to write and have published.
It was even more exciting to envision in the hands of readers
curled up in bed or on their sofas following the saga of
Trinidad and Dominique Salem.

I have been so blessed to have the opportunity, not only to
write, but to share my writing with people like you. People
who enjoy a wonderful story, watching it unfold, watching the
characters emerge and become more complex with every turn
of the page.

I pray you all will continue to be entertained as I continue
to write. I do enjoy feedback and have several friends who
take advantage of offering their feedback whenever possible.
So, please feel free to email me with your opinion of my work
at altonya@writeme.com.

The response may not be immediate, but I will do my best
to reply in a timely fashion. It's my readers who make my job
possible. I love you guys. Thanks for your support.

God Bless You All
AlTonya Washington

ABOUT THE AUTHOR

A South Carolina native, AlTonya Washington began her writing career after obtaining her Bachelor of Arts degree from Winston-Salem State University in 1994. As a writer, she combines romance with suspense, and enjoys creating passionate and obstacle-filled storylines. In addition to raising her son, AlTonya also works as a Library Reference Associate.